RIN

An Assassin's Tale

Claire A. Brower

To the former high achievers – you don't need to ask permission or beg forgiveness to chase your dreams.

Note To Readers

Dearest reader,

Let it be known that this book is set in a fantasy world very different from our own. Despite this, many similar struggles and themes appear on the planet of Primthera. Those include but are not limited to sex, alcoholism, drugs, violence, manipulation, kidnapping, torture, rape, war, mutilation, child death, and more. For those wishing to avoid or perhaps skip to chapters containing explicit sexual content, those are Chapters 14 and 24. At the back of the book, there is also a glossary of terms and creatures to alleviate confusion or additional questions.

Streyland
Khlofastein
Giananor
Verone
Litholt
Gaela Plains
Wreabarroth
Borreagor
Creagachi Mountains
Boreagor Desert
Savaile Pass
Antissi
Bernitra
Chiotania
Elelia

and
Castlemore Ruins
Freymore Forest
Velreign
Liagheria
eagor City
Balliendon
Eastern Rift Valley
Innesfall Plateau
Eastern Mountain Plateau
Maigfall Cliffs
Reinalie
Temple of
Leaghaire
Usilaede
Lorcaide
Wraithland

PROLOGUE

Isadora Loughley walked along the woodland path just outside town, kicking at the ground and swinging her empty basket in her hand. She was meant to be collecting the gray and brown mushrooms that grow on dead logs that her gram used to help them when they were sick, but she was too frustrated. That stupid Kenneth Matteare had done nothing but harass her all day: pulling her hair, stealing her pencils, telling her she smells like the ash she shovels after school in her father's smithy. He's the worst sort of pest—the kind who has money and status and is good at everything, and he knows it. Annoyance churned in her, welling up until it was a ball of rage. She pulled back her leg to give the rock she'd been kicking a good hard wallop, only to miss it completely and land right on her bottom.

Throwing her head back, she looked up into the sky, letting out an exhausted sigh—too large for a girl her age—when she heard a chuckle in the woods. A wave of heat washed over her as she realized someone had seen her mishap. Turning her head slowly, her worst fears were confirmed when she saw Kenneth not ten feet away leaning on a tree and two other boys from school standing just behind him. A smirk stretched across his face as his dark eyes narrowed on her. Pushing herself up to her feet, she dusted herself off and scooped up her basket, intending to walk away without incident. But of course, he had other plans.

"What you tryin' to do, Dory? Beat up that ol' rock? What's it ever done to you?" he said, striding up alongside her, his henchmen chuckling behind them.

"I've had enough of you today, Kenneth. Go find some frog to torture." She shrugged him off and sped up her pace. But he was at least a head taller than her, and with his long legs, he easily stepped in front of her.

"Oh, come on," he chided. "I was just having a bit of fun with you earlier. You get so worked up and turn all red." She rolled her eyes and stepped around him, but he moved to block her path again. "Just like you're doing now." His smile was wide, his eyes twinkling in delight. She thought momentarily about punching him in the nose and giving those eyes purple rings around them.

"You're an idiot," she seethed, making to move around him yet again. He blocked her path, and the boys behind him chuckled more. Electricity began crackling at her fingertips as the anger in her built. She would have liked nothing more than to wipe him off the face of the earth. Pulling at her magic, she began building it up inside her until she felt strong and confident.

His eyes widened at the change in her demeanor, and he opened his mouth as if to speak, but nothing came out. Instead, he had gone eerily still, his mouth agape. She paused, listening for the sounds of the woods that were silent as well.

"Don't you dare!" The strangled voice of her grandmother cut through the silence from behind her. Whipping around, she looked between the two other frozen boys and saw the hunched form of an old woman ambling down the road toward them with beguiling speed. "Isadora Marie Loughley." The woman spat her name like a curse. "Just what do you think you are doing? You know what, no, don't say a thing, not yet." She waved a hand, and the boys blinked. "The lot of you had better scram if you know what's good for you," she shouted at them.

The three boys looked at each other, confusion etching their faces.

"Now." Her grandmother's voice turned deep and angry, causing the boys to run away without question. Left alone, the older woman stared down at the young girl with her hands on her hips, eyes blazing with anger.

"You know better than to be pulling at your magic in front of people," she said, her voice now carrying only a slight edge.

"It's not fair," the girl whined. "They are nothing but brutes, and I could end them all with a wave of my hand."

"You know damn well that's not the way of it." The older woman shook her head and turned, motioning for the girl to follow. "You'd be putting not only yourself but your siblings and your ma and pa in harm's way if you'd done it. Not to mention the stain on your own soul for using your magic through hate."

"Our way is stupid," the girl huffed, feeling her anger well up again. "How is it that humans have become the kings and queens of the world? We are Witches. We have magic." She was nearly shouting now. "And-and Elves have their strength, and the little people, and the water folk, and the beasts. The humans should all be dead, not forcing us to hide our magic."

"Because killing is not our way." The older woman gave her granddaughter a soft smile and put out a withered hand. "Have you forgotten our history, youngling?" she asked with a raised brow.

A moment passed as they walked in silence, the girl sulking. Then, she slid her hand inside the one offered. "I haven't forgotten," she said, her eyes downcast. "But maybe I need to hear it again."

Her grandmother's smile widened.

"It was long, long ago on the coming of the third moon that the Elves came, flying in on moon dust." She waved a hand over the forest in enthusiasm. "They had such power and intelligence. They taught our ancestors how to harness magic, but they didn't teach just anyone. There was a divide between the Elves who thought everyone should have magic and those who wanted to keep it to a select few.

"Eventually, the divide became so great that a war started. The Wraiths, as they called themselves, believed that all beings should have magic and included mostly lesser Elves and other beings, while the Elven nobility banded with the humans who worshiped them. When the Elves won, their king, Eldrid, banished the Wraiths and all other beings to the island they now inhabit, warded by magic to keep them there." A couple of squirrels skittered across the forest floor, chasing each other and making Isadora jump momentarily. Her grandmother smiled at her warmly and continued.

"The Elves continued on the continent for some time until they disappeared. One day, the Elves were here, and the next, they were gone, their halls empty and their stewardship missing. The humans floundered for a short while, eventually settling on kings and breaking up the territories as they saw fit. Some were taken over by the few half-bloods or Elven-blooded that hadn't disappeared with the rest.

"Over the next ten thousand years, the stories of Elves and wraiths became legends. The human kings began to fear that those with magic would come for their power and began their own war on magic, driving it from the land.

"They say on the twelfth return of the third moon, the Elves will return from hiding, and there would be a great battle of light and dark. A human will be the one to end the reign of Elves. Then, we will be free once again." The older woman stopped, taking a moment to breathe. She looked down into the innocent, gentle face of her grandchild, knowing the child would face untold dangers as the third moon neared once again.

"I know it's hard to see with the fire of youth, girly, but someday you will understand what it is to stay safe, what is required of you to protect your loved ones, and why those of us with magic still hang on to the old stories," she said, squeezing the child's small hand.

"Yeah, and when I'm older, I'm going to blast those old men who spent their lives killing the magic." The girl grinned up, meeting her grandmother's gaze.

"Sure, girly. We'll see what you do." The old woman smiled to herself as they continued their walk home.

CHAPTER ONE

I took a deep breath and checked myself in the mirror. My eyes were puffy, nose red, and skin pale—the epitome of the grieving mistress. In truth, the king's death didn't come as a surprise to anyone in the court, least of all me, who had been the cause of it.

It has been my longest mission yet. Taking nearly two years of playing the maid, the dutiful lady in waiting, then the mistress, all to get within reach of King Zakia Agyros of Wreabarroth. Nearly two years of pretending to be a mindless human with no more ambition than to climb the social ladder in this kingdom. Endless days of needlework and gossip intermixed with mind-numbing ceremonies, balls, and the occasional trip to a new castle. I was beyond tired of being stuffed into tiny corsets and skirts larger than the doorways. The regular use of citrus and lye to lighten my naturally dark hair had begun to irritate my scalp, and the inability to use magic at will had begun to irritate the rest of me.

His death couldn't come in cold blood, which was my preferred method. There were too many politics at risk for such a thing, so instead, I had to bide my time until I could get close enough to add bits of various poisons to his food and drink. He needed to weaken slowly for it to appear natural. As a young and virile man, it took longer than I had hoped for them to work, but they did eventually do their job.

Tucking in a tendril of blonde hair that had fallen loose from my coiffure, I pulled a handkerchief from my pocket before stepping out from behind the dressing curtain and back into the sea of mourners. The funeral itself was a drawn-out affair that culminated in the burning of the funeral pyre down in the sands of the desert as the sun set behind the city. Most of the court had just returned to the castle for the feasting and dancing portion of the event in celebration of the king's life. I had hoped for some reprieve from the droning sadness. However, as the king's most recent mistress, many courtiers felt the need to give me their condolences personally, and the conversations were getting tedious. It wouldn't be long now, though, I reminded myself. The job was done, and all that was left to do was plan my escape.

The queen, for her part, had remained stoic in the face of it all, even when Zakia had chosen me to reside by his deathbed in her place. Theirs was not a marriage of love but of duty, something that he often reminded me of in our time together. The queen had tolerated my presence as I'm sure she did several mistresses before me. Like most rulers on the continent, it was common for men of power to take a number of women aside from their bound partners; often, this was seen as a status symbol. Women, on the other hand, were viewed as ruined for the same thing, an unfairness that grated on my nerves.

Queen Isla Agyros was a formidable woman with beauty,

poise, and cutthroat dominance that I appreciated. It wouldn't surprise me at all if there were a bounty on my head before sunrise, but then a fake death would be an easy enough way out of here.

"Excuse me, Lady Elnora." One of the queen's younger ladies-in-waiting appeared before me. Jumping back as if startled, I took the young girl in; she wore a plain black shift dress with her hair pulled back behind a black lace band. I knew her as one of the queen's many nieces, though I couldn't remember which one she was for the life of me. I flagged a passing servant who carried a large bottle of wine and looked back at the girl who stood nervously, wringing her hands and looking anywhere but at me.

"Yes, darling?" I crooned, clutching my hand to my chest.

"The queen, in her kindness, has prepared a wagon to take you back to the Dewhorte family home this evening," she said, still staring at the floor.

"But the funeral has only just ended, and I haven't packed a thing." I tried to make my voice strained, but this was working out all too perfectly in my favor. "It's nearly the middle of the night, for goodness' sake."

"My sister and I would be happy to assist you, milady." She gave an awkward curtsy, and I eyed a gangly-looking girl behind her who appeared very interested in something on the floor. Beyond them, the queen stood surrounded by a group of ladies, a triumphant smirk spread across her regal face.

"Well," I said heavily. "I suppose I don't have much of a choice then." I let my voice crack as I turned away, biting my knuckle and hiding my smile. Unbeknownst to her Highness, she had just secured the easiest escape I had ever had. The server approached with my wine, and I scooped it up as I led the way out of the dining hall, the girls scuttling behind.

***

My private rooms were set on the top floor on the opposite side of the castle, tucked away from the hustle and bustle of court life. The King was a little disappointed when I refused a set of rooms adjoining his but was understanding enough of my need for privacy. The rooms were comfortable and quiet, the most privacy I had ever had in my life. These rooms might be the only part of this entire mission that I would miss.

It was no time at all before cheap wooden trunks were delivered to my door for the three of us to load everything into. They worked quickly and efficiently, barely looking at me in the process, likely out of embarrassment for my predicament. I took care to flit around the room, acting worried and flustered, scooping up weapons I had hidden in various places along with my fighting leathers, boots, and other items not typically part of a noble lady's belongings. Luckily, their averted eyes made it easy to stuff the conspicuous objects in bags and clothing unseen.

The girls took great care in folding the expensive dresses and carefully packing away the jewelry, though I watched them pilfer some of the nicer pieces that were given to me by the king. The queen I'm sure would appreciate them finding their way back to the royal collection.

While King Zakia was leaving behind a vastly wealthy kingdom, he was leaving it without a legitimate heir. He had named his wife his successor, but there was little faith that she would hold the throne long. Many of the High Lords of Wreabarroth did not believe a woman was capable of leading a kingdom, and others coveted the throne for themselves. There would be an internal power struggle that would, with any hope, cripple the country for some time. She would need every penny she could pilfer for the battle ahead.

An hour or so later, the whole group accompanied me down to the stables, where the footmen loaded my belongings onto a dilapidated-looking carriage, and the girls said their goodbyes. Dragging the corners of my mouth down, I swiped a finger under my eye as if dashing away a tear. It was important to remain distraught at the idea of being sent away in such shambles. The girls, to their credit, looked guilty and gave me words of encouragement as I climbed into the cabin of the carriage, still in my mourning clothes. They shut the door on me, and the carriage started its rickety movement out of the city.

We had barely made it out of the castle gates when I pulled out the bag I had stuffed with my gear. I ripped off the ridiculous dress and corset as quickly as possible before slipping into my fighting leathers. It was like coming up for air after diving into deep water; it had been so long since I had donned them. There was some muscle loss, causing the leather to hang loose in places while pulling tight in others. It didn't matter, though; they were enchanted and a moment later they morphed to fit my figure like they were painted on.

Castle Kielossi, the Agyros Families' main residence, was built on the edge of a cliff face overlooking the Borreagor desert. It had been meant to be a place of rest and relaxation for the ruling family several generations ago, but people had flocked to the home, and the city of Bernitra grew up around it on the high rise of the grassy cliffs overlooking the desert.

To protect its citizens, the rulers built exterior walls with large gates at each entry point. By the time we reached the outer walls, I was strapping my collection of weapons into their various places and pulling on my hood and mask. Waiting patiently until we passed into the darkness of the forest beyond, I pulled the curtain back, discreetly checking that there were no guards following us. That would have been something the real Lady Elnora Dewhorte would have fretted over, but I was pleased about it. Pushing my magic out, I felt for any presence surrounding us but was relieved to find only the two men seated at the front of the carriage.

Before popping open the door and reaching for the roof, I pulled the mask over my nose. Swinging myself around to the back of the carriage, I landed gracefully, my feet easily finding the back ledge. Over the curve of its roof, I saw the two men, one driving and the other looking around the corner to see the door bouncing on its hinges. Moving quickly, I leaped onto the roof, took a step, and dropped down onto the foot bar beside him. He looked up at me in shock, unprepared for the knife I drove into his gut.

Without stopping, I pulled myself onto the roof again and plopped down on the bench between the two men. The driver was already reaching for a weapon on his side, but I was faster, slipping a blade across his neck and pulling. The force snapped his head away from me, and he rolled out of the carriage in a spray of blood, reins still in hand. I had to lunge for them as he fell, to keep the horses from being yanked backward. The commotion spooked the horses, and I took a moment to steady the reins.

There was a flash of metal in the moonlight beside me. Turning, I saw the first man had brandished a sword. He looked green in the face and slow-moving with one hand holding his stomach where the hilt of my knife protruded. I continued to coo to the horses as I watched him, his movements slow and labored. It was amazing that he could even hold up a sword in his condition, and I felt bad for him. Reaching out, I swiftly pulled the knife from his stomach, and a stream of blood and bile followed it. The knife dropped onto the floorboards, and his head slowly slumped to the side, eyes following me as it did. I felt the presence leave his body as it brushed by me, sending a chill down my spine. No matter how many deaths I witnessed, the feeling still hit me.

***

It had taken more time to carry the men's bodies into the woods and call in scavengers to do away with them than I anticipated. Then I still had to clean the carriage and ride through the woods to a crossroads to re-enter the city through a different gate. I finally made it to Sayed Street just as the sky began to lighten.

About halfway down the street, there was a large three-story stucco building that housed a seamstress and tailor on the first floor, though no one with any sense came here for those services. I pulled the carriage down the lane beside the building, making sure my hood was still pulled down over my eyes and the mask pulled up over my nose before pulling into a small barn at the back. The two other horses inside snickered and stamped but calmed at the coos of a young boy who popped out of the hay beside them.

He said nothing and took to unhitching the sweaty beasts. I slid off the seat and retrieved my bag from the cabin before entering the building through the back. The door opened up into a kitchen where several women in varying levels of undress lingered, smoking and eating, their work for the evening coming to a close. They barely acknowledged me, aside from one who pushed off from the counter where she was leaning and motioned for me to follow.

As she led me down the dark hallway, I chuckled to myself at the contrast between her bare feet and disheveled hair with the sophisticated dress and string of expensive pearls she wore. I wondered vaguely which of the expensive gowns in the trunks out back she would take. She stopped at the door at the end of a hall and turned on me, leaning back against the wall. Knocking lazily, she took a long draw of her smoking stick and eyed me.

"Come in," said a muffled voice from the other side of the door. The woman reached out and turned the handle, pushing the door open without moving from her spot against the wall. I stepped around her feet and entered, the door closing behind me.

The front room was bright as the light from the rising sun began to creep in through the large windows. Across the room, Sister Adelay sat up from a chaise. She was several years my senior, but magic had kept her looking young and beautiful. Standing and stepping forward, her copper curls bounced as she moved. She was wearing a dress of emerald green, the same color as her eyes. The fabric was as fine as anything the queen's ladies had, but it was pulled low to reveal the top of a front-laced corset and ample cleavage.

I moved across the room in three long strides, placing my hand in hers, both of us slipping two fingers into the cuff of the opposite sleeve, feeling for the single mark that all of the Sisters of Harridan carried: a small circular scar on the inside of the wrist. To anyone else, it looked like a common scar from pulling hot pans out of ovens, but when pressed, the hard, flat presence of the stone beneath it became evident.

These thin stones were inserted into our skin on the eve of our sixteenth birthdays when we reached the age of Ascension. The process was a testament to our strength, as well as a marker to identify who could be trusted throughout the world and the special handshake had become a customary way of greeting.

I pushed the mask down but left my hood in place. "There is a royal carriage and horses in the stable, complete with clothing and jewelry suited for a lady in waiting. Just leave me a few in case there is a need to return."

"The girls will be glad to have them." She smiled warmly and turned to a glass front armoire laden with bottles and crystal glassware beside the door. A moment later, she came back holding one of the darker bottles. "The usual room is ready. Get some sleep, Catherine, and we can discuss your plans in the morning."

"Thank you." I returned the smile and replaced the bottle in her hand with a folded message. "For the tailor." I winked and saw myself out.

The usual room was one that was set aside for my sisters and I when traveling between missions and locations. Houses like this were created in nearly every eastern kingdom on the continent, each having a different front that explained the coming and going of various women like myself. The room here was in the attic space, which offered privacy and roof access, so we could come and go as needed. I trotted up the stairs with my bottle and found the room already alight with candles. The fireplace was empty, but as summer was winding down, the room was more than warm enough.

Minutes later, I was washed clean and lying on the bed in a soft nightgown. The sun had finally crested the distant mountains beyond as I placed the empty bottle by the bed and fell into a blissful sleep.

***

I was woken around noon by Adelay with a tray of food and a hot cup of tea. I stretched luxuriously and accepted the tea with a smile. The older sister came to sit on the foot of the bed, tucking her bare feet beneath her, with the tray between us. Her dress had changed into a blue house dress, a bit more modest than the earlier attire. Her beautiful curls were pulled off of her face and piled on top of her head behind a long scarf wrapped around them.

"The tailor won't be here 'till the day after tomorrow, but you are to stay until at least then," she said, pilfering a slice of apple from the tray.

The tailor was the nickname the sisters had given Rahmious Warder. He was one of the male warders who were in direct contact with Father, in our home on Wraithland. It was a warder's job to not only supply the sisters with our missions from Father but also maintain our training and ensure our safety and health while we worked. Unfortunately, there were only a few warders who could physically cross the wall around Wraithland and come to the continent, so they often traveled between the houses and left the day-to-day management to the Tachdre sisters. Adelay had been the top-ranked Saithe when I came of ranking age and was moved to a Tachdre position a few years later when her skills began to diminish with age.

I shrugged, blowing on the tea in my hands. I had been looking forward to getting home, but none of it was up to me. I would be as comfortable here as anywhere. "How are things here?" I said, making conversation.

"Well enough, I suppose," she sighed. "Not much goes on around here, I rather miss going on missions and training with you lot."

"Is there a place to train here?" I asked, grabbing a sausage biscuit from the tray.

She shook her head, curls shaking with the movement.

"Sometimes I sneak off to the barn in the early morning while the girls sleep. And Rahmious shadowjumps us to the forest for a few hours a day when he's here."

"Maybe I could give you some practice in the barn tomorrow. It's been a good while for me."

She nodded, understanding well, I'm sure, the itch that crawls under your muscles during times of rest after a lifetime of physical activity.

"Are you glad to be going home after such a long time?" Her face was relaxed, but I could see the appraisal in her eyes. My answer to this question mattered, for some reason, I couldn't quite distinguish.

"Of course," I said, watching her over the rim of my cup as I sipped. A shadow passed over her eyes, lasting only a moment before she shoved it away. Was she disappointed that I wanted to go back to our homeland? "I will miss the food here, though," I countered. She smiled, but it didn't reach her eyes.

"Things still hard to come by on the island?"

"Better now that Moreanne has worked herself into a captain position."

"She has, has she?" Adelay's face lit up, the freckles that peppered her cheeks straining. "That's good news for all of us."

Moreanne was a Tachdre who had spent most of her time working with the handful of pirates who were willing to trade with Wraithland. It was a great risk since not only was the water treacherous around the island but many would be shunned by those on the continent if they found out.

"Do you ever miss it? The island, I mean."

Adelay sighed, leaning back against the bedpost. "I miss my sisters. I miss training. But I don't miss having every moment accounted for. There's a freedom in my day-to-day that I didn't know I was missing."

I tumbled the words around in my mind. There was a kind of freedom to be had here, without the ever-watchful eyes of warders and never-ending lists of chores. I had served the crown of Wraithland all my life, following the direction of those above me just as the rest of my sisters did. It was that direction, though, that kept everything running smoothly, kept us together. Father Pterol had taken all of us, his daughters, in and then given us a life on Wraithland that most could only dream of. We were fed well, taught well, and trained well. Physically and mentally, we were exceptional among our people, able to take on the toughest warriors, and the greatest sorcerers, to be champions for our people. All so we could take back what was rightfully ours. We owed everything we had and everything we were to Father and The Society he built.

A shout came from downstairs, and Adelay stood rolling her eyes. "And the work never ends. Enjoy your rest, Catherine." She patted my foot hidden beneath the covers and sashayed to the door.

CHAPTER TWO

The lights from the street hid the recesses of the temple rooftop, where I perched, overlooking the city of Bernitra. From here, I could watch the people moving about their lives unnoticed, seeing and unseen. They had no idea what lay in store for them, but I could imagine it: their reactions, their thoughts, their jobs, anything I wanted. Picking up the flask I brought up with me, I imagined a whole life for the two young lovers who were walking north toward the water's edge hand in hand, the woman's pregnant belly visible. Taking a long swig, I savored the slight burn as the liquid slid down my throat.

I had little else to do while I waited for orders about my return or next assignment. Moments like this were rare. Typically, I would finish an assignment and immediately travel back to Wraithland, where there was always training or work to complete at the manor. There were times, of course, during this last mission, small moments between events, but I was still playing a part. I still had to wear the costume, keep the accent, and complete activities that my persona would do. Now, there were no barriers on what I could do. The idea sent a wave of heat over me like it had in the room with Adelay, and I pushed the thought away, uncomfortable with the feeling.

Another couple strolled away from the water toward the town center. The two men linked arm-in-arm, laughing and talking animatedly. I imagined their conversation; they just had a delicious meal and were headed back to the home they shared together.

Something tickled at the edge of my senses. I took note of the glamoured elf that walked among the humans. He was easy to spot with the ethereal glow about him and the pointed tips of his ears, neither of which humans could see. Seeing magic, even something as mundane as a glamour, was one of the skills I had spent years honing. Not everyone had the ability, and it had more than once given me an edge that saved my life.

The elf was walking with purpose, a stack of papers in hand, his long blonde hair wafting behind him. I wondered vaguely where he was headed. It was rare to see Elves anymore, especially pure-blooded ones. His presence would have been enough to pique my curiosity, but the terse expression and haste with which he moved rang the alarm bells inside my head.

I took another nip of the sweet berry liquor in my flask before sliding it onto the clip on my belt and dropping off the ledge onto a spire below. Carefully, I tip-toed along the edge and hopped down onto another roof. The thud sounded louder than I would have liked it to, but I had been drinking. The elf was a few blocks away now. I had to keep moving.

Dropping down to the ground, I sprinted across the lawn toward the shadow of the nearby buildings. The stone was cool on my hands but easy enough to climb. Once on the roof, I paused and spotted him unknowingly stretching the distance between us. Quickly moving to the opposite edge of the roof, I leaped onto the next, a thatched one that I grabbed onto hard and climbed over. Moving silently from roof to roof was something I had gotten good at in my time here, learning quickly that it was the easiest way to follow people in a city like this without being noticed. Humans hardly ever looked up, and even if they did, they wouldn't see me moving in the shadows with my black leathers and hood.

I closed the distance with ease, eventually slowing to meet his pace. He turned into a narrow lane lined with large stone houses. Rich men lived here, comfortably tucked away from the bustle of the main streets. He dashed up the wide steps of one of the homes, rapping on the door urgently.

A stout, balding man, whom I recognized as one of the powerful men among the advisers of King Zakia, answered. Any amusement drained from his face as he quickly ushered the elf inside. He ducked his head into the street, looking solemnly both ways as he put the cigar in his hand out on the stone rail and slunk back inside.

Every muscle in my body went taut, senses attuned to the house as I silently made my way there. Wrapping myself in a shield of magic so no one would hear or see me, I slipped down the vines that crept up the side of the neighboring home, barely three feet away. I reached out with my magic, willing the sounds from the other side of the wall to reach me. There was a clinking of glasses and a scrape of chairs in a room toward the back of the house on the second floor. Moments later, I perched on the windowsill, listening intently.

A hollow wind sounded in the room, and I could feel two

more beings had entered. Magic had transported them to this room. Shadowjumping was a kind of magic that very few beings had access to, and it made the hair on the back of my neck stand on end to know a being of such power was here on the continent. Following this elf was a good decision.

"You're sure this is all the pages we need?" a garbled male voice I recognized as the man who had opened the door asked amongst the sounds of shuffling papers. I reached deeper into the room with my magic, feeling for the beings there. There were two humans, the elf, and two other beings I couldn't quite place—both held magic, one of a strength and nature I had only felt a handful of times before—but couldn't quite place. I ached to be able to see through the curtains and place their features.

"Of course, it's not." The elf spoke calmly. I pictured him leaning over the table to peer at the pages. "Only an idiot would give us everything, but it should be enough."

"Now is not the time for games, Weilson." A younger male voice sounded smooth and confident. "The third moon draws near. The end of days is upon us. We need those pages."

"You don't know that, Inialos. The prophecy is not clear." Weilson's voice was steeped in venom.

"When is a prophecy ever clear?" Inialos snorted. "And the Elves haven't figured it out yet! In fifteen thousand years, they haven't thought to work on this problem before now. And why bring humans into it? What good are they in this kind of battle?"

My heart stilled in my chest. What prophecy? What being was this Inialos? With his heartbeat so fast, he was no elf, though perhaps Elven-blooded, or some other mixed breed. His voice was eerily calm despite the bitterness behind the words. Whatever this meeting was, I should have known about it before now, before stumbling onto it this way. It begged the question of whether or not father was aware of it. Had this been just a group of humans, it could have been dismissed as nonsense; their religions had so many prophecies and doomsday predictions that it was comical. But an elf in the human realm and these other beings all keeping council together, again, made the alarm bells chime in my mind.

"You forget whose house you are in, boy," the man who had opened the door and who I finally remembered as Garthrold seethed at Inialos. I shook my head in disgust at how long that took me, damning the liquor in my mind. "The prophecy states that a prince of our kind will take down the immortals."

"Sure, by some happenstance, maybe. Or some half-breed of considerable power, but a normal mortal, it can't be," Inialos said. "King Aelthor of the Wraiths is stronger than you think, and he's had hundreds of years to hone his powers."

"Same for Eldred," Inialos pushed back. "I doubt either one is a fan of giving up their power to live under the rule of a human, regardless of what a prophecy says."

"Do not put my king's name in your mouth, Wraith," Weilson cut in with a pulse of magic crackling around him.

I sucked in the air around me. How was I just now stumbling into this after having been in this kingdom for months? Eldred was the King of the Elves ten thousand years ago before they disappeared. It was not possible that he was still alive. None of this was making sense.

"Calm down," Inialos, the wraith laughed. "Are we not here because we are on the same side?"

"Why are you here exactly, young wraith? Besides sowing doubt in the minds of those here." The fourth voice, a female, was gravely and old, ancient even. The magic in it made me shiver, and I tugged at the invisible veil around me to ensure I wouldn't be noticed.

"He's here on my account," the other human answered, his voice deep and smooth. "We need someone who has been to the island, who knows Aelthor." He took a breath. "Intimately. If we have a hope of defeating him."

I had to hold in my laugh. Defeat Aelthor? My king. There was no way these five could accomplish such a feat, even with all the continent's armies at their backs. I could sense their power, and there was nothing special about them. Maybe the ancient one had a trick or two, but even she would be dead before setting foot on the island. What hope did they have? They were meeting in some townhouse in the city, not in the king's castle, less than a mile away, not with generals or commanders or anyone of any real power.

"We should not be too hasty in doing away with the man," the ancient one said coolly. "His considerable power may be needed in the battle ahead as the Immortals approach. If these pages are to be believed, everything here was only meant to be an experiment. The Immortals may have already chosen our fates."

"Aelthor is the more immediate threat to the balance of the planet," the elf spoke with a steady voice now. "He is gaining power despite the wards, stockpiling the strongest magic wielders and warriors. When he chooses to strike, it will be devastating. This same human child that the prophecy speaks of is the key to restoring that balance."

"The balance wouldn't be threatened if the Elves hadn't thrown away entire species of beings on that island," Inialos cut in. "No one can fault Aelthor for wanting vengeance for the thousands of years that they have suffered."

"Some suffering. He's doing, all right," Garthrold spat. "He's sitting on a golden throne, with naked women at his feet."

I rolled my eyes. These men had no idea what life was truly

like on the island.

"That, my friend, is an exaggeration," Inialos drawled. "A vein of gold was found on the island, sure, but not as much as you all seem to think, and no amount of gold could make up for decades of starvation and war on that island. You forget Aelthor's ancestor won that throne centuries after the revolt. It was hard won, and the people of Wraithland still bear the scars from those times."

There was silence. I imagined them looking at the younger man debating his words, wondering if any of them believed it, though I knew it was all true.

"Regardless of the history, the truth is both kings will need to perish. At least according to this."

CHAPTER THREE

It was the darkest hours of the night when I arrived at the room above the brothel and tailor shop, my mind somersaulting with the events of the evening. An evening that was supposed to be easy and relaxing, without work. The group continued to argue about the prophecy well into the night. The pages they had received were apparently copies of the witness accounts of the visions of some Elven seer thousands of years ago. The kind of things that were held behind lock and key in the royal libraries at Verone, a city-state in the center of the continent.

Verone was notoriously neutral in all things, and with its location in the temperate mid-north, it had grown into the continent's center of trade and knowledge. I had only visited it once but dreamed of returning to the place at some point in my life, if only to experience the feeling of serenity that enveloped the whole place.

The stairs groaned softly under my feet as I trod up to the

third floor. My senses twinged as I reached the last step. There was someone else here. Someone who was blocking their scent from me.

Casually, I rested one hand on the long dagger at my hip as I pushed the door open and stepped over the threshold. The blocking spell released, and I scented her before I saw her, lazing in a chair behind the open door. It was Ash.

My shoulders slacked, and my hand dropped. "To what do I owe the pleasure, Sister?" I kicked the door shut and slipped the glass of dark red wine from her hand, as I made my way to the chair opposite her. She narrowed her overly large green eyes at me and I tossed the half-full flask of liquor on my hip at her. She caught it easily and took a sip. Her blonde hair had been cropped short at the chin and slid backward as she tilted her head. She was wearing the same black leathers that I was but had already removed her boots and shoved them under her chair, her legs dangling over its arm toward the roaring fire in the hearth.

Ash was part Naiad, and it showed in the size of her eyes, the sharp angles of her face, and the length of her limbs. She always took care to tuck her fangs behind her lips, often smiling without showing any teeth at all. While she hid it from most, I knew there was a thin webbing that held a green tint between her toes. She was beautiful by most counts, but her physical attributes kept her in the shadows, and often, she would go months without interaction from anyone but our sisters or the warders.

"Leeta is dead," she said flatly, rapping her long-tapered nails on the side of the flask. She stared out the small window that overlooked the city, giving us both a moment before looking at me again.

In that moment, I schooled my face to show no emotion. Leeta was a few years older than us. She was known for her tenacity in the sparring ring. Father adored her, as did most of the older sisters. I was sad we lost her, but it was the way of things for women like us. I took the information in and locked it away. Instead, taking the moment to catalog the room around us. The two chairs we sat in were well-worn but comfortable, with a low round table between them. An open wine bottle sat atop it, with another empty glass. The hearth was in the middle of the room, an addition to the existing chimney. The opposite side of the room held a large bed, another window with another set of chairs, and a battered wood wardrobe. The wardrobe was empty save for three iron hooks. It had the same number of drawers on the bottom. In the top drawer, I had placed a calfskin book with all the notes, papers, and correspondence from the entirety of my time here.

"Daren has come to the continent," Ash said, bringing me back to the present. "You and I are to finish the mission Leeta failed." This was a surprise to me; the only indication of which I gave was a raised eyebrow as I sipped my wine. "I haven't been told more than that," she responded with a raised eyebrow of her own and a shrug.

Daren was another warder who only occasionally accompanied newer Saithe on their missions to ensure their success and training. It had been a decade since anyone had overseen either of our missions. For him to accompany us, along with Leeta's death, meant that this would be a difficult one. I took a breath and changed the subject, hoping to distract myself.

"Have you heard any of this nonsense about the return of the third moon? Or the prophecies around it?" I asked.

She shrugged. "A legend amongst the humans. That the third moon came fifteen thousand years ago, bringing the immortal gods and the Elves, and it was to return with the Elven gods to decide the fate of our world or some nonsense. Why do you ask?" She looked at me directly now, her hair swinging with the turn of her head, eyes twinkling in the firelight.

Ash was the closest thing I had ever had to a friend. Any attempts at friendship when we were growing up were quickly squelched by the warders or the Father. I had only learned of the concept on one of my first missions, while on assignment in Addorial. Learning how to get close to people, and siphoning out their secrets for the first time was a testament to my patience. The relationship with Ash was different, while I knew that she would have my back against any enemy, even another sister, I also knew that she, just like myself or any one of my sisters, would flay me alive if it was commanded of her. I shrugged noncommittally.

"I don't know," Ash sighed. "It all makes sense, you know, fits in with the other legends—how the Elves suddenly appear and then disappear and all that."

"I only heard of it tonight." I debated silently whether I should tell her about the meeting I had overheard, but perhaps this was something that should be discussed directly with the Father. "Seems silly." I rolled my eyes and finished my glass.

Ash shrugged again and picked up the wine bottle. I held out my glass, and she filled it, then the other. "We should get some sleep; we are to meet Daren at the edge of town just after dawn."

I nodded, slugging back the heavy glass. She did the same, and we both rose from our chairs. It didn't need to be discussed where Ash was sleeping. We would share the bed as we had many times over the years. I threw a large log on the fire and unstrapped my weapons, scattering them throughout the room for easy access. Ash doing the same on her side of the room.

My eyes were heavy with exhaustion and wine, but sleep didn't come easily. I lay there for a long while, listening to the steady sounds of Ash's breathing beside me. I thought of Leeta, my gut twisting. I wished I had been told more about the mission. The anticipation of the unknown had always been a nuisance to me, but knowing whatever we faced was enough to end a sister with the skills of Leeta made it worse. If I had been allowed to feel fear, I imagined it would be very similar to this.

***

A pounding on the door woke me out of a restless sleep as the earliest rays of light began to streak through the sky. My body felt heavy in the bed, bones, and muscles crying out as I moved to sit up. Ash jumped out of bed and went to the door, returning with a breakfast of eggs with ham and toast. I reached for the hot black tea first. It was smokey and bitter, not as strong as the roasted stuff we had back home, but I had gotten used to it in my time here.

After eating, we dressed quickly, without speaking. I sat on the end of the bed while Ash took a moment to brush out my currently blonde hair and re-braid it into tight rows that we coiled atop my head. I asked a sister to braid it any chance I got; their deft hands made for good braids that lasted for weeks instead of the days that my own work resulted in. She did not comment on the color; she had seen me in passing a few months ago and knew already I had changed it for this mission. I wondered vaguely if I would be able to find a dye to bring it back to its usual brown while I checked the pages in the calfskin book. I packed it into a small bag and slung it over my shoulder, under the cloak that Ash had tossed me from a bag she pulled from under the bed, along with a plain brown skirt to go over my leathers. The disguise would be enough that no one would question us as we walked through the streets.

We arrived at the designated spot just as the pinks and oranges from the sun's rise began to fade from the sky. Daren met us at a brewer's house near the edge of the city proper. He sat at a table outside, his long body folded into the attached bench as he finished his breakfast. He was easy to spot despite dressing like many of the men here. He had grown his beard out, but his light hair and skin were still a stark contrast to the darker features of the desert people of Wreabarroth. He had glamoured his lightly tapered ears but left nearly all of his other features alone. I assumed we weren't staying long; otherwise, he would have used stronger glamour to fit in better, perhaps dull his handsomeness. He was easily in his eighties but had yet to show it; like most Elven-blooded, he would live much longer than most and retain his youth with it.

Across from him sat a younger man with dark hair that was slicked back and curled around his ears. He was tall like the Elven-blooded, but there was no point to his ears, and I sensed no glamour. Daren motioned for us to sit as we approached. I took the spot to his right and Ash slid into the spot opposite me. The guest looked up at me, grim-faced, from his meal and I was surprised at his handsomeness. I placed my elbows on the table and threaded my fingers under my chin as I gave him an appraising look back. He had a strong jaw with a cleft chin that was accentuated by a dark stubble along its edge. His slate-gray eyes were striking despite being hooded by thick eyebrows, but perhaps most unnerving was the intensity of his gaze and the fact that he made no effort to look anywhere other than directly at me.

"This is Adrien." Daren waved at the man, still intently staring at me. "Adrien, meet Ash, and Brigitta. They are both trained to resist you, so don't bother," he said dryly, using the name I went by at court. It dawned on me that his staring was an act to distract me as he reached into my mind. Now I could feel his presence there, as light as a breath in the mist. Luckily, as Daren had said, we were trained so thoroughly that I couldn't remember the last time I had relaxed the fortress I had forged around my mind, it held now without any effort.

The handsome man, Adrien, grumbled and turned back to his food.

"You are a Mindwalker?" Ash piped up, eying the man beside her. "We've never worked with a Mindwalker before." She looked at Daren, her brow knitted together slightly, echoing my own concern. I hoped Daren didn't notice, or she would be chastised for it later; she had never had courtier lessons and often failed to hide her feelings from her face. I felt it as an invisible wall tightened around us. Daren had concealed our voices in a bubble of air; invisible to the humans around us, but effective in preventing them from hearing us.

"Yes, it's rare that we need their expertise," Daren commented, wiping his mouth delicately with a napkin. There was something about him that always remained regal, even in training, despite sweating and bleeding, he would never remove his shirt or allow his hair to move out of place as if he couldn't show any imperfection, lest it be perceived as a weakness. It was something I admired about him, unlike myself, who turned red at the slightest exertion. Because of this, I had spent much of my youth training harder than my other sisters, doing what I could to build up a resistance to my coloring. As a result, I also became the top of our class in hand-to-hand combat, only falling second to Leeta until now.

"Is that why you've joined our mission? There was not much explanation in my message, aside from where to pick up Gitta." Ash switched between my names easily. Another facet of our training. I could tell she was trying to look bored, but in truth, she was trolling for answers. Mindwalkers were a dangerous lot that needed to be kept in check or they would be likely to take over an entire city, vanishing the minds of hundreds with a flick of their wrists. It was the main reason so many were banished along with the Wraiths. These days, only a select few were allowed to survive in Wraithland, and only after extensive training, under his majesty's guidance. Unfortunately, magic talents didn't always follow bloodlines, so it was possible for Mindwalkers to pop up anywhere at any time.

Daren nodded. "I'm here to ensure everything goes to plan, and I hold the key for this one." He nodded in Adrien's direction. "Our mission is simple, in theory." He looked at both of us females now for the first time. "We are here to extract a girl of extraordinary power. Unfortunately, we were unaware that both her parents also have magic, and have training in wielding it. Her father is a fire wielder and the mother is a Mindwalker. The siblings may have power too, but they are of less concern due to their age."

While I had no idea what Daren meant by key, I assumed it held some kind of control over the man by the way his eyes darkened, finding something very interesting at the bottom of his teacup. Daren went on to explain that we would be traveling most of the day on horseback, arriving in the evening at the family's home.

CHAPTER FOUR

The ride was somber and mostly quiet. I might have enjoyed it if it weren't for the ache in my backside. As the town neared, we ducked off the trail, mercifully tied up the horses by a stream, and moved the rest of the way on foot.

We entered the small town from the woods, avoiding the one main street. As we passed it, I noticed no more than a handful of merchant stalls, a single bakery, a smithy, and only one or two buildings with a second story. Despite the lack of commerce, the town wasn't grimy or even dusty, as if they swept the single cobblestone street daily. The sun had already begun to descend, and while the streets were nearly empty, the regular sounds of life echoed through open windows and cracked doors. It felt like a place of peace and it struck me as odd that something that resided here was powerful enough to destroy one of our sisters.

It was toward the edge of the town center that Daren slowed

his movements, pausing just before the end of the street. "As you know, this will not be easy." He smoothed the front of his shirt and scanned the street before us. "Our goal here is to take the middle girl, Isadora, alive, but if all else fails, she will be killed as well. She has great power that will help our cause, and we cannot leave her alive to avenge her family." Then he turned to us, his large frame stiffening, preparing for battle. Rolling my shoulders, I instinctively stretched my neck while Ash felt for the various weapons on her person. Together, we pulled the sleeve that covered the bottom of our faces up over our noses. "Remember your walls against the mother, and keep your senses honed. Be wary of them all." We each nodded in turn. "Adrien, Ashlynn, you first." Daren waved his hand toward the squat stone home across the road.

The Mindwalker licked his lips and slipped his hands into his pockets. He slunk across the road with hunched shoulders and knocked gingerly on the door. Ash coolly followed in his wake, slipping to the side of the door and out of direct sight. Adrien's whole demeanor had been diminished; he was utterly unremarkable.

The door opened, revealing an older man with deep-set eyes and a broad chest. Adrien only came up to his nose and had to look up at him when he spoke. I didn't hear what he said as I focused on building walls around myself and reaching out my senses for other disturbances around us. I felt the presence of the other four people in the two-room house. A woman and three children, all seated around a table to the side of the main room. They were slowly moving away from the table, trying to sneak into the back room or root cellar, I supposed. Feeling a back door, I launched myself across the road, skirting the view from the door to the narrow space between buildings. I dashed around the corner just in time to see the back door open, a small boy and girl pushing each other through it, stopping short when they saw me. In the shadows behind them, a woman looked startled, and an older child grabbed at her siblings.

They may not have seen the smile on my lips, but they certainly saw it in my eyes as I stepped toward them. The scent of terror enveloped me as I crossed the threshold. It emanated from them all despite the gritted determination that had overtaken the woman's features. I felt it as she stretched her magic toward me, feeling the fortress I had built around myself. She didn't flinch in defeat, though; only pulsed more magic toward me. Beside her, I saw the oldest daughter building her own power, a soft brown pulling in from the air around her. It was a rare gift to see the magic as I could, one that had garnered me more respect than I deserved at a young age but also propelled me forward into the position I now held in the sisterhood.

I struck with ease using base magic to close her in a cocoon and stop her from building more than a whisp that fizzled against my wall. The smallest, a little boy with big eyes and a smudge of dirt on his cheek, ran at me, pulling violet magic into the movement, trying to throw me off balance. These children were better trained than we had anticipated. I sidestepped and dodged, grabbing him by the collar before he knocked himself out on the stone of the wall. I hadn't even realized I had done it when it hit me that I wasn't in complete control of my movements. I whipped back to the mother, still holding the middle child, as I fought to find her presence in my mind. How had she broken in? That was the thing about mindwalkers, theirs was a magic I couldn't see.

A crashing sound, a yelp, and the unmistakable sound of a fire wielder's vortex flying across the room thundered on the other side of the house. There was more commotion and I saw the illumination of fire out of the corner of my eye. I ignored it and gently set the boy down of my own accord. I had never harmed a child. In my mind, they were innocents, even if the Father said this one girl was dangerous. I looked at her now. She had dark brown eyes that were big and round like her brother's. Her blonde hair was half braided, the other half falling in soft curls down her back. She couldn't be more than six and barely came to my middle. She stood firm in front of her mother and sister, who had collapsed to the floor gasping with the effort it took to break my cocoon.

You will not be taking my children, a silky voice resonated in my head. She was deep inside, and I felt my stomach drop with the realization.

Only the one, I responded in my own mind.

She shivered and looked down at the girl, Isadora. She knew her one child held more power than the others, though the girl had yet to show it. She had probably been schooled on control most of all. I felt a force pushing against my muscles. The mother was trying to take control of my body, but years of training meant I was not an easy target. The little boy was coming at me again, violet whispers of magic sliding toward him. I was still battling mentally against the mother, who had pushed the two girls behind her and was staring me down intently. I took the hit from the boy to the stomach that nearly knocked the wind out of me. I stumbled back, muscles straining from multiple directions.

Looking up, I saw Adrien appear in the opening between rooms, flames licking at the rafters behind him. His hair was a bit disheveled, but his eyes were bright and locked on mine. His presence brushed against my mind as he stepped forward. I directed my own mind back at the mother, trying to push against her, as the boy wound up again, and brown tendrils of the older girl's magic twined behind him.

A single movement and Adrien slipped his hands around the mother's head, snapping it to the side. She crumpled to the ground, the force wrapping around my muscles dissolving with it. I caught the boy in midair, plopping him on the ground beside me. The older girl was screaming now, tears streaming down her face while she shook her mother's corpse as if she could simply wake her. The middle child, whom I surmised must be Isadora, just stood beside her, looking down at the twisted remains of her mother.

Golden yellow smoke began wisping toward the girls. This had to be Isadora's power. It was building quickly, swirling around her. Her sister halted her crying long enough to skitter away from the girl, grabbing up her brother in the process. They both backed away toward the corner nearest to the door. Isadora just stood there, staring at Adrien, her eyes blazing, flashes of the same golden yellow sparking through them.

With a swift movement, I sliced my hand through the air, coming in contact with the side of her head. I knew the spot for adults and figured it couldn't be much different for children. She dropped instantly into my awaiting arms, the golden mist dissipating around us. Daren appeared in the doorway behind Adrien and I moved toward him with the girl in my arms. Behind him, the flames had engulfed the front room. In the middle of the room, the children's father was sprawled in a bloody mess on the floor. Ash was catching her breath against the wall nearby, flames licking at her boots as they spread across the house. It was done. We had completed the task for which we had come. I loosed a sigh of relief as the girl's weight left my arms, and Daren took her from me.

"Kill them," Daren said, looking directly at me before turning on his heel, walking the girl through the flames and out the front door. Ash gave me a nod of acknowledgment and followed gingerly behind.

My mistake was clear when I turned around and realized that I had moved too far away from the door and the children, still cowering in the corner, could have easily escaped. I moved quickly, but they saw the opening and dove for it. Luckily, I was quick enough to grab the boy in the lead, and they both fell back toward me. Pushing them into the room, I drew a dagger.

The two kids held on to each other and looked at me in utter terror. The scent of human waste wafted by me and I realized the boy, who had been so brave earlier, had wet himself. His big brown eyes were strikingly wide, and I couldn't tear myself away from them. The edges of my sight began to close in as I stared at those eyes. It felt as if my heart would burst through my chest as the darkness grew and I was transported to another place, another time.

"Run, Catherine!" a girl around ten with the same big brown eyes and lush brown hair as me yelled. Her dress was ripped and muddy, and in her hand, she held a kitchen knife. Behind her, I saw myself, but perhaps older, struggling with a man twice her size. He had sandy-blonde hair and a scar that ran under his right eye straight back into his hairline. The woman turned, shouting something over her shoulder at us. She wasn't me; she was my mother. My mother, with the golden-brown eyes wide with fear. The girl shoving me away was my sister. I looked down at the knit doll in my chubby hands. Red liquid spurted across the dingy surface of the doll, and I felt warm flecks splash on my face. Looking up, I saw that it was blood. My mother's blood. The man had slit her throat. He turned, looking directly at me and my sister, not an ounce of feeling in his gray-blue eyes.

A cry from one of the children in front of me brought me back to reality, to the task at hand. Killing children was not something I had ever done. I looked at the knife in my hand and looked back up to the children, my knees going weak beneath me. The crying had stopped, and now the children stood before me, unmoving, glassy-eyed, almost as if they couldn't see me standing in front of them with a knife in hand.

A hand wrapped around my own, and I looked up into the formidable face of the Mindwalker.

"What have you done?" I whispered, my voice suddenly hoarse.

"What you couldn't," he answered smoothly as he slipped the knife from my hand. I didn't even flinch, just letting him take it from me. Like a stone, I stood there, my head spinning as I watched him slit their throats in two quick movements. They tumbled to the ground on top of one another. Their little bodies entwined, eyes unblinking, until the light seeped from them. Adrien turned from them and dropped the knife into my still-open palm before striding out the back door.

CHAPTER FIVE

It took a moment for my body to respond, to move out of the house and away from the fire that was closing in on me fast. I paused outside, leaning against the warm stone to catch my breath. Tears were threatening to shoot out of me like a torrent, and I had to get control of myself quickly.

Looking out at the yard I counted the rows in the garden, some of which were already tilled and mulched ready to sleep for the impending winter. There were two rows of carrots, their tops pointing to the sky. Three rows of potatoes, another of cabbage, and two more of some greens I didn't recognize. Along the fence line were patches of herbs. I listed their names and uses in my mind as I scanned down the row. I wiped the tears from my eyes before they could fall and took a deep breath before pushing off the wall.

Adrien was there as I turned the corner, shouts ringing from the street he had come from. The villagers had heard the commotion and were gathering in front of the house. Wordlessly, he pushed me in the opposite direction, past the garden, and into the narrow alley to the far street.

We cut diagonally across the street and moved east toward the outside of town. Luckily these streets were still quiet as most of the residents finished their meals. Adrien paused at an alleyway and looked back over the street suspiciously. I nearly scolded him for acting so blatantly when he took my hand, a mischievous smile spreading across his face, as he pulled me into the alley. He was playing a part; if anyone saw us duck into the alley, they would hopefully think it was too young lovers looking for some privacy. I was shocked by the sudden change in his usually taciturn expression. While he had been handsome before, the smile had transformed him into someone almost impossibly good-looking. A wave of tingles washed down my spine in response.

The sun was setting quickly, and as soon as he pulled me into the shadows of the alley, his face changed. As one arm wrapped around my waist, his expression drifted back to the usual sternness. For a moment, I could have sworn his eyes darted down to my lips, but just as quickly, he turned to lead the way out of town. I chided myself for my body's response, my emotions suddenly getting the better of me.

My mind spun as I obediently followed Adrien through the streets and alleys back to the woods where the horses were tethered. I assumed Adrien would divulge the fact that I had hesitated to follow direct orders, and I needed an excuse for my actions. There would be no pity for pausing to kill, even an innocent child. To say that the mother's magic had disrupted my thoughts would make me weak and useless. The last thing I wanted was to lose the freedom of my current position. The idea of spending my days at Lockheed Manor washing pots or training others was disheartening. Before I realized how far we had come, we were stopped in front of the horses, and I still had no good reason for my actions.

"We need to move," Adrien said as he untied his horse and climbed on.

"Is the evidence gone?" Daren responded from his place beside Ash's horse. They had contrived a sling of sorts to adhere the girl to Ash's chest like women often do with new babies, though larger. The little legs wrapped around Ash's waist, and her head was tucked against her shoulder.

"The fire was nearly over them when we left. The townspeople won't be able to move quick enough to save the bodies, and we had to go," Adrien said, simply turning his horse to the road. Daren and I quickly untethered and mounted our horses, and we began the journey to the coast without so much as another word.

***

We arrived at the inn of another small town late in the night. Dismounting quickly, I took the child from Ash so she could dismount as well. She grimaced and rubbed her back as we entered the raucous dining hall. Daren made the arrangements with the voluptuous barmaid and led the way up the narrow stair to the side of the main room.

He used a key to open the door to a large room on the second floor. Pushing it open, he stepped aside and gestured for me to enter with the girl. It was nicer than I expected from the look of the first floor. It had a sitting area, a dining table, and a large bed. A smaller trundle bed was pulled out from beneath it, ready for a guest with pillows and blankets. I set her there gently, and she roused slightly, a moan escaping her little body. I looked up at Daren. He motioned to Adrien, who stepped forward, pulling a bottle from the saddlebag over his shoulder.

"Just a few drops will do," he said as he handed it to me. Carefully, I lifted her and dribbled some of the dark purple liquid into her mouth. Tilting her head back, I watched her throat to ensure she swallowed it, before laying her down. It was a draught that would keep her asleep for the duration of our trip. I had used it occasionally when transporting prisoners. It kept them from not only waking but also falling ill from lack of food or water. They would wake at the manor with no recollection of anything prior to the draught being administered. I pulled the covers back over her shoulders and stood.

The others were making themselves comfortable around the room. Ash tossed logs into the fire and used a spark of magic to ignite it. Adrien set the collection of bags he carried by the door while Daren placed his own on the larger bed. A set of maids appeared at the door with trays of food and wine. With a nod from Daren, they sauntered in and placed them on the table. They were dressed in the usual style of barmaids with flowing linen skirts, aprons, and low-cut corsets that revealed the edges of their open chemises. They were clean, though, and smelled of perfume, with hair that was tied up in just a way that several loose curls tumbled down on their shoulders. It was rather fancy for a place like this, as was the room, making me wonder what other sorts of businesses went on in this small town. I stood and watched as the girls, both attractive in their own ways, bent over the table, removing the plates from the trays and opening the wine. Daren and Adrien noticed as well. I couldn't stop myself from rolling my eyes at Ash, who only stifled a smile as she swiped a freshly poured glass of wine from the table.

The girls finished their work and made their way out, making sure to sway their hips and give extra-long looks to the men in the room. Again, I rolled my eyes and pulled out a chair from the table. I hadn't eaten the hard cheese and bread that Daren had offered during our trek through the evening, my stomach too unsettled at the events of the day.

Usually, I enjoyed the silence, but tonight, the images that appeared in my own head in that fiery house plagued me. I could taste the blood, my mother's blood. I could smell the scent of my sister, rosemary, and earth as she pushed me to run, her eyes so wide with terror. A terror that she pushed down for me. Me, a child just like Isadora. Looking up from my half-eaten plate, I saw her little feet pointing up under the covers, her face obscured by the larger bed.

Is that what had happened to me? Was I taken from a loving family as she was? Could everything I had been told about being given up for a greater good, to use my powers for the betterment of our people be a lie? I had never had a memory of my past, never seen my mother's face, but somehow, I knew that it was real. That vision had happened. It happened to me, to my family.

I hadn't been paying attention to the discussion around me, but now Ash kicked me under the table. I looked up, eyebrows narrowed. She tossed her head in Daren's direction as he stared at me, lips pursed, a glass of wine poised in the air.

"Apologies, I was thinking of something. What was it you wanted?"

"The other children, did they exhibit anything special?" Daren drawled, swirling the dark red liquid in his glass. He was trying to appear bored, but I knew he was deeply interested. I could tell by the glint in his eyes.

"Magic, sure, but nothing supremely as special as this one." I nodded in the girl's direction. "What's more, they were afraid of her power. They knew when she began to summon it and moved away." Adrien nodded beside me as he continued to eat. "Why, though, may I ask, did they need to die?"

Daren scoffed, putting his wine down. "We leave no witnesses, you know this."

"They were children," I said a bit too quickly and with a bit more force than I intended. This was not the kind of conversation to have in front of outsiders.

He put his fork down and looked at me across the table, licking his lips. He inhaled deeply through his nose as he placed his elbows on the table, interlacing his slender fingers over his plate. "They were human children," he said with disgust. "Human children with magic. They would hate us and our kind until the end of their days. It is not a risk worth taking."

I pushed my plate away and stood up. Something in me had to see the girl's face. I stalked to the other side of the room, clenching my fists at my side, and biting my lip. A fire was building in me that would erupt soon; I could feel it, and I was struggling to control it. I wanted answers for the questions swirling in my head now, questions about this girl's future, my own past, and the past of my sisters. It was as if everything I had ever known had ceased to exist, and I was left with more questions than possible.

"Since when are humans any kind of threat to us?" The girl looked angelic in her sleep. A few wisps of hair had strayed from her braid and fell across her face. I saw a resemblance to the little girl of my memory. My sister. This girl could have been her, she could have been me. "What happens to her now?"

Daren had turned in his chair to face me, his arm draped over its back. His blonde hair fell into his face as he studied me. "She goes to the dormitory and we begin her training." His tone was dry as if it was of no consequence, but he watched me with intensity. The pieces of the puzzle that had been plaguing me since we left that house began to fit together.

"Just like we did as girls."

Ash stilled her fork, dangling it in the air midway to her mouth. Did she understand the gravity of what was being revealed to us with this mission?

"No." Daren waved it off but stood, taking a step toward me. He was much taller than most, even the Elven-blooded, and he towered over me despite my own considerable height. "Your parents left you with us because of your considerable gifts to serve the realm and help us to take back the freedom we deserve."

It was a line that we had heard so many times throughout our lives. We were given, chosen, or found abandoned, but we had considerable gifts, gifts that could help our people if we chose to do so. But had there ever been a choice? This girl didn't have a choice. "How is it that a child who is a threat, as this one is, could become of service to us? What could you possibly say to her after what happened today that would make her want to help our kind?"

He took a breath, his mind calculating, deciding what to say. I could see the thoughts rushing through his brain. I had spent more time with Daren than any other warder, and I knew him better than most. He was holding something on the tip of his tongue, a secret. We all had them, he more than any of us. Warders weren't supposed to get close to any of their wards, but there had always been something between Daren and me. My mind flashed back fifteen years, to a time when he was tasked with training us to withstand torture. It took everything he had to push us to our breaking points and then past them, to build up our defenses to the point where we were unbreakable. It had pushed him past his own breaking point. I had pushed him past it, and at that moment, in the dark dungeon of Lockheed Manor, we broke together.

"How many of us have you stolen from our families?" I shot before he could respond and before I could stop myself.

"Enough," he growled, raising a hand to halt any movement in the room.

I had stepped too far, knowing so as soon as the words left my mouth. I shouldn't have pushed him, not in front of the others. There might have been hope for truth between us before, but now that was not possible.

"These humans," he sputtered. "These beasts are nothing more than chattel. They do not deserve your attention. Nor mine." He ran his fingers through his hair and sighed heavily. "Leave us."

Without hesitation, both Ash and Adrien scooped up their plates and glasses and scuttled from the room, dragging whatever bags were theirs with them as well.

Neither Daren nor I moved until the door closed. He swept across the room, and the lights dimmed slightly with his movement. Stopping in front of me, he caressed the side of my face. I kept my eyes locked on his, knowing what was going to come next. "These things happen, not often, but they do, and we do the best we can to deal with them. It's not perfect, but we both know that the Father has a plan and we must trust in him." His smile became feline as his fingertips traced down my neck and across my shoulder. "Let us move past this." He pressed down gently, and I knelt, keeping my eyes locked on his, the way I knew he liked it. "It's been so long," he purred. "Remind me why you are my favorite."

My mind slowed, calming at his touch, as it always did. He

was right, the Father had a plan. I had been in the presence of humans too long, and they had twisted my thoughts. Perhaps that image was one the mother had implanted after she broke into my mind, her last defense to try and break me. I reached for the buckle of his pants, keeping my eyes upward, and did, in fact, remind him why I was his favorite.

CHAPTER SIX

Daren was finally satiated a little before dawn when he dismissed me to the room I was to share with Ash. I didn't look at the girl, lying drugged, motionless on the trundle bed throughout our entanglements. Dressing quickly and slipping into the hall as he fell asleep in the large bed, I held my cloak and boots in my hands so as to not make a sound on the wood floors. At the end of the hall, I made my way up to the third floor, passing one of the barmaids from earlier, in more disarray than even I was. She averted her gaze from me and hurried past. At the top of the stairs, Adrien was leaning on the open doorway, arms crossed in smug self-satisfaction. He was barefoot, his shirt open at the top, and his hair disheveled. As if that wasn't enough, I was smacked with the musty scent of sex that emanated from the room. He was clearly trying to parade his conquest to anyone who would notice. I was overwhelmed with annoyance, not just from his posturing, but that he would now see me slinking back to my own room. The guilt another vestige of my time here.

"Ahh, the poor victim Daren had screaming all night." A smile twisted across his face as I rose to the top step. "Tell me, do you do it to please him, or are you really so loud?"

"Fuck you, Mindwalker," I spat, moving down the hall past him.

He scoffed. "You dug your own grave, hatchwoman." I spun on him, fuming at the derogatory name, but halted for a moment. He stood there unbearably handsome with a smirk plastered on his face. "No one forced you to say those things," he said quieter, tilting his head to the side as he did so.

I swallowed, recognizing the game he was playing at, and took a few steps closer to him. He faced me, propping one arm above the door frame. He was only a few inches taller than me, so I needn't tilt my head back far to look into his eyes as I said in a breathy voice, "Is there something you would like to force me to do? Adrien."

He pulled a sharp intake of breath through his nose and bent closer to me. So close I could feel the warmth from his breath on my neck as he whispered.

"I wouldn't take Daren's leftovers for all the gold in the world, Brigitta."

I hid the hurt behind my own wry smile as I let my nose just barely slide down his jawline. "No, I imagine a night with me would ruin any fun you could have with those sad little barmaids," I whispered back, my lips almost grazing his, before I turned on my heel and strode away.

Finding my room was easy, merely using my magic to feel for Ash's presence behind the closed door. It was only a few steps away, and I could feel the Mindwalker's eyes on me the entire time. They bored into my back as I turned the handle and continued to stare even after I had shut the door on him.

Ash was fast asleep in the bed, head thrown back and mouth wide open, the sheets tangled around her. She didn't move as I slid into the bed beside her and collapsed into exhausted sleep.

***

Morning came far too soon, but Ash let me sleep as long as she could, tossing me a tin of salve to rub away some of the soreness between my legs. Daren had not gone easy on me. I hadn't expected him to. We both knew the harsher he used me, the more distracted from my own thoughts I would be. It mostly worked, as it had been the deepest sleep I had been able to achieve in nearly a week, despite its brevity.

I did not look forward to another day in the saddle but there were 3 days ahead of us. Then, it was a short trip by boat until we reached the way-gate that would transport us home to Wraithland.

We ate a hearty breakfast downstairs in the main dining room. All of us were cordial and kept to light chit-chat before collecting our things, including the girl from upstairs, and loading the horses up.

Again, the ride was quiet, all of us lost enough in our own thoughts. We spent that night camping in the woods, rising early to set off again. By evening, we came to another small town and found the local inn near a crossroads on the way out. Dinner was served in the dining hall as the rooms at this location were only large enough to hold a bed and a fire. We took up half of one of the long wooden tables that were lined up in front of the large fireplace and ate in near silence. The food was fine, if not bland. The ale was better, though I would have preferred wine. Most people barely paid attention to us, which was expected. The town was about a day's ride from the coast, meaning it was a usual pitstop for travelers despite its small size.

Soon after dinner, Daren rose, stating his intentions to sleep, and gave Ash's shoulder a squeeze as he left. We exchanged knowing glances as she, too, excused herself and followed him down the hallway to his room. He was looking for an escape and didn't want Adrien to get the impression he picked favorites. Without similar distraction, I motioned to the barmaid for another ale for myself and reached across the table to scoop up what was left of Ash's. I could feel Adrien's eyes on me, as I had several times over the past few days.

"What?" I grumbled at him while I sipped my pilfered ale.

"Your mind hasn't rested for hardly a moment since we took that girl."

"Stay out of my head," I snapped, looking away toward the hearth in the middle of the room.

"I don't have to be in your head to see it working." He took a drink of his own mug, slate eyes watching me over its rim. "What happened in that house?"

"Nothing." The barmaid appeared at my side with two more mugs of ale. I pressed a coin into her palm, and she left just as quickly as she came.

"I know you saw something," he pushed. "A vision? A memory?" I ignored him and continued to drink. A moment went by, and I reached for the new drink, having finished the other. I watched him chew his lip out of the corner of my eye. I was not interested in continuing this discussion, and there was nothing he could say to keep it going. He had to have known because, after some time, he finally chose a different tact.

"Does it bother you that the warders take a different sister to bed every night?"

My head snapped in his direction, not because of the accusation but because of how he said it. "They are not your sisters."

He put his hands up in surrender. "Noted," he said, looking thoughtful. "But does it?"

"Why would it?" I turned back to the fire, bored.

"There's no jealousy between, uh, women?"

I rolled my eyes. "Why would there be? Sex is useless for us. It's the men who need it all the time. Besides, most of us wouldn't be alive, let alone where we are today if it weren't for Father Pterol and the warders." While we called him the Father, most on the outside called him by his given name, Pterol. When I looked back, I noticed something pass over his face before he scooped up his mug, and while he may have hidden it well, I was not in the mood for games. The last several days had exhausted me, and I wanted nothing more than to drink myself into a nice, deep sleep. I raised an eyebrow at him and asked, "How is it you know so much about us anyway?"

Most people, even in Wraithland, our home, had no idea the Harridan Society existed. The entire society was a secret hidden in plain sight. None of us used our real names in public if we were allowed in public at all. Brigitta Rehault was the name I took as a teenager entering Aelthor's court. She had been the daughter of some backwater lord who was happy to accept a bribe and pretend that I was the daughter he had lost to illness at twelve. For this man to know enough about us to ask such a question raised my suspicions.

Adrien leaned back in his chair, pointing his mug at me. "We are similar, you and I, for I was raised in a home like yours, but for men, like me. Trained to use my powers to serve the king." He said it simply, but I didn't miss the biting way he said the word king.

"That doesn't answer my question."

"Well, when you have been around as long as I have, you pick up a few things. This isn't my first mission with your society. With things moving the way they are, I doubt it will be the last."

I looked into the empty mug in my hand, disappointed, but Adrien flagged down the barmaid before I had the chance to. That was the problem with ale: it took too much to feel anything, a waste of money.

"How old are you then?" I asked, putting the empty mug on the table.

He blew air out of his mouth and leaned forward on the table. "Oh, I suppose I'll be about one hundred and six this year. I'm not interested in doing the math right now." The barmaid set another round of mugs in front of us, though I noticed Adrien hadn't touched the last one she had brought.

"Elven-blooded?" I asked, my eyes dropping to his rounded ears as I scooped up the new mug and took a long swig.

"Something like that," was all he offered. It didn't matter much; everyone in Wraithland had some sort of mixed blood, though most announced their blood estimations with ease. Magic did help many of us live a more youthful life, only showing our age in the last few years of it, but only the Elves had been blessed with truly long lives, and their descendants to varying degrees.

The silence strung out between us, becoming awkward. It was rare that I found myself in the company of someone who knew who I was, what I was, and wasn't also a warder or a sister. I knew how to charm a courtier, or how to steer a conversation for my interests, but Adrien had nothing to offer me. There was no need to charm him or get information from him, and I wasn't even sure if I'd ever see him again. What then was there to say to this man?

"Do you come to the continent often?" It was a pathetic attempt at conversation but it was all I had at the moment. I took a big gulp of my ale, attempting to speed up the process of drinking so I could leave the awkwardness behind and go to bed.

He shrugged, looking as bored of me as I was of him. He turned to the fire. "I've been a scribe in Ontanio for the last twentyish years." I nodded. Ontanio was a large port city on the border of Wreabarroth and Liagheria. As a scribe, Adrien would have access to thousands of important documents possibly to both countries, and with his Mindwalker abilities he could attain just about anything. "You?" he asked, not turning from the fire.

"I've been at the main court of King Agryos for the last two years." My ears heated the moment the words left my mouth. I had never divulged so much information about my mission to anyone other than the warder I was assigned to check in with. Even sisters didn't share such information for the protection of everyone involved. Adrien barely registered the admission, still staring into the fire.

"Will you be going back?"

"Doubtful, but I don't make such decisions." I shrugged, taking another sip. "And you?"

He shook his head. "No, my mission there is complete." He ran a hand under his chin and finally looked up at me. "Can I tell you a secret?" I leaned in with a smile playing on my lips. What could he possibly have to tell me?

"I hate being a scribe." I nearly snorted out my drink as I giggled unexpectedly. The ale must have finally been taking effect.

"It's a shame we don't get to pick our own stories, isn't it?"

"And what would you choose to be if you could?" He looked

at me now, cocking his head to the side, that captivating smile beginning to slide across his face.

Laughing, I finished the mug and reached for the last one. "Nothing that requires a corset, I can tell you that much."

Adrien laughed abruptly, nearly spitting his drink onto the table. "Females wear corsets on Wraithland, too, you know." He wiped his face with the back of his hand.

"None with any sense. They are far too restrictive."

Another moment passed before Adrien became contemplative and asked, "And what if you were to choose your own profession? To not be a Harridan at all?"

A wave of heat washed over me; such a question felt dangerous. I owed my very life to The Society and to the Father; imagining my life outside of it seemed blasphemous. "I don't know that I have the talent for anything other than what I am." I eyed him now warily. "And you?"

He licked his lips and shrugged. "I'd like a house in the mountains, away from people, maybe with some sheep and a wife."

"One love until the end of days," I drawled, taking another large sip. "How very human of you."

"I don't think so. There are plenty of beings that mate for life. The idea of having one person to count on, to share with, it's a far cry from the solitude demanded of us in this life."

"Speak for yourself. I'm surrounded by my sisters."

"But how many of them know everything about you—the things you've done, the places you've been, the feelings you have? How many of them know the you behind all the training?"

He locked eyes with me and held them while he waited for my answer. This conversation had taken a turn I was not comfortable with. These are the kinds of words that could cause trouble for us both. Everyone had secrets, and they stayed secrets because like locked doors, they protected us from ourselves and from each other. Should any of us be taken down or come across a man like him, we would have only our own secrets to share and no one else's.

"There is no other me,'" I said simply. "I am everything you see before you and nothing more." I finished my drink and stood. "Goodnight, Mindwalker."

He looked up at me from under his thick lashes, like he had more to say, but instead, he held up his mug in salute.

"Goodnight, Brigitta," he said solemnly.

***

The following morning, we hired a carriage to take us down the coast to Reinalie. It was a welcome change of pace from traveling on horseback for most of us, though Ash complained of boredom. She had always been the feistiest of us, unable to sit still through lessons, but excelling at physical training and athletics. Another reason why I became the courtier while she remained in the shadows.

Reinalie was one of the few Wraith strongholds on the continent. As a large town just outside the waygate it allowed us to travel to the warded island that contained it without detection. A local shuttle man brought us to the island, avoiding the jagged rocks and rough waters that surrounded it.

The waygate itself could not be seen with the naked eye and was skillfully hidden within a temple on a treacherous island just a mile off the coast. The difficulty of reaching the island safely and the unpredictable weather had successfully deterred even the most devout humans for the last several thousand years. Now, both the temple and the boarding house for pilgrims to the island were run by agents of Wraithland, living in hiding amongst the humans.

Having been constructed in ancient times by the Elves to honor Leaghaire, God of the seas, the temple was simple yet magnificent. It hung off the cliff of the island's far side with columns that dropped down into the water. Below the surface, there was rumored to be a larger temple where the Naiads and other Waterfolk could come and pray to their god—beings that the continent thought they had eradicated.

On the surface, the temple was a simple rotunda supported by eight large pillars on which beautiful carvings of mermaids, Naiads, and long-gone ancient beings sprawled. Each pillar represented a different species of the Waterfolk. Between the pillars, massive windows arched toward the central dome, which was painted in a deep blue. The windows themselves were cast in small blue and green panes that spider-webbed out from the corners. Inside, sunlight filtered through them, causing the polished gray stone floors to dance like water reflecting light. In the center of the rotunda, a freshwater pool fed by magic in the rock below bubbled quietly, spilling over the far edge into a stone trough that led to the back of the chamber. There, a set of stairs led down, the water flowing along the edge of the stone on its way below.

Following the steps around, they would continue to the surface of the sea some fifty feet below. However, after only ten feet, a large opening appeared, cut from the very cliff that the rotunda sat upon. The roof was pock-marked with stalactites that hung down and dripped occasionally. Looking up, we could see the glass bottom of the pool above illuminating the cavern. The water we had followed down the stairs glided along the stone floor and back up the body of a glass statue of a bare-chested women carrying conch shells and re-entering the pool above.

Stepping past the statues, we moved to the back of the cavern. It was utterly empty but for the symbol carved into the stone near the roof. Daren reached up, using his considerable height to trace the symbol with his hand. Behind us, a swirling vortex, a few feet wide, swept up from the floor. Despite its movement, not a speck of dust in the room moved. In the swirling air, I could see the hazy shadows of my home, the green of the grass scattered with rock, and the gray of the sky where it meets the sea beyond. Together, we stepped into the vortex.

CHAPTER SEVEN

The wind whipped my hair, wrapping around my body as we were transported through the space between worlds. It was impossibly dark, so dark I couldn't even see my hand in front of my face; everything swallowed in blackness. The ground, solid under my feet, was the first thing I felt. Then, steadily, light and color returned, like the sunrise on a summer morning. My eyes adjusted quickly, registering fuzzy shapes beyond the whipping wind surrounding us. Slowly, it died down, and we were home.

Taking a deep breath, I pulled the scent of salt-licked grass into my lungs. It had been so long since I had been home. I took a moment to savor everything. The scent, the air that felt almost electric, the sounds of the far-off city, the braying of cattle nearby, the crash of the waves on the craggy coast. There was something about this place that was wholly different from any place I had ever been on the continent.

A roll of my shoulders and a shake out of my limbs brought

me back to the present. Ash smiled at me over the bundle of child in her arms. She knew me well enough to know how I was feeling. The waygate on this side was a simple stone in the middle of a farm field at the tip of the island, and we would have to walk back into the city from here. Nothing more was ever designed to mark its location in order to keep it as secret as possible from the rest of Wraithland. There was a small footpath that led from the field and into a small patch of woods, maintained by the crown for cover. On the other side of the wood, the capital city of Lorcaide sprang up, the castle wall mere feet from the forest's edge.

A huge monstrosity, the castle had massive walls lined with downward-facing golden spikes that gleamed like a serpent's scales in the sun. Above them, the stone towers and turrets stretched toward the sky, creating an ominous ensemble. There were no entry points on this side of the castle, so we had to take the narrow guard path around to the front gate.

The sandy path opened up into a stone roadway as we neared the front of the castle, the city of Lorcaide rising up out of the windswept grass, just feet from the base of the walls. The roadway quickly became crammed with the bustle of bodies and I was overwhelmed by the sounds and stench of the city. Amid the usual shouts and commotion, music bellowed in the city center, the scents of roasting meats and smoking herbs wafting about. It was some kind of celebration. My mind ticked through the dates and nearby holidays, but I couldn't piece together what this event was for.

Wraithland was home to various beings, most notably Elves, Witches, Naiads, Goin Elves, and Gasyters. The latter groups having been banished with the others out of fear and prejudice more than anything else. Gasyters made up the majority of the population. They were physically intimidating, reaching the same heights as Elves, but with bulging muscles, a blue hue to their skin, and two large horns that curled back from their foreheads.

In addition to their natural features, their warrior culture also resulted in markings on their skin that were designed to intimidate. These same markings sparked a similar culture with all the beings here on Wraithland thousands of years later, but instead of intimidation, they denoted achievements and rank in society. Whether scars, brands, or tattoos, the markings were typically given by the Markers, a class of Witch that trained to use their magic to read an individual and place the markings. Those without markings were viewed as lower class, weak, and often treated as such. After more than ten years as one of Harridan's Saithe, I should be covered from head to toe in markings. Even if you discounted the deaths caused by poison, considered by many a weak form of death, my sisters and I would still be some of the most marked on the island. The warders, for the most part, wouldn't be far behind. Unfortunately, markings were not something that was known on the continent, and it would interfere with our work.

Barely anyone even gave us a second look as we moved through the throngs of beings, which was typical due to our apparent status. Soon enough, we were stopped by the crush of bodies gathered near the front gates. Daren was unable to flag down a guard who might recognize him, and we were forced to duck into a side street. If we could get to the main roadway, there was a chance we could move with the crowd toward the main gates.

The side streets were narrow, and the alleys more so. The city had grown quickly in the last few hundred years, forcing homes and shops to be built jammed together. Daren and Adrien led the way while Ash carried the girl, and I followed up in the rear.

Unfortunately, every alley we passed was just as packed as the last. Eventually, Daren chose to just push his way through; while the humans and Witches moved aside easily enough, one particularly large Gasyter held his ground, eying the elf with distaste.

The large Gasyter was covered in markings, including two lines under his right eye and several over the same ear where his dark hair had been shaved back to reveal them. Markings on the face and head were reserved for great warriors, giving him the confidence to ignore our markless group as he crossed his hulking arms and turned back to the street, blocking the path. Daren leaned in and said something I couldn't hear into his ear. The Gasyter reared back, shoving him away, but Daren didn't move. His feet were firmly planted on the ground, with his hands balled into fists at his side and a smirk plastered on his face.

He was leaner than the being before him, but years of training with the Harridans had made him strong and capable. The male Gasyter had no idea what he was getting himself into. I didn't even hide my smile as Daren cocked his head to the side and assessed his prey. The next movements were a flourish of fists and snarls. The crowd parted immediately, shouts of encouragement rising from the other beings. Adrien appeared between me and Ash, ushering us along the outer edge of the crowd and onto the main street.

"Go, we will catch up," he said, launching himself between the two already bloody beings.

Turning to the main street, I saw a band playing music in the back of a carriage as it rolled slowly to the front gates. Behind them, beings danced and threw wildflowers to the bystanders while several men carried a large dragon skeleton. They moved in practiced steps that made the articulated beast seem alive, though the last dragon had left thousands of years ago. Children shouted and squealed with delight at its movements. Looking back down the street, there were several more spectacles that made up the whole parade as it moved toward the castle. I urged Ash along with me, making our way out in front of the carriage with the band. There, a group of guards was leading the way, pushing the crowd back. We were halted there for a moment before Daren and Adrien appeared beside us again. Daren scooped up the girl in his bloodied hands as if she were a rag doll, looking barely worse for the wear I noted. The guards recognized him immediately, and we were ushered in front of the parade.

We followed obediently as Daren stalked ahead, clearly still riled by the encounter. The crowd parted in front of his handsomely haggard appearance without effort from the guards around him.

If the sheer size of the castle wasn't foreboding enough, the front gates were flanked with statues of the god Wraithen. The statues were so detailed that even the black swirls of markings he bore across his chest and arms were included. On the left, he held a great sword over his chest, his eyes closed, and head bowed, with the horns curling back from the top of his head on full display and his hair falling over his shoulders. The other with his arms wrapped around a faceless female, who was pressed against his muscular torso, his eyes looking out toward the entry almost followed us as we entered. Both images were fitting for the god of love and war as much as they were for the court that was held inside.

In the courtyard, Daren called for a guard to prepare a carriage immediately, handing off the child easily. Then turned to us and doled out our tasks. He had always been curt, but now he snapped out orders like a man at war, his eyes hard on us. I knew that he sometimes resented that his place in the Harridans prevented him from markings and the underlying social status it implied. He did not like having his authority challenged or having to prove himself, especially when he was one of the potential candidates for succession to the throne.

"Ash will take the girl to Lockheed by carriage," he said, pointing to the stables. "You will deliver her to Leon. Brigitta will remain here. Father Pterol is staying here to attend the ball tonight, and you will make yourself available for debriefing." He nodded to me and shooed Ash away with his hand.

She turned away with nothing more than a nod to me. I didn't allow my disappointment to show, but I had hoped to return directly to the manor to see my sisters and train in the arena. Staying here tonight meant I would have to dress and attend the ball, prepare to debrief Father at his convenience, and retain my ridiculous court persona. At least in Wraithland, I could get away without a corset.

Daren continued, motioning us to follow as he led the way into the castle. "Adrien, you and I are to attend the king directly. You will have time to wash up for the ball after our debriefing. Brigitta, I trust you can find your way to your rooms and decent attire for tonight." He threw me a look over his shoulder that made me roll my eyes. After so many years, I knew what he meant by decent, and there was nothing decent about it.

We climbed the stairs and crossed into the entry. I couldn't help the sidelong look I gave the Mindwalker, wondering what he had accomplished in his time on the continent that would make him so important to both the Father and the King. Daren paused, turning toward me and I handed off the calfskin binder with my notes to him. He continued to lead us through the massive iron doors to the main hall, where we went our separate ways.

The hall was easily larger than any other I had seen on the

continent by at least double. Large stairs led down onto polished stone floors where a mosaic of designs that depicted the five elements entangled with Ether, the largest in the middle. The central part of the large room was flanked by a row of large columns on either side that held up the immense glass ceiling. At the far end, a raised dais held the king's black iron throne. It was simple, cold, yet dominating. I watched Daren and Adrien stride to the right of the dais, where a door led to the king's private chamber. The former turned, giving me a wry look as he entered. My heart fluttered a bit in response.

I tamped it down and scolded myself for such a girlish reaction before scooting along the outer edge of the hall. I ducked into a passage that led to one of the main stairways. Our room was a private one on the third and top floor of the main part of the castle, in a wing farthest from the main hall.

Few single women were given their own rooms, but as a favorite of both the king and Father Pterol, I was awarded a small space to use, at least that was the arrangement to the public. The location acted not only as a place to keep my courtier clothing but also for any of my other sisters who worked or attended events in the castle. It was a place to hide, stash gear and weapons, or hold clandestine meetings. I touched my hand to the door knocker; it easily recognized my essence and unlocked the door.

***

The room was a good size, with a large fireplace, a sitting area, and a four-poster bed large enough for four to sleep in comfortably. There was a large storage room tucked behind a tapestry to the left of the bed and a separate bathing chamber on the right. A sigh escaped my chest as I looked around the tidy room, a fire already in the grate and several dresses laid out on the bed. It was a nice room by all accounts, and I often preferred it to the shared room I used at the manor, but after so many months away, I yearned for the close quarters and sounds of my sisters scuttling about. Pushing the thoughts away, I began stripping off my worn clothes and made my way to the bathing room.

A few hours later, I had sufficiently scrubbed the filth of days of travel from my skin. A servant brought me some strong coffee to help dye my hair back to its usual brown. While I could, of course, use magic, the cost of a constant glamour for something as silly as hair seemed unnecessary. Letting it dry while I ate a hearty dinner of roast and pasta, I then tied it up in a loose bun and allowed several stray pieces out to frame my face. Makeup had never been something I enjoyed, but I still lined my eyes with dark kohl as many in Wraithland did, along with a touch of white powder to accentuate my paleness. A red tint on my lips was enough to complete the ensemble.

I looked in the mirror, admiring my figure. Months on the continent had weakened me physically, but I also noticed the hard edges of my muscles softening and creating a more feminine figure. Growing up, it was made obvious to me that I was pretty, but it was sometimes contradicted by my height, broad shoulders, and powerful thighs. I was built to be a warrior, and that was fine with me, but in the last few years, I had gained weight in my chest and lost the firmness in my stomach that I had in my twenties. These developments, coupled with the lack of training opportunities on the continent, had resulted in a rounder figure. Here, such changes would be looked down on, but I appreciated the more feminine appeal it gave me.

The dress I had chosen was made of deep red lace and it accentuated my assets with wide straps and a plunging neckline.

The fabric gathered at my hip, flowing down over my thighs and away, with a tall slit that stopped at the top of my thigh. It glittered as I turned in the light, and the small beads scattered throughout caught the light. Instead of heels, I slipped on a pair of black sandals that laced up over my calf.

The rap at my door told me Daren had arrived to escort me to the ball. When I opened it, he was leaning on the door frame, looking down the hall, both hands in his pockets, trying to look casual. The metal rings and spikes that he usually wore had returned to his ears, lip, and left eyebrow, along with the small silver chain he wore around his neck. He'd donned a fancier outfit than usual for the festivities, pants, and a leather vest over a shirt, all in black. The shirt had been left open at the top, showing a hint of the markings hidden beneath. His blonde hair, always a stark contrast to the rest of his appearance, had flopped into his dark blue eyes, adding to his handsome roguish look.

He turned his head toward me and sighed, his body almost sagging with relief as he took in my appearance.

"You look like you need a drink," I said, turning from the door, giving him a view of just how low-cut my dress was in the back.

"I'd prefer something else, but I doubt there's time for that," he drawled. I mixed up a set of strong drinks at the bar beside the sitting area and turned back to find him brooding in one of the chairs by the fire. I handed him the drink and sat opposite him.

"Does this have anything to do with whatever important business you and that mindwalker had with the king?" There was no point in hiding my disdain, Daren knew me well enough.

"Don't tell me you are as infatuated with him as Ash was?" He looked up at me, face impassive, but there was a hint of jealousy in his tone, his body stiff in the chair.

"I don't trust him," I responded honestly. "I want to, but there's just something about him that sets me on edge."

The tension melted away as he leaned back in the chair. "He's loyal enough for a man who doesn't have a choice in the matter." Daren sighed again. "It's what he found that's concerning." I raised an eyebrow, waiting for him to continue, and biting my tongue about whatever he meant about Adrien's choice in the matter. He took a drink, clearly debating how much he should say. Then ominously he said, "There might be a way to break the wards."

A wave of shock rolled over me, my mind reeling with the impact of that statement. This had been what we had been working for, us, our ancestors, working for hundreds of years and thousands of lives toward this one goal. I knew we were close; that's why I was sent to Wreabarroth, but to hear it out loud was stunning.

"Everything is going to happen now. Hundreds of years in the making, all coming together, now, in our lifetimes," he said, looking at the wall beyond me like he could see the future there.

"Is it really so simple?" My voice came out unexpectedly hoarse, and I took a sip of my drink to smooth it over.

"Is it ever?"

He looked at me, his eyes full of emotions that I couldn't read. There were so many questions, so many unknowns, that it was impossible to pick a spot to start. I opened my mouth and closed it again, biting my lip in frustration.

"We should go," I said, finally handing over my nearly full glass. Suddenly, I felt the need to keep my wits about me. He threw it back easily and rolled his shoulders as if willing his body to relax.

CHAPTER EIGHT

The music could be heard halfway across the castle, its rhythmic thudding filling my chest, and begging my aching bones to dance. Balls on the continent were nothing compared to the debauchery and excess of those here. It was lucky I had chosen not to finish my drink earlier since the energy around me was intoxicating enough. Daren led me down the hall silently, nodding occasionally at one courtier or another. He was still lost in thought, the implications of the news having far more effect on his immediate livelihood than mine.

For me, it would be as simple as waiting for my next assignment. If we were to truly go to war, then my services would surely be needed in more ways than one. I would need to get back into shape quickly, but that could wait until tomorrow. Tonight, there was a ball.

We stepped through the main door of the hall, looking out over the melee before heading down the steps and into the throng.

The ballroom had been transformed from its usual austerity, decorations peppered the walls and columns, while magical orbs of light bobbed and bounced among the party-goers. Large cauldrons placed around the room were alight with columns of purple flames. Between the pillars, half-naked dancers of all sexes writhed to the beat of the music, each painted with illuminating paint that reflected the light around them. From the entry, it looked as if the stars were alive and dancing with us.

Across the room, Daren nodded to the King, who raised his glass to us. The iron throne that usually sat atop the dais was replaced with cushioned couches, a low table, and a plush chaise where the king himself lounged. Beside him on the couches sat Adrien, Father Pterol, and Maleathe, a Gasyter, and the king's general. Around them, relaxing on scattered cushions on the floor and steps of the dais, were several of the king's champions, along with barely clothed beings plying them with wine, food, and flirtation.

A servant stepped in front of us as we moved down into the hall, offering tall, stemmed glasses of wine. Daren waved him away and pulled me into the center of the floor, where most people were dancing either as couples or small groups. He spun me around twice before pulling me in close and swaying in time with the music. He was a practiced dancer and swept me around the dance floor as if I weighed nothing. For a moment, I felt the tension in my body ease, as if all my unanswered questions had vanished and I was simply existing in the moment.

The song was over too soon, and in the moment of quiet between songs, Adrien appeared beside us, directing his attention to Daren. "The king would like a word."

"He didn't get enough of me earlier?" Daren grumbled.

"I get the feeling he will be keeping us both close these next few days."

"Months more likely, Mindwalker. Things have been set in motion now." He turned, bowing to me. "Excuse me, Brigitta." He winked and disappeared into the crowd.

"You clean up nicely," Adrien said, taking my hand. He had cleaned up as well, wearing a gray jacket embroidered in blue swirls that brought out the blue in his eyes and matching pants. I let him lead me into the next dance as I debated on what to say, but Adrien beat me to it. "How does it feel to be back here after so much time on the continent?"

"Shouldn't I be asking you that? You were gone much longer."

He shrugged. "It feels different, as I'm sure you know the life of a scribe is not much to speak of, especially compared to this." He waved a hand around them.

I hummed noncommittally. We continued to dance, moving in time to the music without speaking. I still wasn't sure what to say, my thoughts continuously rolling back to his mission, whatever he had done to grant the king the ability to break the wards.

"Did Daren tell you, or did you spy on us in the king's chamber?" he said finally, his eyes narrowing on me.

I looked back at him incredulously, but there was a possibility he had already been in my mind and knew everything anyway. If the mother's powers were strong enough to obliterate my walls, his were likely greater. He might be able to enter my mind without me even knowing. I reminded myself that Daren had said he was trustworthy enough; he was on our side, after all.

"What difference does it make?" I said, keeping my voice flat and uninterested.

"None, I suppose, except the king will be furious."

"Only if he finds out."

"For a Saithe, you are far too easy to read."

"No one has ever said that to me." I laughed. "Though I doubt anyone ever had your, um, skill set."

"My skill set has made me an asset to this country," he said with a raised brow.

"So I hear." I made sure there was a hint of sarcasm in my voice. Our previous conversation in the tavern replayed in my head. There was something about him—things that might have seemed benign from anyone else, but in his voice, they grated against my nerves, putting me on alert.

"You don't appear to be wearing a corset tonight," he said, breaking the silence, his voice softer, his eyes roaming.

"This particular dress doesn't require one," I said sharply.

"Have I done something to offend you?" He looked down at me earnestly, his eyes twinkling as an orb of light bounced over us.

"What is there to offend?" I tried to say it sweetly, but it came out more facetious sounding.

A sneer crossed his face. "So, because I'm not easily manipulated, you can't be bothered to even be civil to me?"

"What reason would I have to manipulate you?"

"None, except it's what you do. It's how you Harridans maintain some semblance of control over your life, a life that you, in fact, have no control over."

"What is it you want with me, Adrien?" I said, pinning him with a look. I could feel the anger beginning to boil inside me. Again, we were crossing a line of conversation I wasn't comfortable with. This man might have thought he knew my sisters, but he didn't know me, and I didn't like being treated like an idiot. He spun me in time with the song. When I came back around, he pulled me in and held me firmly against him so that I could feel the corded muscles under his shirt and coat.

He looked at me intently, and I looked back just as intently, not willing to back down. Never in my life had a man pinned me into a corner I couldn't get out of. Not even Daren. I didn't care that this man might very well be able to squish my brain with his power. I was not going to back down.

"I saw something in you in that house." He pulled me tighter, his voice but a whisper in my ear as we continued to move with the music, no one near able to hear over the din of the bass. "That mother was the most powerful female mindwalker I had ever encountered. Almost as strong as me. She broke down your walls without trying. I saw it. I saw it on your face, and I saw it in her mind. It was only a second, but it was enough to know that you are not like the others. I—"

"Don't," I snapped, frustration gnawing at my nerves with every word. "I told you to stay out of my head."

"I wasn't trying. I was in hers. What I saw was only what she saw in you, and she hesitated because of it." The words tumbled out of him in a torrent. "She could have killed you in a moment, but she hesitated, and it cost her her life."

"Enough." I threw magic out of my skin at every place our bodies connected. No one else would see it, but he would surely feel it, like a zap of current pricking him. "You and your kind are a plague on magic wielders. Taking what does not belong to you." I turned to pull away, but his grip became vice-like, his hand on my back like steel as he moved me across the floor still in time with the dance. He spun me again and then pulled me close against his chest. I ran through the options in my head, all the different ways to handle this that wouldn't cause a scene, but half the people in this room were as well-trained as me. They would sense the commotion no matter what I did. For now, I had to play along with whatever game this was.

"You think I asked for this?" he whispered in an icy voice. "You think I want to beg at the feet of the king for the mere right to live? Almost everyone like me is dead, murdered in their cribs because they fear us, what we can do. Those that are allowed to survive are kept on a leash so tight we can barely breathe. Don't fool yourself into thinking your training could stop me. If I wanted to break into your mind, I could with barely a fight; I've done it plenty of times with your kind. In that way, you are no different than a slug that crawls along the ground." He took a shuddering breath and stepped away, releasing me. The song still played and dancers around us still moved to its beat. He stood, looking me up and down, with a blank expression before turning and leaving me alone.

CHAPTER NINE

It wasn't more than a second before a handsome half-Gasyter scooped me up. Trying his hardest to charm away whatever argument had just occurred. I let him spin me around and pull my backside tight against him with the gyrations of the music for several songs. Eventually, Father stepped in, artfully guiding me away from the central part of the hall. Outside, the columns, tables, and booths were placed to allow for private conversations, gaming, and whatever other debauchery the guests had in mind.

"Tell me, darling, how was your trip?" he asked casually, placing my hand in the crook of his elbow as we glided toward the edge of the festivities. Father Pterol was tall and lean, with looks that strongly resembled Daren and his brother, King Aelthor. Most everyone in the Aellonson line had a strong resemblance. With the dwindling number of Elves on Wraithland after the wars, males took to siring as many sons as possible with as many women of Elven-blood as possible, resulting in dozens of closely related offspring. While the identity of royal offspring was a close-guarded secret, it was impossible to deny the features that the former King Aelward had passed on to his progeny. They all had the same sandy hair, square jaw, and pale blue eyes. Father, however, had a set of markings that ran under his right eye and into his now-receding hairline.

"All went well enough," I responded, not sure how much he wanted me to divulge in such a public place.

He lowered his voice and bent slightly toward me to avoid being overheard. "I haven't had time to read your notes, do give me the short version if you can."

"Oh, of course," I laughed as if he had just whispered a joke in my ear, then lowered my own voice, letting the words tumble out of me quickly. "There was a misunderstanding during one of King Zakia's trips to Chiotania last year that raised tensions between the two allies. Shortly after, the Chiotanian ambassador died under mysterious conditions. The paperwork for a new ambassador was mishandled, and a new one never instated when King Zakia fell ill a few months ago. He died recently, heir-less, and left rule of his kingdom to his wife. Though some say that she couldn't hold on to her husband in his lifetime, how could she be expected to hold on to a kingdom? Of course, there were other less important events, but I do believe the goal was achieved."

We passed by a group of pirate merchants, the only type of men who dared to bring goods back and forth to Wraithland. Moreanne sat amongst them, skillfully beating them at cards. Her eyes flicked up to me briefly, the only acknowledgment that she would give of our relationship. She looked even more the part of a pirate since the last time I saw her: in linen breaches, a man's shirt, and a captain's hat with a few visible marks on her dark skin.

Her once beautiful curly hair was subdued into locks that were tied back from her face. She had become Wraithland's most notorious smuggler—ruthless and smart, she was able to get goods and information from anywhere. Little did anyone know how much the Harridan Society aided in her quests. I very much looked forward to an evening sipping wine and listening to some of her tales.

Father paused on the threshold of the veranda and turned to observe the crowd. The cool night air caressed my heated skin.

"There is one more thing that was not included in my notes, Father," I said before I could think better of it, my voice hushed. He inclined his head toward me in a silent command to go on, and I felt the rush of air as he wrapped us in a cocoon of privacy. "On my last evening in Bernitra, I observed a clandestine meeting. The group was debating documents about a prophecy that stated a boy would put an end to the Elven kingdoms of dark and light. I believe they thought Wraithland was the Elven Kingdom of Dark and the Kingdom of Eldred to be the Light." I could see his interest waning, the silly legend of humans of little importance, but I pushed on, saving the best for last. "Father, there was a pure-blooded Elf in attendance who spoke of Eldred as if he were still alive."

Father's handsome, scarred face remained impassive, but it was impossible to miss the darkening of his eyes and the stiffening of his body beside me.

"You are positive the tips of his ears weren't even slightly shortened," he asked, watching me intently. I nodded calmly, having expected the question. He put a warm hand over the top of mine and turned his head toward the dais. The king's eyes found us immediately as if Father had pulled on some invisible tether and he beckoned us with a soft wave of his hand.

Adrien was again seated on the dais beside the king, the small smile playing on his lips faded as we neared. Maleathe noted his change in demeanor and turned, giving us his full attention. Again, the rush of air that signaled a magic barrier slid around us.

"My Saithe has witnessed the presence of a pure-blooded elf on the continent," he said without preamble. Gesturing me to sit on a couch opposite the king, who sat up slowly, trying not to draw attention from the champions and servants surrounding the dais.

King Aelthor had grayed with age, his beard only holding hints of the red and brown that once colored it. His light hair fell forward over the gnarled marking that encircled the crown of his head. It shimmered with the tiny silver thread pierced into the skin with it, the marking only allowed to the king, worn in place of any man-made crown.

"Brigitta, a pleasure." He smiled broadly, showing a set of straight white teeth. "Do tell us in detail what you saw." I glanced hesitantly to the left, where Adrien and Maleathe sat in rapt attention. "I assure you they would have to know sooner or later. Please, tell us everything."

I reiterated my story exactly as I had for Father. Noting each of their reactions, none more surprising than Adrien, who didn't seem shocked to hear any of it.

"There hasn't been even a half-blooded elf on the continent in generations; where could he have come from?" Father commented from his perch beside me on the arm of the couch.

Aelthor shook his head, "If there is a pure-blooded Elf alive on the continent, it changes everything." His eyes narrowed on me, the teardrop-shaped markings under his eyes scrunching with the movement. "We have a gift among us that can corroborate her story." He looked over his shoulder at Adrien. An icy chill entered my veins, as I realized he was asking Adrien to enter my mind.

"My Liege, you know as well as I that my girls are loyal beyond measure." Father put a reassuring hand on my shoulder as if my well-being actually mattered. He was worried about the secrets I held, secrets that could cost the lives of many.

"It's not a question of loyalty," Aelthor spat, his body going taut. "We must be absolutely sure of what was seen before we act on this information."

A whisper echoed through my mind. My eyes shot daggers at Adrien, who was staring back intently, his face serene, calm.

I won't enter your mind, Brigitta. His voice brushed the back of my skull in silky softness.

Then what is this? I answered back through my own mind.

A conversation, that's all. I don't have to break your walls; you can pull the memory and show it to me in the Ether between us. I don't have to go any further than this.

And the king?

He will never know I did not violate you.

The other three men were still speaking to each other animatedly, but I couldn't hear them. I took a deep breath and closed my eyes, searching for the image of the elf as he ran through the street, blonde hair flying behind him. Unsure of my next steps, I simply willed the image away, picturing it floating in the black space behind my eyes. I heard the sharp intake of breath in my mind, and my eyes flew open.

Adrien's eyes were still intent on me as he spoke loud and clear over the voices of the others. "I've seen it. Tall, blonde, eyes turquoise like the sea, and ears sharper than any I've seen in this life."

A hush settled over them. The moments stretched out like hours as I continued to stare into those gray-blue eyes.

"Maleathe." Aelthor was the first to speak, his voice husky and commanding. "Gather Daren, Talrick, and the other council members and sober them up. There is work to be done," he said, standing abruptly, causing us all to jump up around him.

"Adrien, take your rest while you have it; we may have use for you sooner than we thought." The king extended a hand to my lower back, curling his fingers gently against my bare skin there and ushering me toward the opposite couch. "Perhaps the lovely Brigitta could keep you company. I've noticed the two of you can barely keep your eyes off each other," he said, stepping behind me and down off the dais.

The king had no love of matchmaking; rather, the suggestion was a veiled command for one of us to keep an eye on the other, the target of the command unclear. Plastering a light-hearted smile on my face, I took Adrien's outstretched hand and let him lead me off the dais.

We moved silently through the hall, passing all manner of being, and all manner of debauchery. I caught Daren's eyes following us even as he danced with a beautiful Elven-blooded girl, her blonde curls bouncing with the movement.

***

In the corridor outside the main hall, we passed several beings copulating in doorways and recesses like animals. Keeping my eyes ahead, I followed Adrien's lead toward the stairs, and up to the second floor. Passing through one hall and then another, he eventually paused at a door.

Opening it, he gestured for me to enter without looking at me. Was it possible that he was nervous? I shrugged off the thought and entered. His rooms were the mirror of mine, but larger, with a bay window so large the arched windows touched the ceiling. I made a show of looking around the rooms as he followed me in and headed straight for the bar. A moment later, he found me leaning on the sill of the window, looking out over the treetops to the ocean beyond. The drink he handed me was dark and strong, scratching my throat as it slid down, exactly what I needed.

"Thank you," I said earnestly, turning toward him and resting my hip on the sill. He was close enough to feel the heat coming off his body. He smelled like parchment and damp earth after a spring rain, my face flushing at the thought. I pushed my magic out, feeling for any presence, magic or otherwise, that could overhear our conversation.

"For what?" His voice was husky in my ears.

"You lied to the king on my behalf."

"There was no lie in my words."

"The implication was there."

He sighed, touching my elbow lightly. Looking up, his eyes shimmered, searching my face. "There is a fine line that I walk with my gifts. Certain lines can only be crossed at a great cost, not just to others but to myself. I did it as much for me as for you."

The honesty was refreshing, but I wasn't here for pleasantries. It was my duty, as implied by the king, to perform. I leaned in closer, setting my drink on the sill with one hand and letting the other trail up the buttons on his shirt. Slowly, I arced it upward around one button and then another until I reached the top, where I hooked my finger in his shirt and pulled him close.

His lips were soft and warm. They parted, inviting me in for more. He leaned toward me, one arm snaking around my middle while the other trailed up the bare skin on the back of my arm. My skin prickled at the touch, heating with a need I hadn't felt in some time. Sliding closer, my knee traced the inside of his thigh.

A strangled growl escaped his chest, and he pulled back, bringing his hand up to cup my face as he looked down at me, his eyes alight with desire. He shook his head, pulling away slightly.

My face scrunched in confusion, gently pulling him back.

"Forgive me, Brigitta. It's nothing to do with you." He scooped up his drink and stepped past me. Running his fingers through his hair, he looked back at me wryly. "It's more that I have a hard time being aroused when someone is commanded into my bed."

It was like being doused by ice water, an immediate shock followed by the drain of heat that had built up in me. I lifted my glass from the sill and took another hearty sip. It was rare that anyone elicited such a reaction from my body. Shaking the thoughts from my head, I leaned back on the sill.

"There was no command to do anything other than keep you company." I crossed one arm under my elbow, holding my drink aloft. "In any case, I can't be sure which of us is truly meant to keep an eye on the other.

"The implication was there." He parroted back to me with a smile. "But regardless, you should stay the night if only to save my reputation."

I laughed. "As if anyone would notice one way or the other."

"Daren would," he said, watching me, gauging my response. I pursed my lips. He was bold but not entirely wrong. "I'll leave you the bed." He pushed off the banister and set his drink down beside the couch. He pulled his shirt over his head in one fluid motion, revealing a well-muscled torso and biceps that had been hidden until now. The dark ink of a large marking in the shape of a serpent carved its way from the bone of his left hip, up his ribs and chest, and over his shoulder, where the serpent's eyes stared out in a vicious smile at me. I took another sip of my drink, my mouth suddenly dry. He tossed the shirt with a smirk and scooped up his drink again. I caught it easily.

"There's no point in being chivalrous with me; I've shared beds with enough men, alive, dead, or otherwise." I shrugged.

His laugh filled the room. It was genuine and bright, and I felt the muscles in my shoulders relax slightly.

"I suppose I can't argue with that," he said, striding to the bed and flopping on it with a flourish. His smirk now more of a grin. He crossed one ankle over the other and threw one arm over his head to rest on it.

I smiled demurely and made my way around the other side, setting my drink on the bedside table and tossing his shirt onto the bed before slipping the straps of my dress off. It fell to the floor in a puddle, leaving my naked body on full display. Two could certainly play at this game.

His lips parted slightly in surprise. My nipples went firm at the sudden chill. I bent low, scooping up the dress to hang on one of the hooks by the bed, and then turning slowly to give him the full view. I heard the ice in his drink clink behind me and turned back. He was watching me, teeth resting on the edge of his glass as if he stopped mid-motion. Bending again, I climbed onto the bed beside him as if I wasn't able to reach the shirt from its edge. Then, I reared back on spread knees to pull the shirt over my head. When his shirt was finally in place, I licked my lips and flopped down on the pillow; my face screwed up in a triumphant evil grin. If we were playing games I was going to win.

He hadn't moved until the moment I stopped. When he finally lowered his glass, his lips parted, and let out a heady breath. Our eyes met across the bed, and I had to purse my lips to hold in the laugh bubbling up inside me, my face reddening with the effort. Then he let out a laugh.

It was a full-bellied, no-holding-back kind of laugh that made my heart leap in my chest. I couldn't stop myself from laughing with him. My body was electrified with a sheer glee that I hadn't felt since I was a child. He had to set down his drink to wipe the tears from his eyes. Taking a deep breath, he tried to calm himself, only to erupt again, this time in more of a giggling, choking laugh. A laugh that cracked something inside me that I didn't know was buried there, and I cackled. I cackled so hard I coughed and sputtered until we both ended up wheezing in the bed beside each other.

"They certainly teach you well in Lockheed," he said finally between coughs and giggles.

"They do certainly teach us many things," I said, catching my breath and lying back on the pillow, arm behind my head. "Though I still find it hard to believe you know so much about us. Aside from Aelthor and Maleathe, I was unaware anyone outside The Society was permitted to even know of our existence, let alone such intimate details. I feel like you know everything there is to know about me. Tell me about the place you hailed from. You said it was a place like Lockheed? Does that mean there are more like you, men with your gifts, trained like us?"

The smile on his face died, and I regretted my question immediately. We had had a moment of complete freedom and I had ruined it because, of course, I had. That was something that was never trained out of me. If there was a way to ruin a perfect moment, I would find a way to do it.

"No, no, there aren't any surviving members of my society." He sighed, rolling onto his side. He gazed down at me with an open, earnest look. He was going to tell me the truth, and it was going to change something for me. I knew it before the words even came out of his mouth by the look on his face. I had seen it so many times from so many lovers and marks. It was my job to lure them into this place of safety, of comfort, so that they would share the darkest parts of themselves, giving me the keys to control them. This time, I hadn't asked for this, and I hadn't conned it from him; he was offering it up of his own free will, and he knew it, and that scared me.

"Aelthor had them all executed. The manor closed, its Father murdered in his bed." He blew a large gulp of air between his teeth. "Likely by one of your sisters. All when he realized we could not be controlled so easily. When he saw that by seeing into people's minds, we could see their motivations, their manipulations, their deepest desires, and we could then bend them ourselves. We became the manipulators, the controllers. Having spent our youths counting every cruel thing they did to us when we found ourselves capable of turning the tables, we gave it back tenfold."

"In the end, only a few of us were left alive." He rolled onto his back, staring up at the fabric of the bed above. "I survived because a man like Daren cared for me. He saved me by giving the king the one thing that would stop me from ever breaking my oath to him. And because of it, I became the king's servant 'till the end of my days, even after the rest of my brothers were taken from me."

I held my breath, not daring to ask what that one thing was, not sure I even wanted to know.

"My mother and sister."

His family. The key that Daren spoke of when we first met. That was the thing that hung over his head, keeping him dutifully working for the crown. Loyal enough, Daren had said.

Scared enough, should have been what he said.

CHAPTER TEN

We continued to talk into the night, albeit about much more pleasant topics: the places we had seen, the food we had eaten, and books we had read. All of it trivial but comforting; I hadn't been able to speak my opinions freely for so long. I woke up feeling refreshed despite only getting a few hours of sleep. The sun streamed in through the large window, illuminating the dust as it floated sleepily in its rays. The drink I had from the night before still sat on the bedside table; half gone. I couldn't remember the last time I had fallen asleep without the weight of drink or exhaustion of sex to pull me under.

Rolling over, I realized Adrien wasn't in the bed beside me; the sheets chilled as if he had left long ago. Sitting up, I searched the room to find him happily sprawled on a couch with a steaming mug of tea and a large book in his lap. The low table in front of him was topped with an array of breakfast foods. He still had not bothered with a shirt, and the view was pleasing to the eye, at least.

I sat up and stretched wide, running my hands through my hair only to realize I had never let it down last night. I took a moment to pull the pins out and let it fall over my shoulders. I ran my fingers through it quickly and tied it back up sloppily.

"I supposed being in the king's good graces has its benefits," I said, rolling out of the bed and making my way over to the couch opposite him.

"What makes you so sure it isn't you he's trying to spoil."

"It wasn't me sitting on the dais with him at the start of the evening," I said, purposely keeping my response vague.

"Well, either way, I'm happy to share." He gestured to the feast in front of us. There was a plate adorned with various pastries, another with fruit delicately arranged in the shape of a bird, and several others that contained cured meats, soft-boiled eggs, fried potatoes, and stewed beans. This was a wildly wasteful serving for just two. While this would be expected of the nobility on the continent, here in Wraithland, beings would kill to eat this well.

I hesitated, taking in the abundance, guilt washing over me. What would happen to the leftovers if we didn't finish it all? I debated the logistics of sneaking it out in my dress but was interrupted from plotting by Adrien.

"I asked the maid who brought it all and she said the leftovers go to the kitchen staff or others who work at the castle, but it won't go to waste." My eyes shot up to his as I mentally checked the barricades I had in place. "Don't look at me like that." He closed his book with a snap. "I grew up here too, you know. It's been a while, but I haven't forgotten how it is here, I don't need to read your mind to know how you're feeling, because I've never been served this way, and I'm feeling it too. You, on the other hand..." He shrugged and sat up. "I'm surprised to see hesitation."

"You think the king would treat me like this?" I scoff. "The best breakfast I've been served in this castle is stewed sausage and beans on day-old toast. Whomever the scribe was that you killed must have been an important one."

He leaned forward, grabbing one of the dainty pastries and stuffing it in his mouth. Perhaps he would not be so easy to goad into sharing information. Not that it mattered. He was not a mission for me, and his information had no bearing on my actions, but for some reason, I wanted to know. Pulling my eyes from him, I found an empty plate and began to load it up with meats and fruit, my favorites.

"I wasn't sent to kill anyone," he said finally, reaching forward again, this time pilfering a sausage from a nearly toppling tower of them.

"What then? You just provided information for twenty celibate years."

"Scribes are not celibate by any means."

I lifted an eyebrow and took a bite of tropical fruit that was sweet and juicy. I didn't remember the last time I had anything so delicious.

He cleared his throat. "Considering your position, I suppose it doesn't matter if I tell you that the king sent me to find a very old book—or a section of it anyway, that had the keys to unlocking the wards on the island."

"And it took all twenty years to find this book?" I said, sucking the juice out of another piece of fruit.

"Most ancient things have been washed from the continent. Any mention of magic destroyed, except for in the legends of gods and Elves. What few relics remain are closely coveted by their owners, or hidden in forgotten places. I wasn't the first or only one on this mission. I just happened to be the lucky one."

I licked my lips, thoughts, and missions coming together in my brain. "If it was so unclear when Aelthor would have this book, if ever, what business did Father have sending me to disrupt things so badly in Wreabarroth and Chiotania? Seems like a waste of effort and money for something so unsure."

He shrugged. "I had been closing in on the book for some time. I knew I would have it this year or next." The silence stretched between us as he watched me continue to put food in my mouth. I set down the plate, chewing and swallowing my last bites, before reaching to pour myself a cup of tea from the steaming pot.

"So, you find a way to bring the wards down. My sisters and I break the kingdom's ability to respond to a threat. Seems like all is in place for the whole of Wraithland to rise up and take back the continent like it's always been planned." I took a hesitant sip, letting the silence prickle. Something in the back of my mind won't let go of the idea that I couldn't trust the man across from me, despite his frankness, despite how he is in the king's inner circle, despite his promise not to enter my brain, despite even the time we had spent lying next to each other talking last night. Despite it all, something gnawed at me that I could not put a finger on. "Then I see a pure-blooded elf, and now what?"

"That's for the king and the council to decide."

"And the prophecy about the boy?"

"I don't think that's anything to worry about," he said quickly with a wave of his hand as he reached for another pastry, appearing to have relaxed. "The humans have hundreds of prophecies, Aelthor has known of this one for a long time."

"And you, I assume, have heard of it before now?"

He nodded, taking a sip of his tea. The silence returned, and I picked up my plate again. My mind was whirling with the implications of the elf. Even if the prophecy meant nothing, a pure-blooded elf doesn't just come out of nowhere. Was it even worth it to try? The Elves would likely fight us if we tried to take back the continent. Would it be possible to just break the wards and become another country on Primthera? Wraiths would then have the freedom to travel and trade in the open. Then there was the question of the human's disdain of magic. Would they look down on beings different from them, like the Waterfolk, or the Gasyters? I shook the thoughts from my head. This is why there were people like Aelthor and Father in power. People with wisdom and foresight that could guide the rest of us through the murkiness of politics. None of this was my mission.

"What are you shaking your head at?" Adrien smiled at me over his mug. His eyes twinkled like a child.

"Nothing." I took another bite of food, and then before I could think better of it, I added, "What was it that you saw in my head before that made the other Mindwalker pause?" The words fell out of my mouth like a pile of shit. *What a subject change,* I chided myself silently.

He had just taken a bite of something and paused mid-chew, his eyes dimming. He swallowed hard, his brows furrowing.

"Are you sure you want to know?"

"I think you were going to tell me last night, before…before I said those things." I had called him and his kind a plague on magic wielders.

Certain types of magic had the power to destroy people from the inside out. It was that kind of magic that the humans feared, but it was also that fear and hate that had entire races of beings locked away on this gods-forsaken island. And the same magic and fear that had ended his entire brotherhood. I had said them in anger, and it was unkind.

He sighed heavily. "It's your soul."

I coughed, setting down my plate and reaching for a glass of water on the table.

"You can see someone's soul?" I asked when I recovered myself.

His face pinched into a wince and he scrubbed his hand down his face. "Not exactly. A person has many layers, but at the core, you can see what truly makes them, *them*. I don't know if it is a soul exactly, that's just what I call it."

"And at my core?" I put my hands on my knees, bracing for whatever may come, expecting a fiery pit or the inky blackness of death or something terrible. I had spent my life taking the lives of others, and while it was for a good cause, the future of our people, it didn't mean that it was a good thing to be doing.

He took a long inhale, blowing the air out heavily between his lips. "Brokenness," he said softly. While I had expected something much darker, more sinister, this small admission felt like a punch to the gut. I was a broken being because, of course, I was; how could anyone fuck, and kill, and walk away with a smile on their face like me?

"Compared to many of your other sisters, that's a good thing," he added quietly.

"You've seen in my sister's heads?"

Nodding, he sat up straighter, looking me directly in the eyes. He spoke slowly like he was speaking to a child. "There was a time when Pterol wanted to know if his training techniques were working as intended. It was after my brothers were slaughtered; they wanted to know that it wouldn't happen again with the Harridans." My stomach began to churn angrily.

"So, they had you go into their minds?"

He nodded, his eyes glistening. "It was before your time. I had to assess every single one who had completed the Ascension and then the assigning. It was one of the worst times of my life. To violate them like that, day after day, and lay them bare in front of Pterol. These powers, they can be terrible, and horrifying, and it's no easy task to stay on the right side of them." He took a deep, steadying breath. "For many of your sisters, there is nothing but blank space. Any individual thoughts have been pushed so far down there is no finding them. They only know how to follow orders, without thinking beyond the immediate moment."

He stayed quiet for a moment and I realized I was clenching my teeth so tight my jaw would begin to ache soon. I rolled the words over in my mind, each one a crack in the foundation of what I thought I was.

"And is that what they intended?" The last word left a foul taste in my mouth.

"Yes"

"But, I'm not that." My voice was not my own; it was deep and raw. Father intended for his daughters to be blank vessels, to have their very sense of self ripped out of them.

"No, you are much more." He moved beside me, clasping my hands in his own. They were warm and calloused. My stomach churned again; a lump forming in my throat. "Broken means you can be fixed—er, pull yourself together, make decisions about your future. It means you have a choice."

"And my sisters don't have a choice."

I didn't look at him. My mind was hurtling between the past and the present. Between moments when we blindly followed orders without question, any pausing beat out of us early. Don't think, just act. Thinking will get you killed, fall back on your training, and your instincts, they will lead you.

"You know what it was like growing up there. The choice was

beaten, raped, and starved out of them." There was a softness in his voice that did little to comfort me as it yanked me back to the present, to the man beside me who was telling me that I was broken and my sisters were mindless soldiers.

"But why not me."

"Your layers were stronger."

Father intended to break us; his daughters, women he found collected and raised, but daughters nonetheless, to the point that we were nothing but hollowed-out shells of being. We owed him everything, that's what they told us, and we did owe him. They fed, clothed, and trained us. Their methods were harsh, but we were given the best trainers on the island, the best tools, the best food, everything so we could be the best, the strongest, the fastest, the most cunning. And we were. We had grown into an army of women who were so capable, but it had cost us everything. And we continued to give even our lives over to him, to his cause. The debt was overpaid.

The cause wasn't all his, though; it was the cause of the thousands of Wraiths on the island. The freedom we all deserved. The same freedom that was forcibly stripped from women and girls like me. From Leeta and Isadora, the beautiful little girl whose family did nothing but bring her into this world and try to protect her. My mind was warring with itself.

I pulled my hands from Adrien's grasp and pushed them into my hair. My head was threatening to explode while my stomach turned over and over again. Everything he said made sense, but I couldn't bring myself to believe that Father, or King Aelthor for that matter, would become so desperate that they would consciously strip the very life from children. The same young girls who put their trust in them and the same young girls they stole and lied to about it. Everything made sense and everything contradicted all at the same time.

It was possible that Adrien was making it all up, that this was some manipulation, but to what end? We had spent the entire evening together, but there had always been that nagging feeling that he wasn't entirely telling the truth, that I couldn't trust him. Now was no different, but how could I ask him for proof of any of this?

Standing, I moved to the bed and pulled my dress from the hook. There would be no show this time.

"I need to get some air," I said simply, going to the door as I pulled the dress's straps over my shoulders and scooped up my sandals. There was no need to let on about all the feelings going on in my head. "Thank you for last night," I said, closing the door behind me.

CHAPTER ELEVEN

The sun was just reaching full height as I arrived at Lockheed Manor. It was just as I remembered it. The narrow dirt drive that snaked between the rises and juts of rock, as the grassland gave way to the handful of small mountains beyond. The manor itself was a plain stone building with four stories and turrets on each corner. It was surrounded by fields of grazing lands for cattle, the main source of income for Father Pterol, or the whole of Wraithland really.

I left the horse I had borrowed from the castle in the barn with the novice and made my way into the front door. The main floor was set up like any other manor home, a useful facade at least. It included ballrooms, dining halls, kitchens, a guest residence fit for the king on his rare visits, as well as ancillary rooms mostly for entertainment including music, art, gaming, and the like, such as the usual business of a manor. Above that, the second floor contained Father's private quarters, his office, guest rooms, and a parlor. The third floor was reserved for the warders and the sisters who remained at the estate full-time. The fourth and final floor was where one would typically find the servant's areas and also where our dorms were. It made sense, seeing as the sisters and novices managed all of the house's needs. Even visiting nobles from other corners of the country were none the wiser when staying in the house, that it was truly a working school, training facility, and more for the Harridans.

The front door opened to a round entrance hall that was flanked on either side by a set of grand staircases spiraling toward each other and the second floor. I stepped over the threshold to find Ash, lounging on the curved rail of the left-hand stair, cleaning her nails with a knife.

She was dressed in full fighting leathers with various weapons strapped over her, including two sword handles that poked out over her shoulders. Sisters were rarely allowed to spend time on the main floor, let alone in full battle garb, but then, Ash had always been one to push the boundaries of propriety. There was no stifling my smile as I approached her.

"Someone is in trouble," she sang from her perch as I approached, drawing out the syllables in the last word.

"Me? What could I have possibly done?"

"You left the freaking castle without permission." She sat up, eyes wider than normal, her face pinched in shock. While she liked to push back against the rules, I had always been a dutiful follower of every single one. My brows furrowed as my mind traced the last few hours over. I had not, in fact, asked for permission to leave.

"Shit." I bit my lip.

"I guess all that freedom on the continent really does go to your head." She laughed, hopping down to the floor.

"How did you know?" I asked as she slung her arm around my shoulder and led me around the corner where the hidden door to the lower levels was.

"Markham," she said, punching the space in the wall that unlocked a hidden door behind it. The door opened to a dimly lit stairwell below the main floor. "Daren sent word to let him know if you showed up. After you left the castle. You were supposed to wait there for your next mission." Of course, Daren would know I had left, and of course, he would have sent a firenote. How had I even done that? The punishment would be severe. I blanched. It would be severe because I was supposed to be a mindless warrior without feelings or thoughts of my own, not thinking beyond the mission, which, least of all, was to stay in the castle until needed.

"What?" Ash paused with me at the top of the steps, eyebrows pinched in concern.

"I just can't believe I did that."

"I'm sure it will be fine; Leeta and Tris have done it before, too, after a long trip. A light whipping can be a good welcome home." She laughed. I forced a smile and let her lead me down the arcing stone stair to the levels below where we had spent most of our lives.

The stair led down to a large, bright expanse, supported by columns of stone. In the center, a large glass ceiling that was the base of the reflecting pool above allowed the sun's rays to penetrate the darkness. Around the edges and dark corners, small holes coated with gold reached up to the surface to reflect the sunlight, illuminating the space.

We didn't hesitate to walk out to the deserted training arena. Most sisters who were staying here would be working chores or enjoying midday meals now. I picked up a sword from the rack and tossed it a few times, giving it a swing or two, becoming reacquainted with the feel of it in my hands. Beside me, Ash began walking through the steps of a warm-up with one of the swords from her back. We fell into a practiced rhythm and were soon sweating, me more than her.

My arms quickly tired from the movements at the fully weighted swords, but I pushed through, my head still churning with what Adrien had said. I had no recollection of him being here, but then again, he was older; it could have easily been before my time. *Your layers were stronger*, he had said. If he was telling the truth, did that mean that there could be others like me? Others that still had a choice. But a choice of what?

"What do you think you would be doing if you weren't a Saithe?" I asked between gritted teeth as I swung the sword fluidly in front of me.

"Like a Tachdre or a Braithe?" she asked, naming off other positions sisters could hold as Harridans. We lunged in unison, thrusting our swords forward.

"No, like if this place didn't exist, if we could just be whatever we wanted."

"Uhhh, what else is there to be? If I wasn't a Saithe here, I would do it elsewhere."

"Okay, well, what if there were no good reasons to kill?"

"What are you trying to ask me, Catherine?" Her tone becoming incredulous.

"If there was peace, no one needed killing, no kingdoms needed to be stolen from, nothing like that. What would you do?"

"Well, we both know I'm shit at just about everything besides this, so I supposed I'd have to start fighting for sport like they do in the city."

We continued the prescribed movements, thrusting and

swinging the swords in unison. Grunts and heavy breathing blew out of me, reminding me how out of shape I was.

"Let's spar." Ash rolled her shoulders and turned to face me.

"Sure." My arms were already sore, and my legs were beginning to burn, but diving in head first was the best way to get back into it. "Don't go easy on me," I huffed.

"Wouldn't dream of it." She gave a smug smile back.

I ran at her and she dodged, slicing her sword toward my middle, a little too close for comfort. Facing each other again, she cocked her head to the side with a raised eyebrow, baiting me. I charged again, this time our swords clashed, ringing throughout the arena. I raised my foot to take out her legs, but she jumped to the side and charged again. We went back and forth like that for some time, always having been a close match.

"Have you seen Isadora?" I said, putting a hand up for a quick breath.

"Who?" Ash stuck her sword in the sand and rested on it, finally breathing heavily as well.

"The girl we took from Wreabarroth."

Her face crinkled in confusion. "No. I took her to the infirmary as directed and that's the last of it. It's not my job to watch after younglings and novices."

"And you aren't the least bit concerned for her well-being?"

"Should I be? This is not the first child I've brought here; you know."

"It's not?" I said, not hiding my surprise.

"Where do you suppose all the new sisters come from?"

"Most of us were orphans already, yeah?"

"And how many of them do you think last here? You and I both know only the strongest survive, and the strongest need to be sought out." She picked up her sword and dusted it off, inspecting the edges. My heart plummeted to the bottom of my stomach, my hands suddenly itching with tension.

"And this is of no concern to you?" I said, rolling my wrists.

"Should it be?" She sheathed her sword across her back and crossed her arms. Her tone had turned venomous. "This is our duty to our people. We are the lucky few who prevailed, proved our worth, and the crown rewards us for it. Children in the streets die every day from starvation and disease while we were cloistered here, safe, fed, and trained to fight for them, so they can have a better future." She looked at me with those wide eyes like she didn't' recognize me. "You have been on the continent too long. Go walk the city, get your head right, so I don't have to tell Father you need re-training." She shook her head and walked past me, giving my shoulder a squeeze as she left.

I stood there in the ring for a moment, my mind whirring over and over again. Everything she said was right but ultimately also wrong. Killing one child to save another grated against my being. Perhaps despite her willingness to balk the rules and propriety, she was still broken, beyond my reach. The mindless soldier I was supposed to be.

Cheerful voices echoed from the hall opposite where Ash had left. I stuffed my feelings down and lifted my sword again, immediately syncing my breathing to my movements as three of my sisters appeared out of the darkness of the hall.

They stopped short at the sight of me. Breathing heavily, I finished the sequence and stood facing them. Then, one by one, they each smiled, coming toward me. Affection wasn't something any of us were accustomed to showing, but a big handshake, a clap on the back, or a punch to the shoulder were the normal greetings after such a long time.

"We heard you had been home for only a day and were

already causing trouble." Tristee, whom we all called Tris, gave me a conspiratorial wink. She was the tallest of the group, matching me in height, but where I was softer, curvier, she was muscled and firm. She had dark tawny skin and chestnut hair that was cropped to her skull on the sides, with the longer top flopped over one ear.

"I'm surprised there wasn't a warder waiting for me." I laughed, rubbing the back of my neck.

"Everyone knows you are a favorite around here. The worst you'll get is a tongue-lashing." Gretta shrugged a shoulder. She was the smallest of us but tough and more cunning than anyone. She narrowed her dark eyes on me. "What's different about you?"

A wave of heat washed over me. My mind flashing through any of the things I had done wrong, anything I might be hiding. I had questions, sure, but could she see that?

"Your hair looks terrible," she said finally. I laughed out loud, mostly out of relief.

"Yeah, I spent the last two years washing my hair with lye and citrus to lighten it. I only just dyed it back."

"Ugh, that sounds horrible." Chelsea strained her voice to sound exaggerated before clapping her hands together and hopping up on the tips of her toes. "Now tell us all about life as a noble, did you get to wear fabulous dresses and fuck fabulous men?"

"Something like that," I chuckled.

"Well, tell us while we practice, or Leon is going to have our heads." Tris pointed her chin in the direction of the mezzanine above us, where Leon, one of the warders, stood arms crossed, watching us with a severe expression. He was tall like Daren, but his skin was so dark it nearly blended in with the shadows around him, the rings on his pointed ears glinting with the twinkling of the wall sconces.

"There is nothing much to tell," I said, moving back into position for the beginning round of sequences. I should be done, and my muscles burned with the effort, but I wanted to stay in this space with my sisters, who moved in line on either side of me. "Sure, I wore some dresses and did some things, but I'm none too interested in any of it as you all well know. What about you all? What have you been doing the last two years?"

"Chelsea's been knocking off Navy Admirals and Captains in Chiotania," Gretta said in a voice low enough that Leon, from his perch, couldn't hear. Our missions were meant to be ours, not shared, though we did, on occasion, gossip about them.

Chelsea guffawed on the other side of her. "It was nothing, just an old man who was weirdly obsessed with the island. Can't have anyone looking too closely, you know. But what I've really been doing is drowning myself in the Legends of Lore." Her voice took on an animistic grumble that had all of us turning our heads in her direction. She giggled, a light blush brushing her tan skin. It took us all a moment to get back into the sequence before anyone spoke again, wary of our overseer.

"Are you referring to those silly books you tried to get me to read?" Tris kept her bright green eyes straight ahead, her breaths coming out in concert with her movements.

"And what if I am?" Chelsea giggled again, keeping her body in time with our movements despite her obvious excitement. "They are delicious. Old stories about fated mates, the rebellion and Elves, and just such wonder."

"Perhaps I could borrow some of those. I need some excitement in my life," Gretta broke in with a sigh.

"Liagherian politics not as entertaining as it used to be?" I asked.

"It was never anything more than it is now, just a country at war, with a dozen cousins vying for a throne none of them can handle. It's just reports about the same thing over and over again." She paused to thrust and turn in unison with the rest of us. "The trip back here was more exciting than the last six months have been."

"Ah, your time will come." Tris stood at ease as we finished the movements together. She lowered her voice, glancing at Leon. "Rumor says the king is about to make a move; that's why all of the younger Saithe and Braithe have been called back. Do you realize this is the first time in nearly ten years that so many of us have been housed here together?"

"A move like what?" Chelsea asked, stretching her neck casually.

"Like breaking the wards," I said, spotting Daren lingering in the shadows of the hallway over Tris's shoulder.

There was a collective hush as I met them each eye to eye. This was the kind of secret we weren't supposed to share, the kind that could get us hurt. They knew it, and I knew it. A cough came from above and the three girls moved back into position.

"Looks like my punishment has arrived," I drawled, making my way to the rack to replace my weapon as my sisters began their next sequence.

CHAPTER TWELVE

Daren stood leaning against the wall, arms crossed, fingers drumming on his elbow as I made my way over to him. I kept my eyes trained on the muscles rippling in his forearm, completely ignoring the stern expression he was giving me. He let out an audible sigh as I neared and raised an eyebrow.

"What were you thinking?"

"I wasn't, that was the problem." My eyebrows hitched up, lips thinning in apology, knowing there was nothing I could say to change my fate.

"Walk with me," he said heavily, pushing off the wall and leading me along the space that ran around the edge of the arena. "We have need of your services," he said in a low voice, wrapping us in an air of privacy.

My head snapped up to him in surprise at the lack of scolding, but he was looking at the ground, chewing his lip, his hands now folded behind his back. It was an unusual mannerism for him, and my stomach tightened in response.

"You are going back to Wreabarroth to find that elf. We need to know everything there is to know about the Elves. Where they are, where they have been, what are their strengths, and most importantly, how to crush them. And we need to know as soon as possible." He slowed in the shadow of a column and turned to face me, crossing his arms again and leaning back, against a column. The air prickled around us with unease. Daren had always been a large being, but now he looked more fearsome than I had ever seen.

"It's going to work, isn't it?" I asked cautiously, keeping my face a mask of calm. "Aelthor can take down the wards."

His face remained stony as he nodded almost imperceptibly. I shot a look at my sisters moving through their sequence, knowing full well they were straining their magic to hear despite the cocoon that Daren was holding around us.

"The fear is that the Elves will take up arms once the wards go down and either replace them or protect the humans, for whatever reason. We have no idea what their motivations are after all this time." His voice turned thick with frustration. "But I sincerely doubt they will be interested in being friends, and they defeated us once..."

"And everything we have worked for is wasted."

"Exactly," he said.

"What are my limits?"

"None. If he has left Bernitra, then you follow him. Whatever it takes, the information is crucial."

"And if I fail?"

"Don't come back," he said, looking away toward the arena. Darkness blazed in his eyes as if there was more, he wanted to say but couldn't. The tightening in my gut wrenched, and I felt my chest get heavy with the weight of his words.

"It's been days," I said through gritted teeth. "You know as well as I that he could be anywhere by now if not wholly disappeared."

"There is no failing this," he snapped, pushing off the column and stepping between me and the arena, the shadow of his muscled body smothering me from sight. He was so close I could feel the heat radiating off of him. "Father will not tolerate anything but success. If you come back empty-handed, he will kill you."

The wind blew out of me in shock. Punishment was one thing, but death had never been a threat here. This was supposed to be our safe place. The only place where we could be what we were trained to be, where we could plan, recover, and rest. We earned that right and fought for it with every moment of our childhoods. Every muscle in my body went taut, on high alert. My eyes dropped, hitting the center of Daren's heaving chest, then to his hands, clenched into fists so tight the whites of his knuckles showed. I imagined those hands gripping me, nails scratching the length of my back, slamming me down. My body shuddered with the thought, in need of release.

"Should we finish this conversation in your room?" I whispered, tilting my head up to him. I watched his eyes, impossibly dark, trail down my jaw to the soft skin of my neck, then my collarbone. His knuckles cracked as he clenched and re-clenched his hands.

"No," he growled, sending chills down my spine. "I have other, uh, duties."

"There is something you aren't saying." It took more strength than it should have not to scream. My body was filled with shock, pain, and anger. I needed to sink my teeth into something, someone. Throw my fists into flesh and release some of this energy.

"There is a lot I'm not saying, Catherine." His voice was strained, like saying my name grated on his nerves. "I've spent too much time coddling you, and we both have jobs to do." He leaned back, crossing his arms again, veritably putting a barrier between us. "Father has chosen to send you with Hilda, Tristee, and Adrien. Adelay will join in Bernitra, and Reikka will meet you thereafter."

I let out a long sigh, trying to quell the chaos in my body, forcing my brain to think straight. "Adrien?" I threw the question out with more force than intended. "We have no need of the Mindwalker."

"He can take whatever truths the elf is holding." His words were clipped. He was trying to get this over with quickly now.

"Since when do we need a Mindwalker for that? My knives work just fine."

"Father commands it." His tone was curt, but there was exhaustion in his eyes. I chewed on the words, staring daggers at the man in front of me as he stood there, ready to take anything I threw at him. Like always, except now, there was something bothering him, something he was holding back.

"The elf is likely not even in Bernitra, but Verone." Daren simply raised an eyebrow in response. I continued, "They were after these prophecies, written in some hard-to-get text in Verone."

Daren sighed, "I'll send a firenote to Rahmious. They will scout Bernitra, and you can make a call when you get there."

"His name is Weilson. He's blonde. That's all I know."

"It's enough."

A moment passed between us, the tension crackling in the air of our enclosed space. Daren sucked his teeth and cocked his head to the side, looking at me like he was waiting for something before dismissing me.

"Why aren't you coming on this mission?" I asked finally. "Something seemingly this important should include a warder."

"I am needed here… We are preparing for war. Whether it's the Elves first or the continent, it's coming, and there is too much that the other Warders and I need to do."

"You mean learning to fight in battle formations or some nonsense." My muscles tightened again. This could be my last mission before the battle came. I had never seen an all-out war like what was on our horizon, but I had heard about them. Thousands would die; my sisters, the warders, our allies, all of us were at risk.

"Something like that." His eyes were sad as if we shared the same disheartening thought.

"Does it have to be war?" I ventured, my heart, ratcheting up in some kind of hope. "Would it be possible to just break the wards and send tokens of peace?"

Daren took a long breath, releasing his arms as he ran a hand through his hair.

"It's been ten thousand years, so much has changed," I pushed. "Our people could be happy if we could trade. Gold is nothing here, but on the continent, it's everything. We have so much of it we could buy everything; we don't need to go to war."

"It's not up to us, though, Catherine."

"So, convince the king. Aren't you on the council too? You know, council him?"

"There is no convincing a heart so set on revenge," he said quietly.

A moment of silence passed between us before he nodded his

chin in the direction of the hall. I took the hint to lead the way there, stomping my feet as I went. My sisters likely still believed I was getting a tongue-lashing and now was headed for punishment. Stepping into the darkness of the hall, I spun, turning to face him, feeling that blanket of privacy fall over us as he stalked toward me, stopping only inches away.

"I brought this up last night with the king and he nearly had my head for it." He opened the neck of his tunic and pulled it aside to reveal a welt the size of a dinner plate spread across his chest; the edges raw as if they were burned. I knew the king had many sons and that he treated them like any other subject in his kingdom, but son or not, this was beyond reckoning. A welt like that, hours later with Daren's healing powers, meant he would have been close to death when it happened. The king had threatened his life for simply speaking an opinion he didn't like. My blood went cold at the thought. Had learning to break the wards unleashed something in the king?

"Do not repeat those words," he hissed, leaning closer. "Do not tell anyone what you know. Just complete the mission."

His hand lifted in the air as if he wanted to touch me, but his lip curled up, and instead, he balled it into a fist, slamming it into the wall above my head. Dust and stone shards rained on the side of my face, but I didn't dare break his stare. He leaned in, our lips almost touching, his scent of leather and ash thick in my nose. "Do not give them a reason to doubt you."

I sucked in the words as they slithered in the air between us, filling me with apprehension, and then he pulled away. The cocoon of silence dissipated, leaving me cold and alone.

"You leave at dawn," he shouted as he stomped away into the gloom behind me.

CHAPTER THIRTEEN

I leaned back against the wall, letting out a long breath. My body ached with a tension I had not felt in some time. I wanted to break things, bite, snarl, and draw blood, much like an animal who has been forced into a corner. I pushed off the wall and stalked toward the arena.

"I'm going into town. Find me when you are done," I huffed to my sisters still in the training ring as I skirted the outside and ducked into the stairs leading to the mezzanine level and up to the dormitory beyond that.

The room I usually occupied when I was here was simple and rectangular. It held two bunk beds, two desks, and two small armoires with a singular narrow window. Going straight to the armoire I shared with Ash; I pushed it aside and pulled out the bottle of liquor kept in a hollow in the wall there. Pulling the stopper out with my teeth, I spit it across the room without care and pushed the armoire back into place with a bump from my hip. After taking a large swig, I wiped my mouth with the back of my hand, enjoying the harshness of the burn that trailed down my throat.

I was lying on the upper bunk with the bottle half gone, tossing a knife into a target on the ceiling above my head, when Ash opened the door, her face pinched.

"Thought you would be in town by now." She sauntered in, swiping the bottle from my grasp and taking a sip. "The way Tris says it, you and Daren had some heated words. Said we would find you half in the bag under some Gasyter male." She handed the bottle back to me, and I sat up, swinging my feet over the edge.

"I was waiting for company." I slid from the bunk, landing on the floor with a thud. "Didn't you say I should walk the city and remind myself what we are fighting for here? Fucking show me."

Ash looked at me for a long time before a smile crept across her face. "Let's fucking go then." She took the bottle, downing a larger gulp this time as she made her way to the armoire.

None of us had much in the way of clothing aside from what we used for missions, but we pulled together something suitable. I remained in my leather pants and boots, though I removed most of my weapons, save for a set of throwing knives hidden in a seam on my hip and a single long blade strapped to my thigh. On top, I opted for a smaller version of my usual leather vest that laced up the front with nothing underneath, a sight that even had Ash raising her eyebrows at me. I left my waist-length hair in a loose braid with tendrils that curled around my face. In contrast, Ash wore a pair of loose trousers and a tunic with the sleeves rolled back. She pushed her mass of hair over to one side, and I braided back the loose pieces over her ear, giving her a rakish look.

We had finished the bottle and were about to leave when

there was a knock at the door, accompanied by a high-pitched, "Oh, Dearies." I opened the door to find Tris toting another bottle of liquor with a reluctant Gretta in tow. "Are we ready then?" she said, slipping into the room and shutting the door behind them.

Heading into town wasn't explicitly against the rules, but leaving the manor without permission was. It was a fine line that we had smudged often enough in our youth to know there were only consequences if something went wrong or if someone got hurt or a jealous warder found out. To avoid any discomfort, it was imperative to keep our plans a secret.

"Where's Chelsea?" I asked, slugging back the last of our bottle.

"With Gabe." Gretta rolled her eyes. Gabe was the Harridan's weapons master, and it was well known that Chelsea was his favorite.

"More fun for us," Tris giggled. "Let's go."

***

We snuck out easily enough, pilfering another bottle of liquor from the main dining room on our way to keep us sated. It wasn't a long walk, and with the amount of drinking we had already done, we also opted to skip stealing horses. I could feel the excitement welling up in me as we neared the lights and the sounds of the city. Having been to many places in my life, I knew there was no place like the capital city of Lorcaide. The debauchery and mirth found here were unlike anywhere else. All the pent-up energy I had inside me would be quelled only by what this city could offer.

Ash led the way through the back streets to a row of taverns and public houses. We opted for one in the middle of the row with

113

a loud band playing. Inside, it was dark and gritty, with all manner of beings from silver-haired Goin Elves, scaled Waterfolk, men, and Gasyters, all of which were well-marked. The floor was made of crushed stone, while the walls and furniture were made of rough-hewn wood, much of it sporting gouges and scorch marks from constant use. With the sun long set, the only light came from the orbs of magic light that hung down from the ceiling.

We went straight to the bar, pushing our way to the counter. The barmaid was an attractive young Gasyter with a round face and a deep blue complexion. Her curly hair shot out in all directions around the horns that curved back, arcing around the tips of her tapered ears. She looked young, but the length of her horns proved she was closer to her mid-thirties, like us.

"Four coal wines," I shouted over the din. She raised her brows at me and gave me a once-over. Pegging her with a look of annoyance, I pulled out a few coins and dropped them on the wooden top.

She scooped it up with pursed lips and poured the drinks, which we all threw back in seconds, barely noting the burn of it.

"Four more," Ash shouted from the back of the group, reaching between Gretta and Tris and slamming her glass down. "Make them doubles." This time, the barmaid had them filled in seconds, and I laid a few more coins out for her, which she took with an appreciative smile.

Moments later, we were jammed into a circle on the crowded dance floor when the room began to sway before me. Reveling in the feeling, I let my body take control, moving of its own accord, dancing salaciously with men and women alike. I was unaware of time as it moved over me, as the music changed, and more drinks were put in my hands, then food, and then more drinks, and the night drew on.

I was at the bar waiting for the barmaid's attention when I noticed for the first time that the place had begun to clear. We would be heading back soon, and I had yet to taste the relief I had been looking for. My eyes proceeded to scan the room, looking for just the right target when the barmaid sidled up to me.

"Prowling for something in particular?" She cocked her head and slid a drink toward me. It was then that my eyes landed on the Gasyter beside me; his skin wasn't as dark as the barmaids, but he was massive, with thick horns that curved around his ears and wiped out at the sides. Black hair hung loosely around broad shoulders that were scarred with the geometric swirling pattern that denoted a warrior. Over the top of the rippling scars, a distinctive inked design that resembled scaled wings radiated out from beneath the light sleeveless shirt he wore. A wave of heat rolled over me as I imagined what his back would look like without the shirt.

The barmaid snort-laughed, catching the male's attention. He turned from the hushed conversation he was having with whoever was seated next to him and looked at her, bringing his drink up to his mouth for a sip. The space between his pointed ear and the base of his horn was shaved and marked with a set of lines in dark ink that stretched from behind his ear, over his cheek, and swiped up over his left eye. Cutting through the thick brow, they came to a point on his forehead.

Maleathe saw me out of the corner of his eye before I could turn away. I swallowed, scooping up my drink, and faced out to the rest of the bar. He turned to me fully, hitching one foot up on the rung of the stool below him so that I'd have to step around his knee to escape. Even sitting, he was taller than me. I realized in all my years serving the king, I had never been this close to him. He was more handsome than I had ever considered. His presence was a colossal thing of its own, and it enveloped me completely.

"Now what, pray tell is little Bri—"

"Maia." I cut him off with a look. We never went out using our real names or in my case, my real fake name.

He sniggered devilishly, and I could feel any resolve I had melting away.

"Maia." He tested out the name, rolling the letters over his tongue in a way that made my stomach clench. "What is little Maia doing in a place like this on such an auspicious evening?"

"I suppose I could ask you the same thing, General." I leaned toward him slightly and ran the tip of my tongue over my lips. His eyes darkened in response.

"I'm the only one who holds my leash; you, on the other hand, have the king's right hand to hold yours. I imagine he wouldn't be too thrilled to know his best, uh," His eyes trailed down the curve of my chest, the skin visible at my hip and the swell of my ass before rising back up. "Asset was out here like this."

Now I turned to him completely, leading with my chest. "I'm sure we can come up with an agreement that he doesn't need to know about."

His laugh was low and guttural.

"If only a little thing like you could handle the likes of me."

While I surely wouldn't be considered a large being, no one had ever called me little before. My height rivaled that of more Elven-blooded women, while my breadth was larger as a result of a lifetime of training. He was teasing me.

"Oh, Maleathe," I purred. "You and I both know that I could handle three of you without breaking a sweat."

His smile dissipated into a thin line as he leaned in closer. "Maybe someday, little Maia, but not today. You have work to do."

He stood, slamming back his drink and stalking from the bar, leaving his companion scampering behind. My body slumped against the bar in disappointment. I looked up at the barmaid, who was standing stock still, with eyes wide and her cheeks puffed out like she was about to explode. I raised my eyebrows in concern, looking around at what she was reacting to. Then she burst into laughter.

"For fucks sake." She slammed her fist on the counter, trying to get a hold of herself. "Never, in all my years," she said between gasps and spasms of laughter, "have I seen anyone run the fucking king's general out of this place. Fucking Gods, woman, you have a death wish."

I shrugged, my face heating. "We are, uh—acquainted."

"Call me Sam." The barmaid stuck out her hand, which I shook heartily.

"So, a good show is what it takes to be accepted around here," I chuckled.

A tap on my shoulder pulled me away from the exchange. Turning, I was confronted with another male Gasyter, nearly as large as the general but with shorter horns and fewer markings. His face was smooth and handsome, and his deep blue eyes seemed to glow in the dim light.

"I know it's not the three males you were hoping for, but my friend here and I could probably give you a run for your money." Another male poked his head out from behind the first shoulder and gave a timid smile. My core tightened, my heart slamming against my ribs with renewed vigor.

"Well, I won't be paying, but we can give it a shot," I responded coyly.

Without prompting, Sam slapped a key on the table and pointed to a room on the upper level. She winked at me with a wicked grin as I let the males lead me away.

CHAPTER FOURTEEN

The room was fairly large for a tavern but sparse. The timid one stepped in first, and I followed, leaving the other to lock the door as I wrapped my arms around his friend. The male's lips were soft and warm, his hands needy as they groped my body.

"Don't be greedy now, Grim." The other rumbled as he reached between us, turning my face toward him. He wasted no time thrusting his tongue in my mouth, dragging his calloused hand down my throat. My chest surged, straining against the vest as heat pooled between my legs. I felt his friend, Grim, grip my hips roughly. Gasyter men were not known for their generosity. Any misstep in this little fling could easily cause these friends to butt heads, quite literally.

I pulled at the base of Grim's tunic, and he quickly pulled it over his head while I ground my backside against him. His friend continued his ministrations on my mouth and pulled at the laces of my top. Using my teeth to ensnare his tongue, I ceased his movement, sucking on it hard. He let out a low groan, pulling me to his chest.

"Fuck, Soren." Grim's voice was surprisingly deep and raspy. It sent a wave of heat over me as I pulled away from Soren's kiss, tugging his tongue a bit as I did. I untucked his tunic and pulled at the laces of his trousers. He took the hint and began removing his clothing while I turned back to Grim, who wasted no time relieving me of my open vest and burying his face in the soft flesh of my chest. His mouth enveloped as much as would fit and giving it a gentle suck, flicking his tongue over the tip of my nipple. The sensation sent ripples of pleasure over me.

This time, it was me who groaned as I tilted his chin up and kissed him hard on the mouth. Soren's cock was stiff on my back as he again slipped a hand between us, this time cupping my breast and kissing my neck. Turning back to him, I pushed him away, needing to take control before his jealousy ruined everything.

"Boots, please," I said with an air of authority, picking up my foot and pointing it at him. His eyes narrowed on me as I leaned back, my arms wrapping over my head and around Grim's neck. Soren obliged, tossing one boot, then the other away. He stepped toward me predatorily, but I stopped him with a foot on his chest. "Pants, too."

He licked his lips and undid the laces, pulling them down over my ass. I used my arms around Grim's neck to lift myself as Soren pulled the pants and the small piece of fabric that acted as my undergarments the rest of the way off. Turning, I ripped at the laces of Grim's pants and pushed them down, his large cock springing free. A confident smirk painted his face, causing me to laugh as I pushed him back toward the bed. He flopped onto it with his pants around his ankles. Facing Soren again, I pointed to the floor in front of me.

"Soren, is it? On your knees," I said, turning my silky, sweet voice to a demanding growl.

He did as I bade him, and I rewarded them both as I bent at the waist, keeping my back flat, and kissed him, again pulling on his tongue while Grim got a full view from behind. Easing backward, I reached behind and wrapped my fingers around the shaft of Grim's cock, lining it up with my entrance. I broke the kiss with Soren while sliding my other hand to the back of his neck. Slowly, I eased myself onto the shaft of one male while directing Soren's head between my legs.

Soren paused, staring eye level at my throbbing sex while I took in the full length of his friend, letting it fill and stretch me. My body shivered in pleasure at the fullness. Fisting himself between his knees, Soren's eyes flicked up to mine hungrily. I smiled as he surged forward, splitting me with his tongue. The sensation of his warm mouth on me sent bolts of white-hot fire through my veins. I began to rock back and forth in time with his movements, my orgasm building easily.

Grim groaned a curse that tickled the skin down my back, and I rocked harder. His rough hands slid over my hips, up my ribs, and groped my chest, pulling me down in the same rocking pattern. Biting my lip, I looked down, straight into Soren's enchanting blue eyes as they pinned me to the spot, the lower half of his face hidden under me as I moved on him. I slid my hands into the hair over his ears, easing them back behind the base of his horns, a particularly sensitive spot. Fisting his dark hair, I pulled him harder into me. His groans of pleasure vibrated against the sensitive skin there.

The tips of my fingers and toes began to tingle as I felt myself rising, eyes still locked with the blue orbs beneath me. Grim bit the curved shell of my ear and whispered.

"That's right baby, just ride his pretty face," his voice thick and gravely turned my insides into liquid.

Soren moved then, pulling the bundle of nerves on his tongue into his mouth and sucking. I shattered. My entire body thrashed over and over again as both men continued to work me from different directions, wringing every ounce of strength out of me.

A shudder from behind as I began to come down from the peak of my orgasm told me that Grim had been satisfied. Looking back at Soren, I knew that my job was not done. Reaching between my legs, I gripped his chin and pulled him up. I felt Grim fall back on the bed behind me, but as he made no indication of removing himself from me, I ignored it and took Soren's engorged cock in my mouth. Pushing it all the way to the back of my throat, I had him nearly to the hilt before I pulled back and flicked my tongue over the sensitive head. I tugged at my magic, swirling it on my actions, and by the third pull, he was releasing himself into my mouth with a growl.

When he finished, I pulled myself off and wiped my mouth daintily. Grim's, now partially flaccid member, slid out of me as I stood and flopped over his thigh. I gave them both a look over my shoulder as I bent to gather my clothes. This was the release I had been needing, and now I was going to get some sleep before the next mission started.

Silently, they watched me dress. Soren had stumbled back and was leaning on the wall catching his breath, hands on his knees, his neck purple with exertion, while Grim didn't move from his spot on the bed. His hands were behind his head, legs bent over the bed's side, and his pants still around his ankles. I tied the laces on my vest and turned toward the door. I tossed a thank you over my shoulder as I pulled open the door and left.

CHAPTER FIFTEEN

I was awoken abruptly by a shake from Ash.

"You're off again," she said, her bloodshot eyes narrowing on me as if trying to see me through the blur of an alcohol-rattled mind.

My last recollection of her had been hours before when I had finished my leave with two males. She had been dancing with a set of girls that could have been sisters, their red hair and pointed ears, and voluptuous curves matching eloquently. I remembered calling to her across the bar and her barely recognizable slurring that she would find me before I left.

It crossed my mind that she had probably not been to bed yet. I wondered what the punishment for her would be if she were late to chores as she thudded into the bunk below me with a groan.

I scrubbed a hand down my face and took a deep breath, trying to will some strength into my aching body. The weight of my headache bore down on me before I even sat up, but the motion proved to ignite an inferno in my skull that I was unprepared for. Wincing, I eased myself down from the bunk, every movement another strike of the flint in my head.

My leathers were still in the pile I had left them in on the floor, and it took all my strength to force myself to bend down and retrieve them. Ash snorted from her prostrate position on the bed.

"The drawer," she grumbled, pointing to the small table beside the bed.

Shuffling over, I pulled it open and found several dropper bottles. Selecting a white willow bark and mint blend for the pain in my head as well as a milk thistle, I dosed myself quickly before moving on to Ash. She didn't move from the bed but tilted her head back and opened her mouth like a baby bird, indicating her need with a small whining sound. I laughed and fed her the same dose.

Replacing the bottles, I turned back to see her having rolled onto her side with an outstretched hand. We shook stoically, gently pressing the stones hiding beneath our skin, nodding to each other at the end. She rolled back to the wall, and I went about my business. That was all the goodbye we would share.

***

Dawn was just beginning to paint the sky as I climbed the stairs to the main level of the manor. I carried very little throughout my travels aside from a change of clothes, notes, and food, the only extra thing being an aid kit. On the continent, only medics and midwives carried them, but with the inherent danger of our lives, it was important to have our own means of caring for ourselves, amongst other things. While I could use magic to heal, there were times it was not wise, such as in the company of humans or if my reserves were too drained.

The apothecary was a large room on the first floor of the manor, just off from the solarium. Large windows overlooked the garden and allowed light to filter in between the rows of plants that lined the glass shelves in front of them. Around the rest of the room, more shelves and cupboards lined the walls, overflowing with jars, tins, and ceramics of varying sizes and colors. In the middle of the room, a tall, heavy wooden workbench was laden with tools, supplies, and scattered remnants of herbs. Cara, the official Harridan Society Apothecary, stood weighing herbs on a large metal scale.

She was a robust woman with soft, round features and kind brown eyes. Everything you would expect from an apothecary if you didn't know about her skills with a blade. She was a few years my senior and one of the only sisters who really gave me a run for my money in the arena, next to Leeta. It was quite a surprise when she was assigned to care for the apothecary after Magda's passing. Once she took the post, however, her magic affinities for the task and pure love for it were clear. She was born for this position.

"I heard you were here," she said with a smile, not looking up from her task. "Need something for your head?"

I chuckled, wondering how much gossip had traveled about last night's escapades. "No, thank you, Cara," I said kindly, laying my kit in an open space on the counter and unrolling it for her view. "I need to restock my kit and get some more drought for the coming months."

"I was just told this morning not to stock your drought after this one," she said, her eyes skimming me while she worked.

I didn't bother to hide my shock. A pregnant Saithe was a

useless one, or so we had been told for as long as I could remember. The monthly drought was the only thing keeping us from falling with child. What would be the point of refusing me the thing that prevents such a situation?

"That makes no sense," I stuttered finally.

Cara shrugged, setting aside her herbs and leaning forward on the table. "It's a first for me as well, but I would guess you should take it up with Father."

"Is he here?"

She shrugged again as a novice with long blonde hair pulled into a braid slipped in behind me. With her head bowed low, she scurried to the back wall and began fiddling with some jars there.

"Father just came in with another man I don't recognize," she said over her shoulder.

"You're late," Cara said dryly, her eyes still on me, a wry smile playing on her lips.

"Leon made me stay behind to scrub the kitchen after breakfast," she said quietly. Cara and I exchanged knowing glances. Leon was the harshest of warders, and no one escaped his scrutiny.

"Have him let me know next time," she said simply, turning to the kit I had unrolled in front of her and taking stock of the contents.

"The man you saw," I ventured, causing the girl to turn to me. She held her head up confidently, shoulders pushed back, and hands clasped behind her, a sign of honor for an older sister. "Human looking, with dark hair, light eyes, and handsome?"

"Yes, ma'am." She nodded.

"Adrien," I muttered, unsurprised since he was coming with us today.

"Maitlyn," Cara called to the girl. "Fill this kit." She began listing off tinctures and blends of herbs, causing the girl to scurry about the room, gathering them up in her apron. Moving with alarming speed, the two of them had the kit fully restocked and rolled for me within minutes. I thanked them kindly and left.

I went straight up the main stair and directly to Father's office, passing by the ornate chairs, cases, and paintings that lined the dark wood-paneled halls. My feet pounded the floorboards in defiance despite the potential reprimand that may follow. The muscles in my shoulders pulled together in trepidation at my own audacity. Perhaps I had spent too much time on the continent.

The door to Father's office was open, so I strolled in to find both Hilda and Adrien sitting in plush leather chairs before Father, who stood leaning against the broad hardwood desk behind him. His hands were clasped casually in front of him, but his ever-indomitable expression gave him a sternness that could never be truly relaxed.

"I would like to speak to you," I said, coming to a stop between the two chairs, arms crossed over my chest, in an attempt to appear confident.

His eyes darted between the two sitting on either side of me and then back to me. It was the only sign of surprise he showed at my actions. I made a mental tally of how many indiscretions I had made since my arrival, wondering when the hand of judgment would finally fall on me for it. Without prompting, Hilda and Adrien rose and made their way outside, closing the door gently behind them.

"What is this about me not getting the drought?" I said flatly, not waiting for Father's Invitation.

"Ah," he said with a placating smile drawn on his face. "I had planned to speak to you about it this morning, but it appears you've already visited the apothecary." I didn't bother to respond, simply waiting for him to continue. The smile slipped from his face as the moments dragged on. "To put it bluntly, it would behoove you to bear the Mindwalker's child."

A moment passed before the meaning of this statement penetrated my thoughts. I was to be whored out for the procreation of magic.

"A pregnant Saithe is a useless Saithe," I repeated the mantra he had drilled into me in my youth with a steely reserve.

"In most cases, yes," he drawled, bringing a hand up to inspect his nails. "But things are changing." He spoke slowly, drawing out his words as if he were speaking to a child. It grated on my nerves as I stood there, my mind reeling from the idea that I was to be used in this way. "Mindwalkers are rare, and your particular strength and innate skill with magic are even rarer. A child with either or both of your skills will be an asset in the future."

"And if I don't want to carry a child?" The words left my mouth before I could think better of it. Questioning the decision of the Father was an offense of the worst kind. The muscles in my shoulders pinched together more as I tried to reel in my emotions, keeping my expression even.

His elegant face crumpled in confusion, then outrage, before it was washed over in stoic calm as he fought to control his response. It was rare that anyone aside from the king questioned him.

"It is of no consequence to you." He tilted his head and gave me another smile that chipped away at my decorum. "There are only a few months where you won't be able to perform your duties, then the child will be removed from your care, and you can return to work. While your magic may keep you young and beautiful, it does not intercede on the nature of childbirth, and your time on that front is limited. If we are to capitalize on it, then we must do it quickly."

I guttered at this, my entire body reacting to his statements—his nonchalance of my potential child, my age, my usefulness to him, and the cause. There was an inherent danger in birth that even the most powerful magic apothecaries couldn't quell. A danger grew with age and grew with the types of power that I possessed for healing, for glamour, for altering the way my body moved and functioned in this world. Any of my missions could be my death, but death at the hand of a sword was an entirely different thing than the pain-riddled death of my body destroying itself from the inside.

"And if I can't perform my duties after childbirth?" I regained my composure quickly. "I could die, or break my hips, or lose my mind."

"We will find a suitable position for you here at the—"

"Then what? You take the child, raise them as you did me?" I cut him off, realizing, to my horror, that I would rather die before I let my child be brought up the way that my sisters and I were. The idea that my own daughter might be forced to fight, to endure torture, starved at times, to undergo the Ascension that was a veritable rape by the man in front of me, then the constant requests of warders. The breaking down of our inner walls that Adrien has so eloquently described until we are nothing but mindless tools to be used and set aside. Bile rose in the back of my throat at the realization. My entire body went taut with white-hot rage.

"Well, yes, of course. We would—"

"What if Adrien doesn't agree? Or it doesn't thrive. What if I don't want this for my child? This is not like other missions. I can't just—"

"Enough!" His booming voice echoed in my ears, bouncing

off the walls. "How dare you disrespect my *decisions*. You have been given a mission, and you will complete it as you would any other. Is that *clear*?"

Taking a breath, I dropped my hands to my sides, clenching and unclenching my fists. Whether for my self-restraint or out of fear, I wasn't sure. Both emotions fought for dominance within me, fanning the unharnessed rage he had ignited.

"This is a child, my child. I have given up my life for this realm, for its people, for you, for King Aelthor, but you cannot ask this of me," I said, my voice steely, and my eyes locked on his.

They narrowed in response, my throat tightening as if invisible hands had taken hold of it. I tried to swallow, but the hands clenched down, crushing my windpipe. I gasped for air as he sucked his teeth in annoyance. I felt a pull upward, my heels leaving the ground. Every muscle in my body was electrified in fear. Reaching for my magic, I found my inner well empty. Father, like the king, had a strength of magic that only came from nearly pure-blooded Elves, and it overruled nearly every other magic wielded by humans or mixed breeds. If he wanted my death, then it would come, and there was nothing I could do to stop it.

My lungs began to burn as my feet fully left the ground, kicking lightly searching for purchase. I tilted my head back, mouth agape, involuntarily begging for air.

"You misunderstand me, Daughter," he seethed; standing, he stepped close to me so that our faces were nearly touching. His expression was cruelly impassive as I continued to hang in the air in front of him, gasping. Searching his light blue eyes for any sign of empathy. "Your life was never yours to give up, but mine to hold. This is the mission I have chosen to give you, and you will complete it. When it is done, you and the child will be cared for as I see fit. You are not to make Adrien aware of this mission, but you will follow through with it, or you will be considered an enemy of the realm."

He stood there watching me wriggle under his magic, his eyes boring into me. Now my lungs were screaming, my vision beginning to darken at the edges. A tingling sensation rose up my hands and feet, the strength in them beginning to ebb away.

A small gasp of air broke through the chokehold, slipping into my lungs, making them ache for more. Spots erupted in front of my eyes like fireworks. Father stepped back, running a hand through his impeccable hair, and another gasp slipped into me, expanding my lungs further. A toe hit the floor, then another, not enough to hold my weight but to remind me that he was in control. Slowly, the tightness around my throat began to loosen, and my vision began to clear.

"Now, Daughter, do you accept your new mission?" Father stood before me, arms crossed.

It didn't matter if I truly accepted it in my heart or not; if he didn't hear the words, if he didn't believe that I would go through with it, I would be dead. He would kill me right here and now. For the second time in as many days, my life had been threatened for things that I may not even have control over. The burning in my lungs was replaced by an ache in my chest. It was like the tendrils of a rosebush, wrapping itself around my heart, squeezing tight. It's thorns piercing the tough flesh there.

The words came out as barely whisper over the remaining pressure easing from my throat.

"I accept."

Father stood there a moment longer, weighing my response. I was oddly thankful his power was still just barely wrapped around my throat, holding me upright. The weight of his statements was bearing down on me with such force that I was sure my legs would collapse without the support. Finally, he sneered, his ever-stoic demeanor slipping for a moment, and walked around me to the door.

"Be in the arena in ten minutes," he said and left.

His magic dropped away as soon as the door clicked shut. I collapsed in a heap on the floor, my lungs aching and my heart pounding. Pushing myself up, I tried to make sense of what had just occurred. The man I had looked to for guidance and protection had just threatened my life as if it were inconsequential to him.

CHAPTER SIXTEEN

Turning, my eyes drifted along the wall of books that ran the length of the office, cataloging titles and dates along the spines, as well as taking note of the inconsistencies in cataloging and the shelf itself. There was at least one door hidden within the mass. This calmed my mind enough to get my feet under me, stand, and walk out of that horrible room.

Flying down the hall, I made my way to an empty office and slid to the floor again, my back against the wall. I took as much time as possible to calm my breathing, slow my heart, and remove all signs of the struggle I had just been through. Luckily, the prior evening's antics had given me a cover for the bloodshot eyes and pale complexion. My throat still felt as if it was lined with sandpaper, but it would ease soon enough as my healing magic took over.

Arriving right on time, I was greeted by Hilda and Adrien at the edge of the arena. Neither one made any indication of what they had seen or heard. Hilda put her hand out, taking mine and running the tip of her middle finger over the hard piece of stone beneath my skin. She was tall and lean, with sandy hair that just dusted her shoulders and bangs that dusted her eyebrows. It had been years since I had seen her, but she still wore it half-up in a small bun, the same dark brown leather, and a light golden tunic underneath that accentuated the blue in her gray-blue eyes. She was Elven-blooded with just a slight point to her ears and my senior by at least one hundred years. As the oldest Harridan and active Saithe, older than even most of the warders, she held a standing well above the rest of us.

"You look well," she said, putting her hands on her hips. Her voice was calm and collected, but her eyes were assessing. Taking note, I'm sure, of the loose braid my hair was in, the fact that my leathers were wrinkled and unclean, my eyes were red-rimmed and bloodshot. I wondered what she thought of me and if she ever needed a drink or a warm body to take the edge off. Hilda had always been the epitome of a good Saithe, easily blending into any situation and incredibly good with weapons.

"As do you, Sister," I responded formally, tipping my head slightly, my throat still scratchy. Behind me, the sound of footsteps echoed as Tris sauntered toward us.

"Tristee," Hilda greeted her. "Hello. Have you been briefed?"

"Hilda." Tris nodded to her. "I'm to be informed when we get to Bernitra." She turned her gaze to Adrien, who had been standing silently beside Hilda with his hands clasped behind his back, dressed as a scribe. The billowing gray robes did well to hide the muscular physique and markings I knew hid beneath. She raised her eyebrows at me and Hilda together as if waiting for an introduction.

"This is Adrien," Hilda said flatly, indicating him with her eyes as she crossed her arms over her chest. He gave Tris a tight-lipped smile and nodded in greeting. "He is a Mindwalker who will be accompanying us. He is to be treated as one of our group."

Tris nodded in response, her eyes trailing over his figure warily.

"Unfortunately, I can only take two of you at a time. So, I'll jump the two of you," she pointed between me and Tris, "to the waygate, where we will cross the wards. Then we will jump to Reinalie and then Bernitra. From there, Rhamius will take me along the reverse path back to here so that I can bring Adrien back without depleting my power. At which point, we can discuss our plans and join with Reikka." We all nodded in unison. She looked at us each in turn before extending a hand to Tris and me. "See you soon, Adrien." Her eyes lingered on him as her grey-black magic began to swirl around us. The darkness soon overtook everything so that I couldn't even see the women connected to me at the ends of my own hands. A gentle breeze swirled around us while a hollow whistling sound filled my ears, and the scent of sea air penetrated my nostrils.

It only lasted a few seconds, but soon, the blackness faded, and we were standing on the grassy shores of Wraithland beside a mooing cow and the waygate stone. The next jump to Reinalie was longer, but not by much. We appeared in the kitchen of an abandoned hut. Hilda took a deep breath, shaking out her limbs before our last jump.

This time, when the blackness cleared, we were in the usual room in Bernitra, where Adelay was relaxing on the bed, one ankle over the other and a glass of wine in hand. For her the evening was just ending. The tailor sat across from her in a green velvet chair, feet propped on the end of the bed. He was tall and lean with broad shoulders and a mop of dark hair that fell across his forehead and over one eye. He had a broad smile that was just a little too big for his face, but it gave him a charm that often made women swoon in his presence. It was not lost on me that those with elf blood always appeared good-looking. Whether it was a result of their magic or simply their breeding, I didn't know.

The tailor, Rhamius, stood, his dark blue jacket and matching trousers falling into place perfectly without a wrinkle. Even so, he smoothed down the front of his shirt and ran a hand through his hair before he greeted us, each by name and a kiss on the hand. Pleasantries only lasted a few moments before his dark blue wisps of magic blended with the dark shadows of the jumping vortex. Moments later, they were gone.

Tris sauntered to Rhamius' vacated chair and flopped down with a flourish, scooping up his half-finished glass of wine as she went. Adelay reached beside her for one of the extra glasses she had placed there and poured me a glass as well. I moved over to the other side of the bed and sat beside her.

"So, we scoured the place the last day and a half. No sign of an elf or even a man of your description." Adelay turned to look at me beside her, handing me the filled glass. "Though, one of our contacts said a man by the name of Weilson had just stayed at his inn for a few nights. Thought he was headed to Verone like you said."

"I suppose that's where we will head then." I nodded and took a sip of the wine Adelay handed me, the thick liquid making my stomach roil. I had to push back the bile rising in my throat, realizing I hadn't eaten anything since lunch yesterday. A soft knock at the door pulled me from my thoughts.

"Come on then," Adelay called. The door opened to reveal a young girl in little more than a slip, carrying a tray of baked goods and cheeses. "Thank you, Annie." Adelay motioned to a spot on the bed where the girl placed the tray and quickly left. I wasted no time reaching for a roll baked with cinnamon and dried fruits, taking a large bite before my stomach decided to upend itself. Meanwhile, Tris dropped her feet to the floor and leaned over the tray, reaching for a slice of toast and a slab of cheese.

"I figured with the early hour, neither of you would have gotten a bite to eat yet." Adelay laughed, her curls bouncing with her movement.

"I think the last real meal I ate was yesterday morning," I offered between bites, pushing the food to the side of my mouth.

"Does it count as breakfast if you haven't actually been to bed yet?" Tris asked, shaking her hair out of her face.

"That's something I don't miss about the life of a Saithe, always on the move, living off apples and stale biscuits." Adelay shook her head. "This room will be busy today, go down and find Christie in the kitchen. She'll find a spot for you to rest in or Hilda will have your hide later for falling asleep while she's speaking."

Tris grunted a laugh and scooped a handful of food. "Thank you, Adelay," she said, making for the door and calling over her shoulder. "Wake me when she's back."

We sat in silence for a moment as I chewed the overly large bite in my mouth, desperately thinking about what to say. My mind was blank aside from running over the events of the last few days. The vision in the burning house, the dead kids, Adrien's words yesterday morning, Daren's injuries, Father's threats, all of it bearing down on me. It was like putting together a puzzle without all the pieces.

"Something on your mind?" Adelay had turned her whole body toward me, tucking her feet up and resting her elbow on the low headboard.

I let out a long breath, not sure what to say or even if I should.

Another moment stretched out between us. I kept opening my mouth to speak and shutting it again, scrubbing my hand down my face in frustration.

"You know we all get worn down after a time. Frustrated, sure. It's okay to feel it, ya know," she said softly. "It doesn't make you weak, and I'll not fault you for it." A small smile tugged at the corners of her mouth, quelling my frustration some.

"And what about your soul?" I asked finally, my voice coming out horse. "How did you keep it from shriveling into nothing?" I wasn't sure she would even know what I was talking about, but after our last conversation, I thought it was worth a try.

Her warm and open expression dropped, her eyes leveling on me with new understanding. Licking her lips, she set down her glass and turned back to me before she spoke.

"I didn't," she said. "It's not possible. Not with the things we are told to do. The lives, the torture, the rape, all of it was designed to do just that."

I put the bread down, fighting the tears that pricked the back of my eyes. My chest constricted, and I felt the tendrils of the rosebush that had implanted itself in me tighten. I shook my head and reached for my wine.

"For what? What is it all for, though?" I took a large swig, the action helping to push down my emotions as I lowered my voice. "To support the whims of the king?"

I watched her reaction closely as she nodded slowly, a hardness taking over her usually soft features. "The king, and his whims, and his thirst for blood, so that he has a little army of dolls to use as he pleases," she said flatly.

"But without him, we—" I started.

"We what?" Her voice came out deep and bitter, causing a chill to rise up my spine. "We wouldn't be here? No, we wouldn't, but how many of our sisters who didn't make it through training would still be alive today? How many of our families would still be alive? There's no way to tell any of it, and sure, we may owe Father for our education, for our knowledge of magic, but does that outweigh what we have given him?"

"What do you mean about our families? I have no family," I said, testing her.

"Sure, neither do I, at least that's what I'm told." The flatness in her voice said it all. She didn't believe for a second that she was an orphan, just like I wasn't given up by the woman with golden brown eyes who was screaming for me to run in my vision with a younger Father standing over her, preparing to slit her throat.

I took another sip of wine, my hand shaking. Adelay loosed a ragged breath beside me.

"I wish I had answers for you. In all my time as a student, then a novice, then a Saithe, and even now as a Tachdre, all I have learned is how to survive. I can't know for sure if the missions we are given are for the benefit of Wraithland's people or just its king. What I do know is that for all the lives I've taken, it spared my own, and now I take in who I can, save who I can with the money supplied to run this place." She raised her hands to indicate the house they were now in. "And the skills and the magic I have at my disposal." She leaned forward, putting a hand on my knee. "You find your peace, your way to make it right, to save yourself from shriveling into nothing, because that's all we can do."

I looked into her big, beautiful brown eyes, noticing the flecks of green in them for the first time. They were full of sincerity, and it made me wonder if that was it, if saving some innocents on street corners and giving jobs to hungry kids would be enough for me. Would it be enough to save my soul if I let them take my child and make them into a monster like

CHAPTER SEVENTEEN

When Hilda's mist cleared, a few hours later, Adrien and I found ourselves in the simple, if not sparse, room of an inn. The only indication of this was the familiar raucous sounds coming from the other side of the wall. This was one of the establishments managed by The Tailor that allowed the Harridans to move easily throughout the continent. We were in Borreagor, a city that lay on the northernmost edge of the Borreagor desert and marked the border of the kingdom of Liagheria. It was something of a sister city to Bernitra, in Wreabarroth, that lay on the desert's southeastern tip, creating a well-worn path through the desert. Unfortunately, Hilda's shadow-jumping abilities only allowed her to move to familiar places, and she did not have enough knowledge of Verone to jump us directly there. Instead, we intended to meet Reikka here and travel by land to the neighboring city-state of Verone.

Having made the first trip with Hilda, Adelay, and Tris were digging through a large closet hidden behind a bookcase. Tris pointed to a note from Reikka that lay in the center of the large bed while taking hold of the dresses and cloaks handed to her. Skimming the letter, it appeared Reikka had arranged for us to meet her at the duke's castle in the city center. There, one of us would be introduced as her non-existent sister-in-law, Lady Lenna Vongale, to the Liagherian Princess Ameria. The princess had already planned a visit to the neighboring city-state of Verone, and we would join her as Lady Lenna and company. While I was surprised at the swiftness of these arrangements, as we had only made the decision to head to Verone that morning, Reikka was possibly the most tenacious sister of us. I handed the note to Hilda, who read it with a frown.

Adelay tossed a collection of dresses on the bed and placed her hands on her hips, assessing us as if we were her troops lined up in front of her. She seemed to decide something in her head, nodding to herself in confirmation, her curls bouncing as she did.

"Catherine has had the most recent experience with courtly styles and manners, so she will play the part of her ladyship. That leaves the two of you." She pointed between Tris and Hilda. "To play the parts of her guards. I can be her lady-in-waiting, and you, Adrien, are clearly ready to be a royal scribe or something." She gave him a raised brow.

"After a few decades in the libraries in Ontanio, I don't have much else in the way of clothing," he said with a shrug and a sheepish smile.

"Perfect, that can be your cover," she said, picking up a dress and handing it to me.

Neither Hilda nor Tris had any complaints about the arrangements since they would be allowed to keep their leathers as usual. I, on the other hand, did not look forward to stuffing myself into more corsets and gowns over the next several days, possibly weeks, to find this elf. However, there was no arguing with Adelay's reasoning, and as a senior sister, I had no choice but to follow orders.

I sighed, looking at the pile of clothing, so similar to everything I had left behind in Bernitra, in hopes of passing many moons before needing to don such attire again. I felt Adrien sidle up next to me, his deep, musky scent preceding him. He smelled of earth and parchment, like a cozy basement library that I could curl up in. He cleared his throat, thankfully pulling me back to the present, and I threw him a look over my shoulder.

"Catherine?" he asked in a low voice.

"The name my sisters use," I said, untying the laces of my leather vest and pulling it over my head. "My given name."

"Right." He scrunched up his nose and turned his back to me only to come face to face with Adelay's ample cleavage, newly released from her corset. "I suppose I'll go find a carriage or something," he mumbled and headed quickly for the door. Adelay gave me a wink as he left, and I stifled a chuckle in response.

"This is amazing," Tris said from her perch on the foot of the bed. She was braiding her hair back on top of her head. While the shaved sides would still stand out here, it would be less obvious if it was all pulled back. When none of us answered, she looked up, arms still woven in her hair, and smiled wide. "I have never been on a mission with more than one of my sisters without a warder. I feel like it's a vote of confidence." She scrunched her nose. "Unless Adrien is meant to be our warder, but he's certainly not acting like it." My eyes shot to Adelay and then Hilda, unsure of what to say. This situation was a first for all of us, I'm sure, but instead of excitement, it left me with a feeling of trepidation.

"Could be," Hilda said evenly. Taking a few steps across the room, she shooed Tris' hands away and took up the braids herself. "Or it could also be a sign of desperation. We are on the verge of war, and the warders need to prepare for it. This mission is integral to the future of our people. Who's to say what any of this means?"

Her words hit home as I looked between my sisters. This mission could change the course of the war and our lives with it. Taking on the humans would be hard enough with their numbers and the dangerous crossing of the Aellon Channel, but to also take on the Elves whose skill and strength were as legendary as Aelthor himself might very well be suicide.

"No stalling, the nights half over," Adelay chided from her spot by the closet where she was forcing her endowed chest into a light blue dress that gave her a regal look as if she was a queen herself.

***

As it turned out, Reikka had also arranged a carriage to take us to the castle, where there was a small dinner reception taking place in honor of the princess. At this point, we would miss dinner but could arrive in time for introductions and some dancing. Leave it to noble humans to make everything an event. There were many things I liked about life on the continent, but the social requirements of the ruling classes were not one of them.

The castle at Borreagor was one of the most ornate in the kingdom of Liagheria. It was of ancient construction, dating back to the time of the Elves' rule. With spiraling towers, its shining white walls were carved with interlacing designs of vines and trees that gave it an ethereal look. It towered over the city's mud-brick buildings and thatched roofs. Unlike Bernitra's cliffs, this side of the desert slowly gave way to vegetation and was often the victim of violent winds and electric storms as they battered against the changing landscape. Despite the odds, the city and its inhabitants flourished as a direct trade route between Liagheria, Wreabarroth, and Verone. I'd had the opportunity to visit a handful of times in the last few years, and even so, the grandeur of the castle shining against the sunlight still managed to take my breath away.

Inside the castle gates, we were quickly ushered by well-dressed livery men into an ornate entry, where a finely dressed courtier took my name. Offering his arm, he led me through the entry and to the ballroom, where, with a booming voice, he introduced me as Lady Vongale to the room before bowing sharply and leaving.

Here in the ballroom, I realized my chosen style of dress was a little out of place. In the courts of Wreabarroth, women styled themselves after the queen, a native to the desert region who preferred loose flowing gowns with wide sleeves and their hair styled up on top of their heads. Here, the dresses were larger and heavier with tailored sleeves, and most women wore their hair down or half pulled back, all straight as a pin. It never ceased to amaze me the lengths humans would go to gain influence, even if it was something as silly as a hairstyle. At least my dress gave the appearance of a small waist without needing the corset too tight. Looking around, it appeared that many of these women were walking around breathless in the name of fashion. Luckily, no one seemed to notice my introduction, continuing with their conversations, and dancing regardless.

I looked through the crowd, scanning the room for anyone from the previous court who might recognize me. It had been long enough that I doubted the regular court that resided here would remember me with my dyed hair and the dusting of makeup that gave my face a slightly darker tint. Behind me, Adelay and the others slithered in at the side doors, trying not to draw attention. I spotted Reikka moving toward me.

Reikka was tall and lean, showing it off with a dark green dress that hugged her figure before splitting at the thigh and pooling behind her. While this would be considered mild attire in Wraithland, here, it would be scandalous. Her long red-black hair, so deep in color it looked almost unreal, was left loose with just a few pins to keep it from falling into her face. She was the epitome of savage grace, and guests quickly jumped out of her way as she cut through the crowd. If it wasn't her attire or demeanor that scared them, most of the guests here would certainly be aware of her reputation on the continent.

Here, Reikka was known as the queen of the underworld. She had a hand in nearly every illegal and unsavory dealing on the eastern half of the continent, all while maintaining the guise of a human. This particular position had been very beneficial to the Harridans over the years, providing information and transport for specialized activities. It also provided her with power to wield over the nobility of several courts, many of which were indebted to her in one way or another. The building of her vast empire had kept her away from the manor for many years, so I had only the briefest interactions with her, but her notoriety was not lost on me.

Lifting the skirts of my ridiculously large dress, I made my way down the steps to greet her. She gave me a quick peck on the cheek before turning and offering me her arm. Adelay and Adrien fell into step behind us while Tris and Hilda took up posts along the outskirts of the room. Wordlessly, Reikka led me back into the crowd.

A wisp of cerulean magic danced across the path before us, piquing my interest. Keeping my steps fluid and my face impassive, I trailed it with my eyes before it dispersed into nothing. Magic was nearly eradicated on the continent, except for a few hidden pockets, making it very surprising that anyone would dare use it in a castle, let alone the castle of Sir Lounton Markest, the Duke of Borreagor. While more tolerant and benevolent than most noblemen in other matters, Duke Markest was staunchly against magic. Even now, thousands of years after its annihilation, he sent out regular war bands to search and destroy any signs or relics of it.

Reikka slowed to a stop near a curtained alcove, and the others casually approached us. As a woman of few words, Reikka simply nodded to each of them in turn as a welcome.

"Her Highness has been convinced to move her trip up a few days and accompany us on the morrow. It will take a few hours for her people to prepare her, but we will leave at noon. Arrive here then." Her voice had a husky lilt that seemed fitting for her.

I nodded and scanned the room again, seeing another few wisps of the same cerulean magic curl toward a man with his back to me. Adelay said something to Reikka that I didn't quite hear as the man's head shot to the side as if someone had called him. He bowed quickly and moved away, revealing an incredibly elegant young woman in his wake. She smiled to herself, her dainty lips only pulling up slightly. This would be the magic user, and according to the small gold circlet on her head, she was also the princess.

I hid my shock with a sigh, eyes flicking away toward Adrien, who stood at an angle beside me also looking out over the crowd. Something in his face snagged my attention. I looked back at Princess Ameria, then back to him. It was the eyes; they had the same hooded slate blue-gray, the same firm jaw, and the same charming smile. While my brain ran through the calculations of how this could be true, the girl caught my eye and then spotting Reikka, began to make her way over to us.

"Your Highness," Reikka greeted her smoothly. "May I present the Lady Lenna Vongale." I curtsied and put out a hand to the princess as was customary. She reached out, then hesitated. My eyes snapped up, just catching the look of shock that passed over her face. She coughed gently into her other elbow and apologized before finally placing her soft hand in mine. I bent my head, kissing the air over her hand, and let it go gently before stepping back to see Hilda behind me. Adrien, it appeared, had slipped away into the crowd.

"Your Highness," I said, using the higher pitch I often employed in the company of nobles. "It is a pleasure to meet you. I'm just enchanted by the opportunity to travel with you. Have you ever been to the city of Verone?"

It took a moment for her to respond, a moment in which her eyes searched for something on Hilda's face.

"Uh, yes, I have been," she said kindly, finally peeling her eyes from my sister. "Only once or twice, however. It's a beautiful place."

"That's what I hear. You'll have to show me around since I've never been. I'm likely to get lost in such a large city. I hear it's the biggest city on the continent." I giggled, clutching the necklace at my throat and straining not to roll my eyes at myself.

"It is quite large and busy, but I assure you, the people there are the kindest you will ever meet and will easily help you find your way," she said. "Personally, I am excited by the idea of having another woman my own age to keep company with. It feels like I'm often surrounded by stodgy old men or witless young ladies."

I smiled at the compliment. The woman in front of me couldn't be more than twenty-five with a head of thick sandy hair, high cheekbones, and those familiar blue-gray eyes.

"I wish I could promise that I wasn't witless at times myself." We laughed, and I took the opportunity to step back, throwing a look at Hilda, who continued to keep her gaze away from us. A lightning bolt of shock threw me off balance, and I clutched my stomach if only to grab onto something. "I apologize, your Highness, but please excuse me as I am in need of a washroom."

"Of course," the princess said graciously. "Out that way, and down the hall will be a chambermaid waiting outside." The princess waved her hand behind her.

"Thank you, Your Highness." I curtsied low and stepped away. "Helen, attend me." I used Hilda's cover name, throwing the words over my shoulder as I made my way hurriedly out of the room. While I probably should have, at this moment in time, I didn't care in the slightest about insulting the princess. Every nerve in my body was electrified with this new revelation.

Just as described, two young chambermaids were waiting on a bench outside a door not far down the hall. They both jumped up, one opening the door for me. "My guard will care for me, thank you," I said coolly.

Inside the small room, I dropped a protective wall around us before the door clicked shut. Whirling on Hilda as I did so. She stood as an immobile wall in front of me, legs wide, arms crossed over her chest, ready for whatever I was about to unleash.

"What is the princess to you?" I said, keeping my voice as level as possible. This was a woman with years of training and skill over me. I wasn't even sure of the full extent of her powers or her influence with Father.

"It's of no concern to you." She barely moved, keeping

everything about her presence even.

"Should it be of concern to your son?" It was a shot in the dark, but the momentary guttering in her eyes told me I had hit home. I couldn't hide my inhale of shock. He had said that Pterol could harm his mother and sister, but I didn't think she would also be one of us. She winced at my reaction, chewing the side of her lip as she looked across the room, lined with chamber pots that smelled of shit, piss, and vomit.

"Don't involve yourself in things you aren't prepared to handle."

"It's too late for that."

I began pacing, my mind spinning, clicking together more pieces of this insane puzzle that was my sisterhood. Hilda was Adrien's mother, possibly Aelthor's daughter or sister, at least if the rumors were true. No one had ever confirmed them, but she shared the same light features and those hooded blue-gray eyes. My gut twisted.

"What does that mean?" She looked at me now, her face stony as ever, giving away nothing.

"Father wants me to bear your grandchild." Magic flared at my fingertips, all the energy that had built up in me begging for release. I stopped pacing and turned to face her. "Adrien can't know."

"No." She dropped her arms, and silver-grey flames flared upward around her only for a moment, but it was enough to stop me in my tracks. I wondered if she did it on purpose, knowing I could see her magic. The desperation in her eyes gave me enough of an answer. "That child will be more than a weapon to use against you; it will be used against him, and it will be a weapon upon itself with the power that the two of you contain. You can't go through with it."

"Do I have a choice?" I threw my arms in the air. The vines wrapped around my heart, constricting. "Did you?"

"It doesn't matter." She took a step toward me, putting both hands on my shoulders, concern lining her face. "Ameria's mother was my sister—blood sister." Hilda corrected herself. "She was murdered in the childbed while I watched. The girl doesn't know her parentage, and I assume she doesn't know about her powers."

Hilda had a real sister. A queen among humans.

"She knows," I said flatly. "She used them tonight. But why, though? What good is having an Elven-blooded Wraith princess here if she doesn't even know what she is? Why kill her mother?"

Hilda shook her head, releasing me and stepping away. "I wish I knew, but what is done is done. Aelthor has a plan, and we are to follow it."

I paused, taken aback by her need to defend the decisions of our leaders. Adrien's words drifted back to me, the descriptions of my sisters and their inability to see past the immediate moment. Maybe this was how to survive, how Hilda, after decades of following orders, had managed to keep herself together. I could not do that.

"Are we? You just said not to. Hilda, what the fuck?"

She pushed a hand into her bangs and grumbled to herself. Never had Hilda looked even the slightest bit flustered, and to see her barely holding it together rocked something in my core. At well over a hundred years old, she was no more in control of her life than I was. She was in no better place than me, still simply doing what we were told in hopes that it would bring us, what? Peace? Or something.

I took a breath. Then another.

"It doesn't matter. I don't want a child," I said, shaking my head. I would tell Hilda what she needed to know for now while I took the time to figure all of this out. My sisters had always been my solace, but now I wasn't sure I could even trust them, through no fault of their own. Never in my life had I felt the depth of bleakness of being alone, and now, suddenly, I was more alone than I had ever been. "Let's just get through this mission and we will figure the rest out later.

"Yes." Hilda took a calming breath. "We find the elf. Then, we find the Elven stronghold. Then Aelthor can break the wards and take on the continent." She closed her eyes and swallowed hard. A moment passed, allowing me to collect myself before she opened her eyes again, nodded at me, and opened the door. With a deep breath, I stepped past her and back to the ballroom.

It was not lost on me that she had referred to Aelthor taking on the continent instead of our people, as it had always been preached to us. As if one man would retain the glory and the spoils for the work of hundreds if not thousands of people, like us, like the Gasyter army, like Father and Daren and the rest of the council. Because she was not wrong.

CHAPTER EIGHTEEN

The rest of the evening went as one would expect. Courtiers plied the princess and the duke with compliments and gifts while dancing and drinking themselves into oblivion. One thing about humans on the continent, they never seemed to learn how to hold their alcohol.

Aside from a raised brow from Adelay, no one said anything about the abrupt departure to the washroom or the princess's reaction to Hilda. Whether it was for self-preservation or because they already knew the details of the situation, I wasn't quite sure, but I welcomed the reprieve nonetheless. I replayed the scene in my mind: the princess's hesitation, the look of shock, the resemblance between the two, and the way her eyes trailed us as we left the room. She had to know something; the question was what?

We bided our time, fulfilling our given roles until an

appropriate time came and we could leave without suspicion. Back at the inn, which I found was called the Brayflower we retired to our singular room. Luckily, Adelay was familiar with the space and was able to use her magic to conjure up trundle beds and blankets for each of us from the other unused rooms.

The following morning, most of us woke late, knowing full well what sleeping conditions on the road were like, even in the company of a princess. None of us had much that needed to be prepared except for our small satchels of necessities.

Reikka had again organized the carriage and guard as well as the baggage a lady would typically require. As I climbed into the carriage in another corset and fancy dress, I couldn't help but wonder what other forms of female torture she had chosen for me and how soon I could escape them for the comfort of my leathers.

We arrived at the castle at the appointed time to find the princess predictably not prepared. Reikka was there in the courtyard, directing servants and guards in her usual curt manner as if she were the princess herself. Today, she wore a long flowing skirt that sat high on her waist with a blouse and leather jacket on top that stopped short above her hips. Her fiery hair was pulled back from her face and pinned behind her ears. I noticed the way many of the female servants watched her movements with awe. It was bold for a woman, not trained as a guard or working a trade to wear leather, and odd for the style of dress and top that most would consider inappropriately lacking in bustles, slips, and other torture devices. But the way she moved in it, so freely, gracefully, like a warrior in disguise, which, of course, was exactly what she was.

With Reikka's direction, we only set off with an hour's delay, but even so, the excess manpower and baggage of the princess would slow the five-day journey down considerably. I felt the weight of this mission bearing down on me, and I would have preferred the soreness of riding a horse and arriving earlier, but we were already tied in with the princess.

The first day, Adelay, Reikka, Adrien, and I rode in the carriage while Hilda and Tris rode beside us, at least pretending to be on guard. We passed the time playing cards, sleeping, or, in Adrien's case, reading an obnoxiously large tome that smelled like mildew. Apparently, he had picked up an interest in reading during his time as a scribe.

The first stop was, thankfully, in a small town that had an inn with enough space for most of us. We arrived late in the evening to hot meals and beds that were not terrible. The following morning over a lavish breakfast of porridge with sausages and onions, Ameria asked if I might keep her company, leaving the others to ride alone.

As expected, the princess's carriage was plush and luxurious with soft velvet seats, lots of extra cushions, and even a table that screwed into the space between the seats for eating or playing card games. We chatted about mostly trivial things as the morning wore on. She asked about my childhood and my impending marriage to Reikka's non-existent younger brother, whom she had thankfully never met. In return, I asked about her main palace residence, any suitors she might have, and why she was choosing now to visit Verone.

The latter elicited a stilted response that gave me the feeling Ameria wasn't quite telling the truth. She had claimed that the visit was to spend some time in the famed library of family records. Here, the family lines of every noble and even some commoners were recorded as well as all intersecting history. Verone had originally been a spiritual center in the time of the Elves, and later a beacon of neutrality. They were able to avoid the many wars and subsequent destruction that occurred throughout the world growing into a haven for records and books from across the continent to avoid destruction. It had become their mission to protect all texts, maps, and historical artifacts, and was now one of the only places these sacred items were kept.

Most nobles proudly kept their own records of family lines in their homes as well, usually to boast about their Elven or noble blood. A royal family would certainly have that information in their private libraries, which led me to believe there was something else she was looking for that would not be found in her libraries at home.

I let the line discussion slide away as the princess artfully changed the subject to shopping in the city, making a mental note to bring it up again at a later time. It was likely nothing, but my curiosity was piqued, and if I had to spend several days with the woman, it was no harm to use my skills to find out the truth.

The opportunity presented itself to me on the third day of travel. We had stopped to break for the horses at a river crossing and were strolling together along the water, with Tris and another of her guards in tow. She had just finished the story of the Broken House of Castlemore that launched the Thousand Year War that had been raging between Liagheria and their rival Streyland to the north ever since. A moment of silence had passed, and I looked out at the water thoughtfully.

"Princess, what is it again that you are hoping to find in Verone that the Liagherian libraries won't already have? I assume your family tree is quite thoroughly documented, is it not?" I tried to keep my voice calm and almost disinterested. However, when I pushed my magic toward her, I felt a jump in her heartbeat at the question.

"It's nothing really, but my mother was a peasant, so there

isn't much on her lineage. I'm hoping to find some more information on her, that's all."

"Really?" I feigned shock. "And this was allowed. It was my impression that all nobles kept their bloodlines close."

She sighed. "They do, but my father balked at the wishes of his family and married for love anyway."

I smiled wistfully. Considering Hilda's admission about her parentage, I could only imagine the entire love affair had been fabricated and coerced. There was so much innocence in the woman next to me. She was a princess, sheltered from so much, yet forced to grow up amidst the vicious games of a court immersed in a generations-long war. Nothing in me believed this woman who hid her magic so easily was as innocent as she appeared.

"I have heard as of late of a certain prophecy that includes the House Castlemore. Do you know of it?"

Another skip in her heartbeat.

"I do," she said calmly. A shout from the carriages carried on the wind to us, and we turned to head back the way we had come, preparing to set off again. "The prophecy states that a boy of my line will strike down the Elves and restore the balance of our planet."

"If it is a boy as the prophecy says, then he should be born soon, as the coming of the third moon nears. Common logic would say that this boy would be your son."

"Possibly," she shrugged. "It's entirely possible that the boy in the prophecy has nothing at all to do with me. Maybe it's one of my cousins or the Streyland line. It makes no difference either way. I have no intentions of marrying anyone or bearing any children."

My hand went to my throat in shock. "But how will you rule?

No man would willingly bow to a woman."

"Stop it." Ameria's head snapped around to me. "We may not have been friends long, but I have heard enough from you to know that you don't believe that for a second, Lenna," she hissed under her breath. "I don't know what part you are playing here. If you've been sent to kill me or are using me to get into something in Verone, it doesn't matter. I'm not an idiot or an easy target, as your employer might think I am. If Reikka can rule the trade over multiple countries, if Queen Agyros can rule without her husband, then what's standing in my way?" She looked me up and down. "Certainly not you."

And with that, she turned and trudged away. I didn't bother to hide my smile as I followed her into the carriage. She looked surprised when I sat on the plush seat opposite, eyes warily watching my every move. This was a first for me to be found out in this way, but I wasn't surprised; there was something about Ameria that did not meet the eye.

"When did you know?" I asked subtly, pulling my skirts up and pulling off my shoes to rest them on the bench. There was no point in pretending to be polite anymore.

"Before I even met you." She huffed with an eye-roll. "Reikka has never had an interest in me. I have nothing to offer her, being controlled as I am by my father, the cabinet, and the rules of court. Then suddenly, she shows up here while I'm staying with the duke and interjects herself into my itinerary with this unknown lady?"

"I suppose it was a bit contrived, but we are low on time these days," I said honestly. "At least you don't have to worry about me killing you. We just need to get to Verone quickly to handle some business, and yes, crossing the borders with your entourage is a great help in getting past the city walls, not to mention the amenities that come with traveling with royalty." I waved a hand to indicate the carriage we were riding in.

Ameria laughed. "So that's it, you're using me for the cushy ride there? Then what? We go our separate ways?" I shrugged in response, not willing to divulge anything more. "And what if I have you killed instead?" Her eyes narrowed on me.

"Then my people and I will be forced to kill you and the entirety of our entourage to save the mission."

She laughed, throwing her head back, blonde ringlets bouncing in her coiffure. "What mission could be so important that your people would risk an all-out war with the whole of Liagheria?"

I shook my head, giving her a wry smile, appearing utterly unruffled by her confidence. "That's not your concern."

"Oh, but you have made it my concern by involving me." Her voice lowered into a steely flatness that was meant to set me on edge. It was a trick I had used often enough to recognize it from someone else.

"Don't you have enough on your plate with this never-ending war in the north? I'm surprised you even have time to run errands like this when your forces and your riches have been dwindling year in and year out."

I saw the soft cerulean wisps begin to pull from the air around us before I even heard the crackling of power at her fingertips. Now, I couldn't help the twisted smile that spread across my face. I clicked my tongue at her.

"Now, now, princess, magic isn't going to help you when it comes to me."

Her eyes went wide, but the wisps of her power remained slithering around her. I reached out, touching one of them, and twisting it around my finger. She couldn't see it, but she could feel it. They could always feel me pulling the magic out of their hands.

She held her ground, staring me down like a worthy opponent, but I pushed my magic out, feeling her body, the racing heart, the anxious sweat, the tension in her muscles. She was scared.

We were at a standstill. There was nothing I wanted or needed from her, but leaving her alive, knowing about my power, was a huge risk. Then again, so was murdering a princess without explicit instructions to do so, especially a princess that descended from Aelthor.

"Let's just say I'll keep your secret, and you will keep mine." I dropped my hand from playing in the tendrils of magic that wove around us.

"It's not just you I have to worry about," she said, holding her body and magic rigid. "There's still Reikka, and the other women in your company, as well as the scribe. No scribe should have that much muscle under his robes."

My eyebrows hitched up in surprise at the last part of her statement. When had she seen Adrien's muscles? I shook my head, pushing the thought away.

"As I said, we are on a mission that has nothing to do with you."

"And the prophecy?"

"My own curiosity, nothing more."

She snorted a laugh, the rest of her magic sputtering out of sight, showing her lack of control. Another small swirl appeared and wound its way around her hands as if she wasn't prepared to trust me fully.

"Is it a deal, Princess?"

Her eyes traveled up and down my frame before she reluctantly nodded. An awkward moment passed as the last bit of her magic faded, and her heart slowed to normal. I sighed and pushed the curtain from the window to look out at the grasslands that covered this part of the continent.

"Can you show me how to do that?" Ameria's voice was so soft I almost missed it, but when I turned, I saw just how intently she was looking at me. "To halt someone's magic like that."

"Unfortunately, it's part of my innate magic. Not everyone is capable, but it takes many years to master regardless." She nodded, eyes downcast. "Do you not have someone to train you?" I asked.

"Magic is not legal," she said solemnly. "It hasn't been for centuries."

"So, what, you've been teaching yourself?" She nodded, and my mouth fell open. "Not even your father has taught you his magic?"

"I don't think my father has magic."

"He must." I insisted, sitting up now. "All the noble families have spent centuries keeping as much Elven-blood in their lines as possible. That would mean magic, too."

She nodded again, although hesitantly. I could see the wheels turning in her mind as she debated what to say next. I let the time stretch out as she thought.

It was true that the noble families had done all they could to keep the bloodlines thick with Elven-blood; we kept track of every noble and Elven line on the continent as well as Wraithland, and even some on distant continents. I had always assumed they trained their children in the use of magic in secret, only subjecting lesser classes to the law, but perhaps I had been wrong. I made a note to ask one of the warders on my return.

"Some things," she said finally. "Uh, happened to my father when I was young, and it affected his health. I doubt, even if he had magic at one point, that he would have it now."

I nodded in understanding. Many things could interfere with magic, a binding spell, an illness, or even something as trivial as a broken heart.

"Well, I'm not an expert, but let's see what you know so far, and maybe I can show you a trick or two," I said.

By the time we stopped that evening, I had shown her how to blow a candle to light, to move cards and pillows about, and to enhance her senses. The latter was a struggle for her, whereas the former two had been a struggle for me as children. I explained how everyone's magic manifested a little differently and that she would master most things with ease, given her parentage.

We stopped at a small copse of trees along a riverside where the servants pitched tents for us to spend the night. Dinner was a simple stew and bread eaten around the fireside. Ameria was exhausted from testing her magic so much and went to bed early, whereas I found myself restless. Teaching the princess had been exciting at the moment. I had never had such an opportunity to use my magic freely and to show another woman how to harness hers. At the manor, magic use was restricted to classrooms and specific activities.

Now I worried about what it meant that the princess had never been taught about her magic, that I was crossing some line by teaching her about it. Perhaps she would be an ally in the future, supporting magic users and their freedom. If she survived the war that we were going to bring to her door.

The many days of travel and the incidents with Daren and Father began to wear on me again. I could feel my body winding itself up into a tight ball. Unfortunately, most of the alcohol had been finished in the previous evenings. Apparently, the servants were unprepared for the thirst of my party and failed to pack adequately.

Across the fire, I caught Adrien's eye, and I imagined the strong muscles and the vivid image of the serpent marking that I knew lurked beneath the loose gray robes of a scribe. He stood, stretching, before saying good night and leaving the circle of fire. Moments later, I rose too, claiming exhaustion, knowing that I was fooling no one. Both Tris and Adelay gave me heated looks, while Hilda refused to look at me at all. Reikka, per usual, remained impassive, the fire illuminating her red-black locks.

I found Adrien leaning on a tree, looking up at the stars a few yards away from the tents.

"Enjoy the ride with the princess?" he asked smugly, not looking at me.

"It was fine," I said. "She's smarter than she looks."

He turned toward me, a small crease forming between his brows.

"Nothing to be concerned about." I waved him away, holding back the truth. "She just has more to her than daydreams and embroidery."

"She doesn't trust us," he said, looking back up at the sky.

"How can you tell?"

"It's all over her, the way she looks at us all, especially Reikka."

"I imagine Reikka's reputation precedes her in this case, but I think the rest of us are fine." I leaned back onto the tree, my shoulder brushing his. "I do wonder how we will break away from her once we reach Verone?"

"I'm sure Reikka has it all worked out, and we will find out when we arrive."

I nodded, sliding ever so closer to him and turning slightly so that my breath would brush his collar as I spoke in a hushed voice. "She's after something herself in Verone."

"Aren't we all?" His voice came out husky as he turned to me, his face inches away, the air between us filling, mixing with our scents.

I took a breath and leaned in, tilting my head upward. My chest brushed his with every breath I took. "I just hope she isn't after the same thing we are."

His nose trailed down mine, electrifying my skin and causing me to suck in the cool night air. A low growl rumbled through his chest; my core tightened with anticipation of release.

"Oh, Brigitta," he whispered. "Just like how I'm not interested in someone who is commanded to sleep with me, I'm not interested in someone using me as an escape either."

He leaned back slightly, revealing a darkened gaze that made my insides molten hot.

"So, what are you interested in then?"

"I think you know," he said, a muscle feathering in his jaw before he pushed off the tree. He shoved his hands in his pockets, taking a few steps back and letting his eyes travel down the length of me. His gaze was enough to scorch my skin beneath the heavy dress before he turned and stalked off, leaving me cold and alone, yet somehow sated.

CHAPTER NINETEEN

The next several days were spent in much the same way. I rode in the carriage with the princess, where we played cards, practiced magic, and talked over her ideas of how a country should be run if it weren't for the stodgy traditions and insidious ideas of war-hungry men. There was something about her hopefulness, her fire that ignited a fire in me. I commiserated with the idea of fighting back against the men in my life who had controlled everything I did since I was a child, pushing aside the idea that being a success was fulfilling the narrative they had written for me. If only it were as simple as she made it sound, if the lives of others didn't hang in the balance because of my actions.

Often, I found myself looking at my sisters from afar, wondering where they actually came from, were they stolen girls like I had been? Or were they bred for their potential? There was too much I couldn't discuss with them, so many secrets between us that I felt utterly alone. I craved distraction from all the thoughts swirling in my head but found none, no wine to soothe my frazzled nerves, no male company to distract my brain. Even the company of so many of my sisters gave little solace or distraction.

Finally, about mid-morning on the seventh day, we arrived at the borders of Verone, and I felt my salvation within reach. At the apex of five different countries, the city of Verone was the largest on the continent, boasting its own functioning government separate from any other sovereign. With so little land to sustain the thousands of people inside the city, all of the farmland and industry in the territory surrounding it had been put to work. The land was organized in a beehive pattern, with patches of earth separated by streams of water flowing between them. The patches were home to overflowing gardens of vegetables and flowers or livestock. Men and women worked side by side, both old and young, ambled along in their work. Every so often, a small home and barns were situated on one of the patches. As we drew closer, the patches of farmland gave way to patches of industry, with grinding mills and weavers' shacks settled between workers' homes and storage buildings.

The main walls of the city were leftover relics of the ancient Elves. Thick tree trunks, wider than the span of a man's arms, grew out of the earth, their branches intertwining and connecting to create a concentrated base that had petrified into hardened stone. As the walls rose over several stories, the branches became less concentrated and more like a lace weave that allowed guards to walk the ramparts and look out across the plains.

There were five main entry gates to the city, one for each of the border countries. Just outside the wall, a cluster of dwellings and shops had been built to accommodate those waiting to gain admittance into the city. We arrived at a large barn just beside the outer gate and dismounted our carriages, the massive petrified walls looming above us.

The large steel outer gate was thrown open, displaying the bright yellow flag of Liagheria on one side, and the pink and white Veronian flag on the other. Making our way to the gate, we were greeted by a large dark-skinned man dressed as a clerk and several guards. The princess stepped forward, extending her right hand and with it the royal seal that adorned her ring finger. The clerk smiled warmly and offered us all a welcome to the great city. Before we could enter, we were required to state our names, our business in the city, and the expected duration of our trip. We were given stern warnings about the laws of the city and how to apply for an extended stay should our business run beyond the designated time frame. Everyone in our company was expected to sign a document stating that we understood what we were told and would abide by the laws of Verone.

Finally, we were allowed to pass into the outer bailey, a space large enough to contain barracks, barns, training areas, and more, from what I could see. The space between the cities' defensive walls was large enough to house a small city in and of itself, spanning a few hundred yards between the two walls and miles in either direction. The inner wall of the city was similar to the outer one but taller and thinner at the base. The sides housed more openings in the woodstone to serve as windows and doorways, even some having balconies.

At this gate, another man checked the paperwork given to us from the previous before allowing us to enter the city proper. Here, we were allowed to remount our horses and carriages for the journey to the city center and our accommodations.

Beyond these walls, the city exploded with vibrancy and excitement. Despite its regimented design, the buildings had grown into a kaleidoscope of colors and structures that shocked the mind and astounded the eye. Verone was unlike any other on the continent and was one of the few places where cultures and beliefs could converge without strife, and it showed in every pocket of space here.

In the streets, people went about their business like any town, but somehow displaying more joy, more noise, more smells—more of everything. Even I couldn't hide the awe in my expression as I stared out the carriage window. Beside me, the princess vibrated with anticipation.

"It's just as amazing as I remembered it," she said breathlessly.

***

We arrived at the two inns we would reside in for our stay just as the sun began to sink beneath the wall. It took us hours to maneuver through the streets, picking our way through throngs of people, markets, and construction work. Neither the princess nor I breathed a word to each other most of the time, simply staring in awe at the magnificence of the city.

The city center was marked by the castles main gate as well as several inns and homes that were more like small castles themselves in their size and design. The two most ornate structures were mirror images of each other situated on either side of the main road leading to the gate. One of these was to be the residence of the princess and her household while my sisters and I would take residence in a smaller building, a honeycomb over, that boasted a sign reading "The Davenlyn House." While

I'm sure it wasn't as lavish as the princess's accommodations, I was more than pleased to find my sisters and I had a set of interconnected rooms on the top floor that would allow us a level of privacy and freedom to complete our mission. The servants that had journeyed with us would take up residence a floor below and were given explicit instructions not to enter our rooms without invitation by a stern-looking Reikka.

We wasted no time settling into our space before taking to the rooftops. As the rest of our entourage looked forward to their beds after a long journey, we craved something different. Hilda laid a plan of the city before us, assigning us each a sector, and we fanned out in the shadow of dusk. Each of us, even Adrien, dressed in black leathers with hoods and masks, moving roof to roof in concentric circles outward from the Davenlyn House.

It felt good to move like this again. I had only gotten a taste of training with my short stay in Wraithland before the trip began, but now, with my leathers on, high above the ground and its people, I felt the constriction in my chest release, if only a little. I moved with a rhythm in time with my breathing, counting my steps, and assessing the distance from one vantage point to another. I made graceful leaps between tall buildings and swung from the terraces jutting out from their sides. Standing on the top of one building, I leaned out over the edge, feeling the cool breeze as it rustled my hood and the wisps of hair that had escaped my hasty braid. This was what freedom felt like for me, and I reveled in it.

Our efforts resulted in nothing, not a single sighting of the elf, not that any of us truly expected to see anything. We were all just itching to get out and see what the city was from above. My sector was completed before the two moons rose to their full height in the sky.

Reluctantly, I made my way back to find Hilda and Reikka sitting at the communal table with trays of food and bottles of wine between them. I sat, filling a glass and plate for myself as the others trickled in behind me. The rest of the evening was spent reviewing maps of the city and making plans for staking out different libraries, possible contacts, or any place we thought the elf might frequent during his time here.

Eventually, Reikka and Hilda made their way to bed, followed by Adelay, who woke Tris up from her chair at the table and helped her in her drink-addled shuffle to bed. I caught Adrien watching me with a quizzical expression as I chuckled to myself, watching them go.

"What?" I said, eyes narrowing on him.

"It's just nice to see you happy for a change."

"Happiness is a weak emotion. It breeds complacency and gluttony," I said with a roll of my eyes.

"Right, while fear and anger are great motivators," he said sarcastically, and I shot him an annoyed look. He bit the inside of his lip, pausing before he spoke again. "But what if that's wrong? What if they beat that into you as children so you never had anything to fight for? Never questioned your place in the world or the way they used your bodies?"

The way he said the last part made my skin crawl, but they had used my body, my magic, my skills. Once, I might have thought that it was their right after everything they had done for me, everything they had given me, but now, I just felt disgusted. I narrowed my eyes on him.

"Let me show you something," he said, standing and coming around the table to me. I jumped back in my chair, still not comfortable with the idea of him being in my mind.

"I'm just showing you an image like you showed me at the

ball. If you feel anything weird at all, say something, and I'm out of there. Okay?" He knelt in front of me, resting both hands on my knees.

I gave him a last withering stare before closing my eyes, mentally letting him past my barriers. For a moment, it was only the blackness of the back of my eyelids, but then a foggy image began to grow in front of me. It was a field. A lush green field spread for what looked like miles, and it was full of wildflowers, yellows, purples, and pinks. The sun streamed down, and I felt it warming my skin. It smelled of grass, moss, and earth. A giggle beside me had me turning my head to see a little girl, no more than six, with dirt on her face and a huge grin as she tossed blades of grass into the air above her head. It was Isadora.

Beside her, a little boy ran in loops around them, squealing with joy. A playful shout came from a large man, the girl's father. He was sitting on a large blanket with a woman, their mother. It was a picnic. I looked from one person to another, their faces alight with the sheer joy of the moment. It was so simple, just a family enjoying the sunshine on a beautiful day together.

My stomach twisted into a knot.

Isadora put out her hand to me. "Come on, Melly, come on, I want to show you something."

I reached out my hand, but just as I would have touched her, the vision fogged over again, fading away into blackness once more.

I opened my eyes to see Adrien's handsome face looking back at me. He rocked onto his heels.

"That was the last image that Isadora's sister saw before she died. I made sure of it. Not us, not her parent's mangled bodies, but this moment of happiness."

My eyes welled with tears that threatened to spill over. Relief and guilt battling for purchase inside me. "Why show me this?"

"Because happiness gives you something to fight for. It's not about mere survival, or numbers, or even doing what's right; it's about this feeling." His eyes searched mine as he spoke. "They beat these feelings out of you because if you were to ever feel them, you would ache for it. But if you have no hope of joy, then you have no reason to object to anything they say. To them, you are just a weapon they have honed, a possession that they leashed with beliefs that will always tie you to them. This feeling of freedom, it awaits you, you can have it. Those feelings, they are as much your right as anyone else's. You just have to fight for them. If you don't, then you, your sisters, and any like you will just continue this same cycle forever."

His words echoed in my mind, bringing me back to Father's office, to the moment I realized I would not want this life for my own child. I sighed heavily, pushing the tears back. I didn't want to think about this. The tension in my body begged for a distraction, a release. What harm would it be to enjoy some time with the Mindwalker, even if it wouldn't result in the child requested?

"So, if I say your speech convinced me that you are right, will that make you happy enough to finally take me to bed?" I blurted.

To his credit, Adrien laughed, that full-bodied laugh that made my toes curl in my boots. Then he leaned forward, his hand slipping behind the back of my neck, and pulled me in for a kiss. It was gentle and loving and far too short-lived.

When he pulled away again, I felt utterly empty. He stood and reached across the table. "Wine?" He asked with a charming smile.

I shook my head and stood as well. "No, I need to get to bed." I leaned in, making sure my chest brushed against his, and gave him a light kiss on the cheek, my hands gripping his robes at the waist. When I pulled away, I let my hands slide down his body, noting the fire burning in his eyes. If he wanted to play games, I would play them too, especially if they gave me a good distraction from everything else on my mind.

CHAPTER TWENTY

I woke up late feeling a little more refreshed. Slipping into my leather pants and a plain tunic, I tied my hair low on my neck and headed to the Library District. There were dozens of libraries in the city of Verone, but the most esteemed libraries were cloistered in the northeast quadrant close to the castle wall. Each had its own honeycomb of land that included the library, ornate gardens, and scribes' dormitories. They were separated by small canals that ran the perimeter of each honeycomb, with only small bridges a few feet wide connecting them. All nine of the major libraries were surrounded by a larger canal to separate them from the city, with the only point of entry a single bridge that stood between the castle and the libraries. These buildings were perhaps the most coveted on the continent, and the care of them was the sole responsibility of the people of Verone.

Passing over the bridge was like walking into a different

world. Here, there were no horses, carts, or hawkers shouting, which created a place of peace and serenity that was hard to come by in a city of this size. It was impossible not to be in awe of the place, with its towering stone buildings, stained glass, and beautiful gardens; it was like walking in a dream.

My goal this morning was simply to blend in, observe, and make some friends with the scribes who ran the libraries we suspected the elf might visit. If possible, I would try to see some of the log books they kept of who entered the libraries and what books they checked out, if any. I doubted the elf would use the name I had heard before, but it wouldn't be a thorough job if we didn't check.

My first stop was to visit my sister, Nessa, who was stationed at the Esoteric Tomes Library.

All the libraries were of similar construction, with sandstone walls that rose several stories before breaking into separate spires. They had large stained-glass windows on the sides that depicted scenes that represented each library's specialty. The Esoteric Tomes Library contained one of the most detailed designs, including symbols from across the entirety of Primthera and its history. I lingered outside, admiring the work until the chatter of a few young scribes brought me back to myself.

Nessa was easily found at the front entrance of the library. Her mousy brown hair hung in loose waves around her shoulders over traditional gray scribe's robes. Her eyes shot up to me over her glasses when I came through the door. Standing, she set the large tome in her hands down and moved behind a tall desk. She was easily one of the smallest of my sisters, and I hid my smile at her stepping up on a stool to lean over the desk, hands clasped on top of it. Her fine features were illuminated by the colorful shades of stained glass from the tall windows that surrounded the library's front entry.

Her face was impassive, but I felt the slap of a cocoon closing around me as I neared her. I reached across the counter, clasping her hand quickly, before resuming our positions of nonchalance.

"Sister Catherine." Nessa gave me a slight smile, but the wariness didn't leave her eyes. "What brings you here?"

"Official business. There are a few of our number staying at the Davenlyn House. Come to dinner; we would appreciate your company." Her eyes grew wide at this, and she shifted on her feet. "When was the last time I saw you? It must have been five years at least."

She nodded. "About that. I haven't been back to the manor in as many. In fact, I have hardly seen anyone in that time. One could almost forget they were part of something like this."

I took a long look at her, understanding that there was something she wasn't saying. "You will always be one of us," I said earnestly. "I'm sorry you've been sequestered here for so long. Hilda is with us; she could jump you back for a short visit." She stiffened.

"Oh no, no, it's okay," she stuttered. "I like it here; it's just a bit shocking to see you and the others, it's good, though."

It wasn't, though; I could see that clearly. She was afraid to go home, to go to Wraithland, to even see her sisters. My chest tightened for her. She had settled here, just like Adelay had in Bernitra. She might even be happy. I cleared my throat, pushing away the thoughts.

"I'm actually hoping you may be able to help me. We are after someone who was looking for information on an old prophecy. It's likely he or his associates have been here or at the other libraries." At this, her eyes blazed, and a smirk crossed her face.

"What was he looking for?" she said in a silky voice, her

excitement palpable.

It was nearly dinner time by the time I left the library. Nessa knew exactly which prophecy I was talking about, as she had helped the princess look it up that morning. She had been able to easily locate all the others who had accessed the information in the last six months, including the request by mail from the elf under the name Weilson Marstead. At the time, he had them delivered to Bernitra, but the request came by carrier from Shiraleigh. A man by the same name had recently visited to read the prophecies in person, as well as visiting several other libraries, including The House of Familial Ties, The Elven Troves, and just this morning The New Continental Library in the company of an Inialos Breandor. All the information made my head spin.

Questions about the elf's intentions, the princess's interest in the prophecy after her earlier dismissal, and the presence of the Wraith Inialos. Luckily, it seemed to excite Nessa, and she promised to look into everything the elf had, hoping to make a connection that we didn't see. I left with the plan to meet with her at the Davenlyn House later that evening to discuss what she had found.

***

After leaving Nessa to her work, I spent some time strolling through the libraries and their gardens. The peace of the place was unlike anything I had ever experienced, and I wasn't prepared to re-enter the fray of the larger city.

It was in the center green, a space between all the libraries where meetings of large numbers of people could take place, that I happened upon Ameria reading on the lawn by a rose garden, a handful of guards loitering around but giving her some space. The wise choice would have been to walk away, but the woman had captured my interest during our travels here, and instead, I made my way over to her.

"Enjoying your stay, Princess?"

She looked up from the book in her lap, startled at first, then smiling. "Ahh, Lenna. A pleasure to see you." She gave me a once-over that made me squirm on the spot. I was certainly not dressed like a lady should be, but then she had to know I was not truly a lady.

"Please join me." She waved a hand over the blanket she had laid out on the grass. I smiled back, carefully sitting with my boots off the edge of the blanket.

"Have you found whatever it is you were looking for yet?" she asked, closing her book and setting it aside.

"Not yet, but we are working on it." She nodded.

"Does Reikka even have a brother?"

I laughed. "No." I paused, shocked at my own honesty. It wasn't something that came easily, but there was no point in lying about this one small thing, not when Ameria already knew so much. I gave a cautious look to the guards, all of which acted as if they had heard nothing, but I dropped the cocoon of protection anyway. Ameria cocked her head to me when she felt it, a line forming between her brows.

"Just something that keeps people from hearing everything, is all," I said, waving a hand at the men.

"So, what, you are just Reikka's errand girl then? You move around where she can't?" she asked, a smirk playing on her face. "And what of the others? Is the scribe supposed to get you access to the libraries or something?"

"We all have our jobs." I shrugged.

"But Reikka is the leader?" Ameria was in a mood, I could see, shooting questions at me to throw me off balance. It was a tactic I recognized, having used it myself many times, but rarely fell victim to it. This question, however, hit home, making me wonder if I had, in fact, said too much to the princess already. I kept my face even and looked directly into her blue-gray eyes.

"It doesn't matter who is the leader."

"Of course it does," she scoffed. "There are five of you, six if you count the scribe. I doubt he's much use anyway but five women; All of you confident, cunning, strong, and with magic, I assume?" Her eyebrows hitched up, seeking my confirmation, to which I rolled my eyes, not giving in to her. "Any one of you could walk into a court and take it over; together, you could rule the whole continent if you wanted to."

This time, I scoffed. "I hardly think that."

"Why?" Her face turned hard. "Don't tell me it's because we are women. What was the last thing you actually needed a man for?"

My brain whirled, finding the path of this conversation likely had something to do with her current position as an unwed princess who was set to take the throne. Likely some comment or action had taken place suggesting she couldn't handle the duty on her own. I thought back to Queen Isla, wondering how she was fairing with her new role as the sole monarch of the vast country of Wreabaroth.

In truth, aside from the occasional release of physical tension, there was little I needed an actual man for. Little I needed anyone for. Of course, that was by Father's design.

"See, you can't even think of anything," she chided, dragging me back to the present. "Look, Lenna, or..." She paused. "Or whatever your name is. I want to make you an offer."

My eyebrows hitched up at that, but I stayed silent, waiting for her to continue.

"It might be completely stupid of me, but I need women like you and your friends on my side." She looked away, and I felt the weight of her gaze lift, not realizing how much it had affected me. "The next few years are going to be very hard on the court of Liagheria. On possibly the whole of the continent. I am going to need women like you. Women that walk in the shadows, that do the things I can't. And you can teach me to wield my power. Together, we could take on anything."

I felt the space between my shoulders tighten, and I couldn't help but shift in my spot. My mind went absolutely blank. It had never even occurred to me that I had the option of leaving the Harridans, or Wraithland, or Father and Aelthor, but here it was, just like that.

"I don't know what Reikka pays you," she continued, turning that heavy gaze back on me. "But I will pay you more."

"I don't need money," the words tumbled out without a thought from me. I had never needed money; it always found its way to me whether Father paid me or not. Likely I had made more in my time as a Saithe through the favors of men and stolen goods than I would need in all my lifetime, but I hadn't kept a penny of it because I had never needed for anything. Again, by design, if we were constantly at work there was no time to think of wants, just as Adrien had pointed out.

"Then where does your loyalty come from?"

The question struck me like a blade to the gut. My loyalty was to my sisters and my people because they deserved it, but what if the people on the continent deserved it, too? Working for the princess would mean turning my back on everything I had known, but what if it could also open the door to peace between my people and the continent? I was only one woman, could I really make such a difference?

I let out a long breath, realizing the princess was still looking at me, her eyes hard, not with anger or hate, but determination. She had a plan in her mind, and I was part of it.

"Think about it," she said finally. "You know where to find me when you've made your decision."

Without any other preamble, she picked up her book. I took it as a dismissal and rose from the ground, mumbling my goodbyes as I strode away.

CHAPTER TWENTY-ONE

I was just slinking out of the Davenlyn to begin my patrol when I found Nessa lounging on its roof, staring up at the darkening sky. She was shrouded in shadows, but it was clear anyway that she was nervous. I wondered vaguely what five years living in the peace of the library district would do to me, if I would become timid like her.

Her glasses were gone, her hair pulled back into a braid, and she wore black leathers like my own. It was a startling contrast to when I last saw her. I didn't ask why she chose not to come in, remembering her earlier nervousness about meeting with all the sisters together. She handed me a leather binder of notes as I flopped down beside her, feeling the weight of the day's revelations already. I wasn't sure I was ready for more right now, but there was little choice in the matter.

"There are some interesting things in there," she said, sitting up. I gave her a raised brow in response. "I've never known Aelthor to even ask for information on a prophecy, so why the interest in this one?"

"It's not the prophecy; it's the elf. If we know what he's after, we have a better shot at getting him and finding the rest of them." I untied the binder and flipped it open on my knees, skimming the papers inside.

"And what good would that do?"

I pursed my lips and gave her a look. The side of her mouth quirked up in acknowledgment. She knew I was not in a position to tell her, but she was my sister. I was getting tired of the secrecy.

"Aelthor can break the wards, but he's afraid the Elves will come out of hiding to stop us from taking over the continent, so he wants to find them and take them out first." The words came out rough and jumbled but honest.

"So, it's vengeance then," she said sadly, more to herself than to me. A moment of silence stretched between us as I looked at the pages in front of me, not really seeing anything.

"I just wish there was a way to break the wards without war. If we could just live together with the humans, and the Elves could go on with whatever and wherever they are," I blurted out, my body tensing as if waiting for a blow in response. I thought of the bottles of dark red wine sitting on the table just inside the window and how they would make this easier.

"Who's to say we can't?" Nessa bit her thumbnail nervously as she looked at me with big, hopeful eyes.

"All the rulers," I sighed, gritting my teeth. "Aelthor and his vengeance, the human kings and their fear of magic, and anyone who doesn't look human." *All the rulers but America*, I thought to myself.

"Let me show you something." Nessa stood suddenly.

"What?" I said, closing the book and rubbing my eyes.

"You have to see it to understand." She bit her thumbnail again as she looked down at me.

"Okay." I tied the book up and left it there on the roof in the shadow of the eve. She pulled up her hood and mask, taking off at a run, launching herself onto the lower neighboring roof, and I followed.

We moved quickly through the city, not just on the rooftops but also through alleyways and buildings. Nessa had grown to know every detail and pocket of the place. It was surprising to see her strength and agility hadn't slipped in the comfort of her position, as mine had. Landing on the ground with a thud, she put a hand up to halt my movements.

"I talk. Got it?" She paused with a raised brow. I nodded, smiling at the sudden change from the timid woman I had seen earlier. This was the part of her that I had trained with in my youth, the woman I knew I could count on.

She led me into the side door of an older building, down a corridor, and a long set of stone steps. At the bottom, there was a thick steel door, only illuminated by a single sconce on the wall beside the handle. She licked her finger and drew a symbol on the surprisingly clean surface of the door, and it swung open immediately, revealing a cavernous room busy with the sights and sounds of magic.

I followed her into the space as the door swung shut behind us. The space was massive, larger than any of the honeycomb parcels above it, and it was illuminated by hundreds of orbs floating above. All around people loitered, chatting, eating, laughing, and practicing magic. There were shop stalls along the walls and music, almost like a whole town square below the city. All around, hundreds of shades of magic danced together, wisps from one, fog from another, a rainbow of colors colliding in an erratic dance that made my head ache. I swallowed, tamping down my magic. There had always been an innateness about my magic that I had needed to learn to control before it overwhelmed me. This was one of those times.

"There are more kinds of beings here than anywhere else on the continent," Nessa said beside me. "Most stay glamoured when they are above, but here, we can all be ourselves."

A large man with a barrel chest and a bald head spotted us and lumbered over, the various chains and buckles on his leathers jingling as he moved. He was head and shoulders taller than most, giving me the impression he was part of the ancient race of giants that were pushed from the continent after the Elves left. People around him followed his line of sight straight to us, and moments later, I saw the convergence of dozens of threads of magic wrap around us. The threat here was unlike anything I had felt. Even when training magic with my sisters, there were only a few of us wielding it at any given time. It was amazing and terrifying all at once.

People moved easily out of the large man's way as a hush settled over the cavern. He stopped short in front of us, one hand tucked in the chain that wrapped over his chest, the other fingering the end of another at his side. His deep burgundy magic twisted around the chain as he stood there looking us over.

"Nessa, you have brought an unapproved newcomer." His voice was softer than I had expected, much softer than the look he was currently giving us.

Nessa nodded, throwing her shoulders back. "This is my sister, Catherine," she said clearly and loudly so everyone could hear her. "She is visiting, and I put my life on her integrity."

My head snapped to the side where she stood, a wave of

appreciation washing over me. My sister, whom I hadn't spoken to in over five years, was willing to put her life on the line for me. What had I done to earn this loyalty?

"It will be more than your lives if anyone outside our group is made aware of this place," he grumbled, looking me over again. "I require blood."

A roar came up from the crowd around us and I looked to Nessa, who bent her head to me.

"A few drops of blood in a vial, that's all."

"Blood magic?" I grabbed her arm, my face aghast. Blood magic would tether me to the one who carried it for eternity. There was little that was more dangerous than being tethered by blood, especially to a being that I had no knowledge of.

"You will do it, or you will die," the man boomed. I barely held back my wince as the plethora of floating magic around us tightened. There were easily a hundred beings here, and most with magic. There was no hope of fighting our way out of this.

Nessa took both my hands and turned me toward her. She had a small smile on her face, and her eyes filled with sincerity. "The magic is only to pledge the protection of this place and its anonymity, there will be no other tether. Just the protection of this place and its people."

I weighed the risk in my mind. For anyone to have my blood was something I wasn't pleased about, but this was something that Nessa clearly cared about. She had risked it to bring me here. I nodded.

The large man came forward, pulling a knife from his pocket with one hand and putting the other out for me. With a last look at Nessa, I placed my hand in his, palm up. I made sure I stared him in the eyes and held still as he drew the knife across my skin, ignoring the sting of the cut. Next, he curled my fingers around and held my hand in his large ones, leading me back to the door from which we had entered. He said some words in a language that I did not recognize and squeezed gently, letting three drops of my blood slip between his knuckles and onto the ground in front of the door.

A ripple of white moved over the door, then out through the rest of the cavern, as if the space had magic of its own. He released my hand and turned back to Nessa.

"I'll allow it—only once because you, Nessa, have done so much for our cause, but do not risk us again," he said sternly. "And you, Catherine Harridan, will not go unpunished if you so much as breathe a word of this place or its people to anyone outside of our group."

I nodded, but the great man just stood there looking at me expectantly. "I understand," I said finally, and the man turned away with a withering stare at Nessa. Instead of shying away as I had expected her to, she reached up on her tiptoes and planted a kiss on his cheek. The man blushed and shook his head.

"His bark is worse than his bite," she said as she took my arm and led me away through the crowd that still lingered.

I felt the many eyes on us as we moved, Nessa showing me the different stalls where people could sell magical bobbles, herbs, or readings of various sorts. She explained that Veromoine, or little Verone in ancient Giantian, had been a haven for non-humans and magic wielders for generations. Victor, who I came to know as the large man who cut my hand, was one in a long family line that was its keeper.

We were told that human magic users were very rare and that all other beings other than humans and Elven-blooded had been pushed from the main continent to other islands or The Uspines Mountains in the Northwest. The very existence of this place and the volume of people here proved that was not true. Verone may be the largest city on the continent, but it was only one city. How many hidden places like this existed elsewhere? What about the family of the little girl I had helped steal? They had been hiding in plain sight. I thought of Reikka, in her work moving across the continent, with her hands in so many places she must have come across this or others like it. I would have to speak with her.

My head throbbed. I rubbed the back of my neck while Nessa led me around chattering to me and with others. She seemed to know everyone here, and they knew her. While they looked at me warily, they looked at her with reverence. She had another kind of family here. This is why she never came back to the manor, to Wraithland. It was why she was afraid to see the other sisters, afraid to lose this. My ears began to ring now, and I rubbed the space in front of it. Ameria's question ran through my mind. Where did my loyalty come from?

Nessa had just finished her tour of the space and asked me something I didn't hear.

"I'm sorry, Ness, there's a lot on my mind right now. Thank you for bringing me here and showing me this. I swear to you I will keep it safe." Her smile began to fade as I spoke. "I-I just need to get some fresh air, and I'll be back to see you soon. Okay?"

She nodded, her eyes dropping to the floor, and I turned away. Ignoring the dejection on her face, I raced up the stairs and into the fresh night air.

My instincts were to go up, and so I did. I went up and up and up until I found a secluded perch on a fancy Elven temple of some sort. Ripping my mask down and pushing my hood back, I greedily sucked in big gulps of cool night air, trying to calm my racing heart. I swore at myself as tears welled in my eyes.

How had I gotten here? Just weeks ago, I was doing everything that I was supposed to, serving my country, my people to the best of my ability. Now, it felt like a cruel joke. A wasted lifetime serving a selfish crown for a future that might not exist. But who was I to say? I didn't have the gift of foresight; I wasn't privy to the information that Aelthor had. Maybe his vengeance was justified. Maybe places like this did exist everywhere, and its people would join us to take down the human rulers. Maybe this was all part of the plan, and I wasn't aware because I was just a cog in the wheel.

I swallowed, rubbing the damp from my face. None of this was my place, and I had a mission to complete.

CHAPTER TWENTY-TWO

Sweeping my sector took the last dregs of my energy and focus. All I could think about was going back to the house and drinking myself into a deep sleep, but I didn't head directly back. Instead, I found myself on the ground, winding through dark streets, taking in the energy of the vast and complex city around me. Shops and taverns stayed open late into the night, illuminated by roaring fires, candles, and sconces. People sang lively tunes and quarreled in the street while kids played and lovers clung to each other in corners and alleys. It was all the things you would expect to see in a place where so many people lived together, but something about it was mesmerizing to me. These people were all living, working, and loving—all of their own accord. Doing as they pleased with no allegiance and no guilt to anyone but themselves.

I was so entranced in the scene and my thoughts so encompassing that I didn't even realize I was being followed until the presence was close enough to touch me. Every fiber in my being went on high alert as I felt it there, just behind me. I kept my movements smooth as if I was still lost in my own head and kept moving forward while fingering the dagger on my hip. The being took hurried steps to get closer to me, and I prepared to defend myself as it neared.

"Beautiful, isn't it?" A silky voice rang in my ears, stopping me in my tracks. I lifted the dagger and swung around, missing him by an inch, as he ducked below my arm, laughing.

"I could have killed you, Adrien," I hissed, spinning the blade over my thumb before stuffing it back in its holster.

"Hardly, some Saithe you are." He calmed his laughter and slid a hand through his tousled hair to set it back in place. I rolled my eyes at him and turned to continue my walk, but he took my hand, pulling me further into the shadows with him, his mouth a thin line. "What's wrong?" he asked.

I sighed, pulling back my hood and looking away. He put a hand under my chin to turn me back to him, concern lacing those blue-gray eyes. His scent of earth and parchment softly enveloped me as he pulled me close. I felt my body relax as his hands slid around my lower back. There was something in his gaze that I couldn't quite read, he was looking at me, but his eyes didn't hold the intent they usually did. There was a tightness in his stance, in his arms, as my hands moved over them. I pushed my magic out, feeling for anything in our surroundings that would be unexpected, like the slow, steady heartbeat of an elf in the building behind me.

There was no stopping the sudden tension in my muscles when I realized it was all a distraction. He felt it and tightened his grip on me, but I was faster, spinning in his arms just in time to catch sight of the elf known as Weilson. His long blonde hair flew behind him as he ducked into what looked like a warehouse. My training kicked in, and I threw Adrien's arms away, planting an elbow into his stomach. I pulled my hood and mask up as I rushed toward the building, cutting directly across the square, not caring who saw me.

Adrien was fast on my heels, his hands grabbing at my clothes, trying to stop me. He called me, using the court name. The sound made my nose wrinkle in disgust, but I would deal with him later. The elf was my first priority.

The building was a shell; the interior had a wide-open space half-filled with grain sacks. On the furthest side of the building, I spotted the elf, glamoured, but visible to me. He was climbing up a ladder to a landing that ran around the interior of the building. I wouldn't reach him before he made it to the top. Battle magic wasn't something I was well-suited for, but I threw out a bolt of fire anyway. It hit the landing above him, catching it ablaze quickly.

Weilson paused only long enough to toss a look over his shoulder at me before batting away the flames with his own magic. I charged ahead, throwing another bolt of fire and again failing at slowing him down. I was halfway across the building when Adrien plowed into me from behind, flattening me to the ground with a thud.

I threw my hands out in front of me, trying to break the fall, but it was useless. I was too distracted. My face slammed into the ground, stunning me for a moment. Shaking out the pain, I rolled onto my back and pulled a dagger from my chest holster, but Adrien was on top of me in seconds, grabbing my arm. I threw a knee up into his stomach as he came down on me, and it was enough for me to throw him aside and roll up to my feet. Weilson had made it up the ladder and was racing across the upper level now, heading for the roof. He was as good as gone.

I swore, turning my attention back to Adrien. He was standing now, hair disheveled, short sword in hand, and breathing heavily. He put a hand out like he was trying to calm an angry bull.

"Brigitta, stop. We need to talk." His face looked pained, eyes pleading. My brows shot up incredulously.

"Talk? About what? Your treason?" I laughed bitterly as I pulled my own sword from my belt and charged forward, a blade in each hand. He threw his head back, the blade barely missing his chest as he spun away. I swung again, and he blocked it with his blade. We were close enough that I could see the evening stubble on his chin, my heart lurched. I had known there was something about him I didn't trust from the beginning, and despite myself, I had grown attached to the man. An attachment that had to end now.

"Gitta, I think we are on the same side," he pleaded, artfully dodging my blows. We moved into the open space of the warehouse, like dancers weaving in and out of each other's space, circling and circling in time with the rhythm of our exchange.

Something about the way he spoke connected to something in my mind, giving me pause. He landed a punch to my jaw, hard enough to knock me off balance but not do any real damage. Blood pooled in my mouth and I spit it away, launching myself at him again. An image from the ball, only a week gone, flashed through my brain and his words. "I've seen it. Tall and blonde, eyes turquoise like the sea..." The vision of the elf running through the streets slid across my mind; the rooftop was too far away to see the color of his eyes.

Shock seared through my veins, lighting fire to the rage that had been smoldering inside all this time. Rushing forward, I swung both blades, letting my anger flow through my movements. Adrien had to fight back in earnest now, landing blows of his own, lest I kill him, which I was more than willing to do at this point.

"Now is not the time for games, Brigitta." His voice was smooth and confident despite the effort he was exerting. The voice I now recognized as that of the Wraith, Inialos. The being I had heard at the meeting in Bernitra. A being who had close ties with Aelthor and was working with the Elves.

My stomach dropped at the realization, and my rage sputtered. I staggered slightly and he grabbed my dagger hand, twisting it. He kicked my knee to the side, causing me to twist further. The dagger dropped with a clatter. He threw an arm out for balance, and I saw my opening, bringing the pummel of my sword down to his shoulder. He howled, his eyes flashing with pain. Wincing, he threw the injured arm up, trapping my sword hand under his bicep. I kicked with my free leg, but it was a weak blow from my unbalanced position. He let go of me anyway and staggered back.

"Do you want to die, Adrien? Inialos? Whatever your name is?" I pulled myself up all the way, panting, and wiping the sweat from my face. He had just given up the upper hand; it was a stupid move. "Treacherous bastard. Stop pretending to fight."

"Adrien, my given name is Adrien." His voice was so calm and confident like his deceit meant nothing. Rage coursed through me, and I lunged. Again, he threw up a defense, but this time, he took the full brunt of the blow with a grunt.

"Listen, Brigitta, er, Catherine." He leaned in, our faces so close that our breaths fogged the blades between us. "I could have used my power, made you believe whatever I wanted."

"Then why didn't you?" I cut him off, pushing away and coming at him again.

This time I anticipated his movement and captured his arm. He saw the intention and used it to duck below me, throwing the full weight of my body over himself and pinning me to the ground. The wind blew out of me with the force, and I hesitated for a moment before I had the wherewithal to plunge my sword down into his back. He knew it was coming and blocked it with his forearm before twisting my arm and pinning it above me. I threw a punch at the side of his head, which he let land in order to grab my other arm and pin it, leaving me helpless under him.

"I made you a promise," he shouted in my face, eyes blazing. We were so close I could see the gray clouds moving through his eyes, his warm breath on my face, the sweet smell of parchment and earth enveloping me again.

"You are an idiot then," I shouted back.

"I thought you of all people would understand."

"That you are a traitor? Yeah, I got that."

"A traitor to what, Catherine?" The question startled me—his use of my real name, not the one he had chosen for me, startled me. My body tensed beneath him; I needed to get away. I struggled to move, but he had me in a difficult position, and my brain couldn't seem to make my body work.

"Thousands will die if Aelthor takes the continent, on both sides," he hissed. My heart began to thrum no longer with the exertion but with something like dread.

"So what? The people of Wraithland are just left to continue to starve on the island, for another thousand years? How is that okay?"

"It's not," he breathed, loosening his grasp ever so slightly. "But neither is butchering the innocent beings on the continent. There are other ways to free our people." The sternness left his face, leaving behind the heaviness I had seen him carry many times before.

"The king only wants revenge," he said, his voice weary now. "Revenge on innocent beings. Beings whose ancestors are more dust than anything." He paused, letting the words sink in. And they did; they sunk into my skin, my blood, and pumped into my racing heart as it slammed against the binding vines wrapped around it.

"Ask yourself," he continued. "What would a world ruled by the likes of Aelthor really be?"

My mind hurtled back to the children we had killed only weeks prior. To the just and kind ruler I had poisoned before that, the innocent lady in waiting I had killed to get to him, and the dozens more before that. The lives I had taken in an effort to free my people, people who deserved freedom as much as the ones I had taken it from.

My breath shuttered, my vision going black. A gurgling, roiling sound escaped my throat as tears pricked the back of my eyes.

"You don't owe them anything," he pressed on. "They stole you, just like we stole Isadora. They took your freedom from you, just like they did to me and your sisters. It won't stop when we get to the continent, even after the battle. You know it won't. The Aellon line of rulers has always been ruthless and brutal, and they will continue to do whatever it takes to have power. Can you live with that?"

"Fuck you," I screamed, finding my strength and throwing him off. An unbridled rage filled every pore of my being, and I scooped up a sword from the ground, running at him and swinging wildly without thought. My eyes swelled with tears so that I could only make out a blurry shape in front of me.

They stole you. The words rang in my mind. I was thrown back into the vision I had in Isadora's house. The woman, my mother, with the golden-brown eyes, unblinking as she lay there dead on the kitchen table. A younger version of Father standing over her, blood coating his hand. I swung and swung and swung, mostly into the air, but occasionally hearing the clang of steel on steel, or steel on stone, until eventually, all the rage had wrung out of me. My body and mind wholly exhausted, I collapsed to the ground, dropping the sword and pulling my legs up to my chest, sobs wracking my body.

Aelthor wouldn't stop. That much I knew. He would continue to rip girls with special abilities from their families, to train them, to rape them, and make them believe they owed it to him. He would continue to murder anyone whom he deemed unnecessary or unworthy, leaving his people to fight for scraps while he hoarded riches.

A set of strong arms wrap around me, holding me tight. The tears continued to pour out of me until there was nothing left. Still, Adrien held me there against his chest. Eventually, my breathing settled, and I tried to lift my head, but the sudden ache of strained muscles and a crushing headache stopped me. Instead, I curled tighter into a ball against Adrien's chest, breathing deep into his scent and letting it calm me.

I don't know how long we sat there, but at some point, Adrien rose, carrying me in his arms and I fell asleep with the motion of his footsteps.

CHAPTER TWENTY-THREE

I awoke from the heat of the sunlight streaming into the window on my face, immediately blinded by the horrific headache hiding behind my eyes. Trying to roll away, the blankets tangled around my legs thwarting my movements. I could feel the sweat covering them in a damp film. Disgusted I pushed them off, realizing that my mouth felt like I had been drinking sand. Scrubbing a hand down my face and sitting up, I searched for a glass of water, which, thankfully, sat on the bedside table.

I was in my room at the Davenlyn House, with only a vague recollection of how I got there. The memory of Adrien carrying me out of the warehouse flashed through my mind, followed by cropped images of me: shuffling up the stairs to my bed, with little exchange from my sisters, and stripping off my clothes as I went. My leathers lay rumpled on the ground beside the bed as evidence.

Then, all the events of the last few days rushed over me, threatening to throw me right back into the chaotic state that got me here feeling like this to start with. I took a deep breath and looked around the room, cataloging its contents in my mind. The action soothed my frazzled nerves for a moment until a knock at the door pulled me back into reality.

I groaned my acquiesce, and Adrien pushed open the door with one hand, balancing a tray of pastries and tea in the other. He sported a black eye, a large bruise on the side of his face, as well as a split lip, but he seemed to move with the same fluidity as usual. Tenderly, I fingered my jaw, feeling the swelling there. Everything hurt so badly that I couldn't tell what was from the fight and what was just from the strain of the last weeks. At least my magic would heal the battle wounds shortly, but I needed something for the current pain.

Reaching over the side of the bed, I found my satchel tucked just underneath and flipped it onto the bed. Adrien froze in the middle of the room, eyes narrowed on me. His free hand hovered over his side, likely the place where his dagger was hidden beneath his robes. I let my lips quirk up in a wry smile as I rummaged through my aid kit. Pulling out my favorite hangover cure, I tipped my head back with a wince and put two full droppers of it right into my mouth.

He sat on the bed, placing the tray between us, watching me warily. I shoved the kit onto the table beside me and reached for the tea.

"What do they know?" My voice came out in a croak, and I took a sip. The tea was mint with honey and lemon, and it was like a balm for my sore throat.

"We sighted the elf. We were ambushed; he got away." His words are curt, his voice low. I nodded, contemplating this. My mind was fitting the pieces together more easily now that I had had some sleep.

"You've known where the Elves have been all this time, haven't you? Inialos." My voice is hard, maybe even a little cruel, but I can't help it. I felt duped again. Everywhere I turned, someone was lying to me, and my patience for it was running low.

He shook his head. "That's not something I'm privy to at this time. And my name is Adrien. Inialos is the cover I use on the continent with Garthrold's men."

"So, Adrien," I drew the syllables of his name out with a sneer. I wanted him to know how far he'd fallen in my eyes now that I knew he'd been playing me. "You have been working with the Elves and humans this whole time?" He nodded, his face sullen. "To what end?"

He sighed, bringing his feet up to the bed rail and resting his elbows on his knees. "I can't speak for the others, but I cannot live in a world where Aelthor rules all." He ran his hand along his unshaven jaw, the stubble making a rustling sound. "I imagine the Elves want the whole of Wraithland gone, and the humans want us or anyone unlike them all gone."

"The humans revered the Elves once," I countered. "Many will die."

"Men with power are not likely to give it up so easily." Adrien's eyes slid to me with a sideways glance. We both knew he was right. Thousands of lives would be lost for the pride of a handful.

"So, you all kill Aelthor? Then what? Wraithland still stands, and our people still suffer there, except now without a ruler."

"A different ruler, perhaps." He looked back at me. "A ruler who will build treaties with the existing kings to support Wraithland and to allow beings to move freely between the continent and the island."

"And who will that ruler be?" I set the teacup between my legs and cocked my head to the side. "You?"

He gave a weak chuckle. "No, but we will find someone when the time comes, maybe my apparent cousin, the princess." My eyebrows shot up at his causal familiarity with Princess Ameria.

"Does she know about any of this?"

"She knows that we are looking for a way to take down Aelthor and that he knows how to take down the wards now. She was the one who pushed for more information on the prophecy but knows nothing of the Elves. Her involvement is only recent and her contacts are human, aside from us."

"Aelthor can only take down the wards because of information that you gave him," I spat. "If you want to stop him, why give it to him to begin with?"

"I had delayed as long as I could, years even. I only handed it off when we had a plan in place to stall him for a while longer. But then you came out with the elf sighting, and everything changed. We are doing everything we can to slow Aelthor's movements while we look for a way to stop him completely."

"That's your plan? Wait for this boy to show up to take Aelthor down? You are putting a lot of hope into a single prophecy."

"I've been saying that for weeks," he sighed, running both hands through his hair. "We've discussed other possibilities, but Aelthor is a full-blooded elf from an ancient line of powerful kings who's been building his defenses in preparation for this moment. He won't be an easy adversary. There are other options out there, I know there are, we just need more time to find them."

"So, we send word that the trail is cold. That buys us some time." Hilda stood in the doorway, leaning a shoulder on its frame, cleaning her nails with a knife. I had to assume my other sisters were out of the house with how openly they discussed their treason.

"We need years, not days." Adrien looked up at his mother with a thoughtful expression, letting a moment pass before he spoke again. "We say the elf is dead." His voice became authoritative. "Aelthor won't move forward without confirmation that the Elves aren't a threat."

"And return failures? That's not an option," I interjected.

"There will be a punishment, sure, but nothing too harsh." Adrien waved a hand. "Pterol will need you in the future; he won't risk too much harm on you."

"How do we get the others on board?" Hilda stopped cleaning her nails and sucked her teeth. "Reikka is with us, but Adelay and Tris are both unknowns."

"Adelay will be with us," I said, lifting my teacup again. They both turned to me, surprised.

"Does this mean you are with us?" Adrien's lips twisted into a small smile, one that made my heart flutter.

I tamped it down and shrugged. "If I wasn't, you would have been dead before you made it to this bed."

Adrien's face burst into a broad grin, warmth radiating out of his features like I hadn't experienced before. Behind him, Hilda pushed off from the door, sheathing her knife and crossing her arms over her chest.

"You understand what a dangerous game we are playing here, Catherine?" Hilda's voice was steady and clear, her eyes boring into me, awaiting my reassurance.

"I do." I nodded firmly. "But if what Adrien says is true, I can't live in a world where Aelthor rules all either. Where my sisters and our people die for his vengeance and greed. There has to be another way."

Adrien jumped up, buzzing with energy, and began pacing to the fireplace and back. "Then I can just plant the memory in Tris' mind, and we can go back to the island."

My eyes shot to Hilda, the hair on the back of my neck standing on end. Reading minds was one thing, but altering memories seemed like a violation beyond the pale. Would she back such an action?

"You told me you hated doing such things," I said hesitantly.

"I will do what needs to be done." He waved me off as if it was nothing.

"No." Hilda took a step further into the room. "That would make us no better than them. We will not use people that way."

I nodded my agreement when a thought struck me. "And what about the consequences of a failed mission? I was told me in no uncertain terms that failure was not an option."

"There are six of us, his best Saithes and the last trained Mindwalker. There is only so much he can do without repercussions falling back onto himself. It's a risk, sure, but so is everything we do." Hilda's words did little to bolster my fears, but I had to hope she was right.

Hilda and Adrien left me to recover and eat in peace while they contacted Reikka to devise a plan. By the time I had eaten my fill, bathed, and dressed, the three of them had everything in place.

We would continue the day pretending that the elf and his friends got the drop on Adrien and me, something I was loathe to allow. Not only for my pride but also because I was not pleased with lying to my sisters. I would speak to Adelay that evening, relaying everything in hopes she would, in fact, be on our side.

***

After a painfully quiet dinner, we all dressed in our leathers, preparing for another night patrolling our sectors. It was our duty to press on, even if the odds of the elf being visible after the encounter were slim. We had a mission to complete.

I took my time changing into my leathers, letting the others slip out one by one, until eventually, I was alone with Adelay. She knew something was up; I could see her movements slow as well. When I was ready, I went out the parlor window and sat in the recess of the dormer. Adelay came out shortly after and spotted me without trouble.

She pursed her lips in a knowing expression and flopped down beside me.

"So, what is it you've got to tell me?" she said, looking out over the city.

"Am I so obvious?" I attempted to break the tension, watching her out of the corner of my eye. Despite having spent the last several hours rehearsing everything I planned to say, somehow, none of it seemed adequate.

"I have to ask you something that's going to change everything," I said finally. She turned to me, her face blank, ready for whatever I was about to say. "It's going to put your life in danger, the lives of our sisters, and possibly the whole of Wraithland."

She nodded and turned back to the skyline. "I had a feeling last time we met things had changed for you. Once you've spent enough time here, you realize the pain, the starvation, and the constant fighting aren't the only way to live. The question is what could we possibly do to change anything?"

I took a deep breath. "Aelthor has found a way to break the

wards." I paused as Adelay turned to me; her face grim. "He means to take us to war with the continent. The only thing standing in his way right now are the Elves. If they are alive somewhere they may return to fight him, and he wants to take the battle to them first."

"So, what? We kill Aelthor?" she said, giving me a sidelong look.

Her directness startled me, and I had to choke back a laugh.

"Ultimately, yes, but who knows how?" I threw my hands in the air. "He's more powerful than any other Elven-blooded on the island and the continent. And no one has any idea how to do it. There's some prophecy about a human boy, but again, no one knows who he is or if it's even valid. What we need is more time."

"How do we get more time?"

"Well, this elf we are after is supposed to tell us where the rest of them are hiding, right?"

She shrugged. "I wasn't even given that much information. My orders were to find him and deliver him to the mindwalker alive, that's it."

"Of course." I rolled my eyes, letting out a heavy sigh. "Well, I saw the elf in Bernitra and told Father and Aelthor, and now they are afraid that if they break the wards, the rest of the Elves will come out of hiding and attack. They want us to capture him and get all the info he has on the Elves, their numbers, and location."

"Right," she cut in. "So, they can decide if they can win against the Elves. And it's war either way." Now she sighed, feeling for herself the weight of what I had been carrying for weeks now.

"We lost against the Elves once before, and they would have the whole of the continent on their side this time. Even if we won, it's like you said, everything would be destroyed. We think if he doesn't get the information he's looking for, he will hold off until he finds another way."

"So, we lose the elf." She smiled wickedly, and something about it bolstered me, lifting some of the tension in my chest. We stayed there on the roof as I divulged the plan and everything I had been through in the last few weeks. Adelay listened, adding thoughtful comments here and there. At one point, she stopped me just long enough to grab a bottle of wine and some glasses.

By the time the others started trickling in, my voice had turned hoarse again, and we had finished two whole bottles. Releasing all of the information and emotion I had been holding did more than just ease my mind; it filled my soul in a way I did not know I needed it. I felt lighter than I had in weeks.

I was still sitting on the roof hours later when Adelay stretched and told me she was headed to bed. Bidding her good night, I laid back on the roof, looking up at the stars as the last of our company straggled in. Adrien was the last to slink back. He spotted me on the roof and took up residence in the space that Adelay had vacated.

"Adelay is with us," I said in a hushed voice without turning to him.

"Good," he said, and then a moment later. "How are you doing?"

"I haven't changed my mind if that's what you are asking."

He rolled onto his side so that he was looking down at me, the moon carving shadows across his handsome face. "I'm asking how you are doing. This decision isn't an easy one."

"Better now," I said, looking up at him, my eyes tracing the line of his lips.

"I'm glad to hear that." His voice came out husky and deep, sending a wave of heat over my body.

"Well, good, your pleasure is of utmost concern to me," I said, wetting my lips and arching my back ever so slightly. He gave me a wry look, his lips making a thin line.

"Gitta," he sighed. Looking away as he ran his hand through his hair. "I thought we talked about this. I'm not interested in being your escape."

I reached up, cupping his face and turning it back to me.

"I'm not looking for an escape," I said, feeling clarity about something for the first time in weeks. "If I'm walking into my death, I want to know what real happiness feels like."

"And you think I could make you happy?" Adrien asked, his eyes glinting in the moonlight.

CHAPTER TWENTYF-OUR

I didn't have an answer since I still wasn't sure what it was supposed to feel like, but I imagined it felt something like the comfort I felt when I was around him. It probably had to do with the way he made me laugh and the way he had seen my brokenness and not thought less of me for it. Maybe it was the way he thought I could be more than the Siathe I was raised to be, that we could make a change, for us, for Wraithland, and Primthera. It was all so much to sift through. I imagined the field of wildflowers he had shown me, but instead of Isadora's family, I saw Adrien and I lying as we were now, but in the grass. This was what I imagined when I thought of happiness.

My hand slid into his hair, and I pulled him close. Reaching up, I pushed my lips to his in a soft, sensual kiss. His hand went to my hip, gripping hard. He leaned over me, pushing me back onto the roof, his chest pressing against mine.

Every nerve in my body lit up with excitement, from the tips of my toes to the points of my breasts, it was an exhilaration I had never felt before. He pulled away, breathing heavily, and his eyes darkened on me. I bit my lip to keep myself from giggling like a schoolgirl.

"Is the window to your room unlocked?" he asked between panting breaths. I nodded quickly and pushed him off of me, leading the way across the roof and over the other side. This window didn't have a dormer, so I had to dangle myself over the edge and tip-toe onto the ledge before pulling open the window. I slipped through the space easily, Adrien following behind.

Without preamble, I stripped off my cloak and then my hood and mask, tossing them away. I reached for the ties on my leather vest, but Adrien stopped me with a hand over mine. He stood before me with that mischievous grin that made him look so handsome, and I felt my feet curl in my boots. He stood before me in just a plain gray tunic and black leather breaches, having also removed his outer garments in haste.

"No-no, Brigitta." He slid his hands down to my wrists, pulling the ties of the leather cuffs that I wore there. "Happiness isn't greedy." He spoke slowly. His voice was so deep and so sensual that it sent chills down my spine.

I watched his careful movements as he tossed away the cuffs one by one, kissing the inside of my wrists before moving on to the leather vest that I wore. Now I looked up into his blue-gray eyes while he continued to slowly undress me, gently pulling at the ties to loosen them and then pulling the vest over my head. His hands traced the outline of my arms to my shoulders, then over the swell of my breast. He paused, gripping one of them in his hands through my tunic while the other snaked around my back. Bending, he brushed his lips against mine, not quite kissing me as he walked me back toward the bed. My calves hit the runner, and he pushed me down into a sitting position without taking his eyes off me. I wet my lips, watching him watch me.

He knelt before me and worked at the laces of my boots. I could feel my core heating with anticipation as he slipped one off and then the other, setting them gently beside the bed. Our eyes met again as he tossed my socks away, and I reached for his tunic, but he brushed my hands away again and stood.

"Patience, Brigitta," he said, his voice a low rumble. "You need to trust me."

He pushed me back gently on the bed with a hand on my shoulder. Clenching my fists, the molten heat pooling between my legs. I had never had this much trouble controlling myself in the bedroom. Of course, I had played these kinds of games before, but no one had ever elicited this kind of response from my body. All I wanted was to tear the clothes from him and devour him then and there. His slow, calculated movements were the sweetest kind of agony.

"If you truly want to be happy," he went on. The rumble of his voice caused every hair on my body to stand on end. "Then you need to learn to trust in those around you. Those that love you, and let us care for you." With one hand, he snapped the button on my breeches open. I sucked in a hissing breath, pushing my hands into my hair in frustration, tugging at the braids there.

He bit his lip as he pulled the breeches and undergarments off me in one long, slow motion. Pushing my legs apart with his knee, he stood above me, looking down at me lying before him. I reached for the bottom of my tunic and pulled it over my head before he could stop me. His grin became vicious as he took in my nakedness and knelt again.

A whine escaped me, and I tried to reach for him. I wanted to feel him on top of me, the weight and heat of his body on mine. But he reached up with one hand on my chest and forced me back on the bed. I yielded with a grumble and his hand went to my breast gripping hard and then pinching the nipple as he blew out a soft cool breath over the hot skin at the apex of my thighs.

My back arched, and I sucked in a breath at the sensation. His other hand dug into my thigh pushing it wide, exposing more of my hot, wet sex to him. He kissed the inside of my thigh, his breath skittering across my skin and eliciting another whine. He continued to kiss down one thigh and then up the other, leaving my core aching for even a moment of his touch. I arched again, squeezing my eyes shut, hands fisting in the sheets and my hair in agony.

Without warning, he dipped his head and parted me with his tongue. Every muscle in my body went taut at once, and I had to bite my tongue to keep from crying out. It was as if I was engulfed in desire, my mind going completely blank as he worked his tongue over the sensitive bundle of nerves there.

He pulled back, and I looked down at him. He looked up under those hooded eyes, bluer than I had ever seen them, his hair falling forward. He dragged a hand over my center before inserting one finger, again ever so slowly, his breath cool on my searing skin. He bent again as he inserted another finger and began to work me from the inside. I reached down, pushing his hair out of his eyes and twisting my hand in it while the other went to my breast. The pressure inside me was building faster, faster than I was prepared for, and within moments, it was bursting out of me in uncontrolled spasms.

Then, he sped up his motions, holding me at the height of my climax for what seemed like hours. I was lost in the throes of it, letting out strangled moans and screams, wringing the sheets around me. I dug my nails into his hair and shoulders as I writhed and squirmed until finally there was nothing left and all the pressure melted out of me.

I was panting, sweat-soaked, and disheveled when he finally pulled away, slowly pulling his fingers out of me. Our eyes met as he licked them clean of my orgasm, causing me to shiver. I wanted to sit up, to pull him toward me, but my limbs felt leaden. Instead, I lay there, trying to catch my breath as he stood, pulling his shirt over his head and dropping his pants. He must have unlaced his shoes while he was down there because he kicked them away easily.

Standing still for a moment, he let his eyes trail down my wasted body, allowing me the opportunity to observe his for the first time in its natural state. He was slim but with the defined muscles and scars of a warrior. He had a large marking that looked like a sword burnt into his thigh. Around it, streaks of black ink vined away from it like lightning. It evoked a sense of his power—the strength that hid beneath the surface. Eventually, my eyes slid upward to his erection. I wet my lips and pulled myself up, crooking my finger at him to come closer.

He obliged, and I greedily took him into my mouth. Starting slow, as he had done, I moved rhythmically using my hands as well as my tongue. I saw the deep blue wisps of his magic as he used it to release my hair from its bounds, and it floated down gently onto my shoulders. He ran both hands through my hair gripping it, letting out a grunt of appreciation before he hooked a knuckle under my chin, and gently pulled himself out of my mouth. Taking my hand, he pulled me up, his arms coming around me. Our lips met again, needy and harsh this time, neither of us holding back.

We landed on the bed with a thud, arms and legs all tangled

together. He rolled on top of me, pressing his hips to mine. I arched my back in response, grinding myself against him, feeling every inch of his body against mine. My skin ignited where we came together, cooling to frost where we moved apart. The pressure was rising again. He dragged his teeth along my collarbone and pulled his hips away, his swollen cock pressing against my sensitive areas. I moaned, raking my hands down his back. He thrust into me with a force that made my eyes roll back into my head. Bending, he took my nipple in his mouth as he thrust again, harder.

My release came as a surprise, the entirety of my body losing control as I writhed beneath him. He continued to pump into me, pushing me further into my ecstasy until he finally shuddered and slowed, giving in to his own release.

He rested his head on my shoulder, taking a few deep breaths while I gulped down the cool night air and tried to shake the haze from my mind. Gently, he pulled out of me, rolling onto the bed. I lay there, unable to think or move.

Never in my life had I achieved an orgasm with such force, let alone multiple. My body felt wrecked and heavy in a way I had never known. Beside me, Adrien's breathing came to normal, and he rolled onto his side. He trailed his fingers up my bare stomach, the skin there rising into goose flesh. I shivered. Reaching across me, Adrien wrapped his arm around me and pulled my back into his chest, curling his body around mine.

Using his magic, he pulled a blanket from the bottom of the bed up around us. I snuggled into the warmth, feeling the tension in my chest loosen ever so slightly. My eyes grew heavier and heavier with every breath. A thought slid into my head and caused my eyes to flutter open again.

"Why do you still call me Brittiga?" I adjusted my shoulders to look at him. It didn't matter to me either way. I had a million names and was happy to answer to any of them, but he knew the one name that only the Harridans called me. I would have thought he would want to take advantage of that position and use it as the ones closest to me did.

He scrunched his nose and looked to the ceiling. "It's just, it's the name that Daren uses. And Pterol and all the other warders you let put their hands on you."

My brows lowered in confusion. "That I let...put their hands on me? You mean our training in seduction? How else are we to hone our skills and complete our missions?"

"You don't need sex to get close to people or complete missions, Brigitta." He looked down at me. His voice was earnest, but his eyes blazed. "When we take the throne, I'll rebuild The Society to something more useful. Where the sisters aren't slaves to the warders."

"We aren't slaves." I started to defend my society, but Adrien cut me off.

"Let's not ruin the moment. We have years to argue over this." He smiled, tracing his fingers down the side of my face. His touch was so soft, the bed so warm. I leaned into it when our lips met, and I felt the tension ease again, lulling me into sleep.

CHAPTER TWENTY-FIVE

The following morning, we all left the inn as if completing our respective missions to find the elf. At the appointed time, I met with Adrien and Weilson in a building that was undergoing renovations– a space no doubt secured by Reikka, who, as it turned out, also knew where to find an already deceased being to use as a body double for the elf. I chose not to ask how she knew such things and focused on my part of the plan.

I scouted the building before entering to ensure we would be alone, something I'm sure Hilda and Reikka had also done. Some aspects of our training would always be part of us. The building was large but cluttered with construction debris, tools, logs, stones, and the like, making the first floor a maze, perfect for finding and losing a target. I strolled into the selected meeting place to find Adrien seated on sacks of some kind, speaking to Weilson, who stood anxiously nearby. He was shifting from foot to foot while his hands wrung themselves in front of him. Up close and unglamoured, he was more intimidating than I had previously thought.

Weilson was tall and lean with sharp features in the way that most Elves have. So many of the same features I noticed in the Aellon line. There was something ethereal about him, though, that made his presence jarring to the senses, more so than any of the Elven-blooded on Wraithland. Adrien didn't seem to be bothered by it as he sat, chatting with the elf.

I shuffled a foot to mark my presence, and Weilson's head snapped in my direction. Finally, I saw the distinctive turquoise eyes that Adrien had described at the ball. He gave me a slight bow of welcome and introduced himself. There was a moment's hesitation while I fumbled for something to say to this being who had become such a presence in my life the last few weeks, but was interrupted by Reikka and Hilda as they entered.

They were carrying a large roll of carpet that I assumed contained the body we would be using. The two of them laid it on the ground and unrolled it, revealing a man with shoulder-length sandy hair and a long, lean body. While he wasn't a duplicate of the elf, it would be close enough, especially with a glamour. Tris didn't have my abilities to see through such things, but we had all been trained to take note of inconsistencies that can be found with glamours. All we could do was hope it held.

Hilda made the carpet disappear with a flick of her hand and stepped aside next to Reikka. Both of them looked expectantly at the elf. There was never any preamble with these two. He looked at each of us in turn, his apprehension palpable. I noted the turquoise wisps of his power pulling toward him, the same color as his striking eyes. Rubbing his hands together, he took a few strides to the man and drew his hands over his face. The wisps swirled, washing over the man, who now looked identical to the elf standing over him, if not a bit more pale.

He stepped back, again looking at each of us for approval. Hilda nodded and turned on her heel. Reikka pulled a vial from her pocket. Uncorking it, she dropped it beside the body, tossing the cork away and following Hilda out.

"You are aware of your next steps?" I asked, the caution in my voice evident.

"I am to go to the clothing district. Allow the one with the curls to spot me and then lay chase, leading them here, where I will disappear through there." He pointed to a door off to the right that was glamoured to look like the rest of the wall around it. His head cocked to the side, and he folded his hands behind his back as if he was expecting more from me. I could feel my heart beating faster with anticipation, sure he could sense it too. I nodded and turned to leave, before I could give more away.

I headed straight to my sector on the other side of the city. It would be more believable if we were actually where we were supposed to be. Moving from rooftop to rooftop with more speed than was necessary, I could feel myself tightening up. Keeping secrets from my sisters was different than outright lying to them. We all skated around the truth, hiding pieces of ourselves and our missions, as we were trained, but this time we were fabricating a story and flat out lying to Tris.

Adelay had reservations about the plan, but she agreed with Hilda that Tris was young, and her allegiance was still tightly wound around The Society and its leaders. There was only a slim chance she would be with us, if not for herself, but even just out of fear of the repercussions. I had wanted to tell her to try and convince her, but the risk was too great. Now, we were setting it up so that she would unwittingly be a party to our schemes. It was a lie to protect her, but a lie nonetheless. The guilt weighed on me, but I didn't see another way either.

I stumbled on a landing and stopped myself, catching my breath. My lack of exercise began to catch up with me and I was breathing heavily. Looking back, I realized I had traversed more of the city than intended, and I needed to work my way back into the center, of my sector. Shaking out my limbs, I chided myself for my carelessness. Now was not the time to be distracted.

Pushing the thoughts away. I began to work back the way I had come. My mind drifted to the inn, the bed I had shared with Adrien. The way I had woken up more rested than I had felt in years. I had laid there staring at his handsome face while he slept. He had smiled at me when he woke and caught me. It was that genuine, open smile that somehow made my muscles soften and my jaw unclench. I felt it happen even as I thought of him, of the night we shared. It was a night unlike any other I had experienced, and there had been many nights in my past. Even Daren had never evoked that kind of reaction from my body.

I wasn't sure what it meant that he could elicit these kinds of emotions from me or if it really had to mean something. It was dangerous, although a different kind of dangerous than the scheme we were embroiled in now. Getting too close and too comfortable with one person could be a risk in our line of work.

I didn't have time to think any more about it when the call went out. Everything I had been thinking dropped out of my mind, and I sprinted in the direction of the high-pitched whistle that I knew Adelay was blowing. The whistle was a trick that we used on group missions to communicate over distance with ease. The three long blasts we had agreed upon at the beginning of the mission meant come now. We would hone in on the sound and use our training to find each other. My unique powers to sense beings made it easier for me than most, so I didn't even bother to pretend and went straight for the building I had been to earlier that morning.

Tris was the closest, so she should make it to Adelay first. I saw her come around the side of the building as I slowed on a neighboring rooftop. The elf stood at a doorway on the ground level. He caught my eye and threw his head back before ducking into the doorway. I leaped from the roof, pushing off the neighboring building's window a level below, then the next, before landing on an awning and dropping to the ground. Tris was entering the building as I dashed across the street. Following her through the twists and turns of the chaos inside, I was breathing heavily by the time I stumbled into the open room with the dead body. Sweat had beaded across my forehead, and I wiped it away as I took in the scene.

The body lay there, just as it had when I left. Tris was crouched by it, with the vial in her hand. Adelay was just a few feet off, letting out a string of expletives and breathing heavily as well. She was supposed to be the one crouching by the body, the only one to touch it, not Tris. Hilda dropped in from one of the upper levels, followed by Adrien, then Reikka, who had been assigned a sector on the opposite side of the city. Tris tossed Hilda the vial and recounted her finding him here to us all with militaristic precision.

Hilda swore and began pacing silently. Tris looked at me, as I stood there looking annoyed, the way an older sister should. She ran a hand over her hair and looked to the ceiling, probably frustrated that I didn't have an immediate answer for her. Tris and I had spent many years training together; despite her young age, she was a skilled warrior, and I suppose I had become something of a mentor to her. It felt like a knife was twisting in my gut at the thought. Mentors shouldn't lie to their students.

Adelay bent and began to rummage through the man's pockets, claiming to find nothing but a few coins, which she dropped into her own pocket.

"We have to get rid of the body. Do we have any other leads here?" she said, looking between the group of us.

"We could try to find his accomplices or where he was staying, but we have no information on that. I checked in with my contacts when we arrived, and there's no record of the elf, by any names, anywhere in the city," Reikka responded coolly.

"I should have followed the bastards that jumped us or something." Adrien shook his head and looked at me.

"That was my failure," I said flatly, turning and putting my fist into the wall. It was another lie to eat away at whatever conscience was left in me.

"We can't just go home empty-handed," Tris said, her voice strained with exasperation. In all our time together, I had never seen her distraught, but then I doubted she had ever failed a mission. We were supposed to capture the elf alive and elicit information out of him. Now, we would return home with nothing. I had only heard of a few failed missions, and they almost always ended with the death of a sister who continued to try until the end. We knew we had to push through whatever circumstances we faced and that our lives meant little in the face of the greater good. Only now did I suspect that not all those sisters died during their missions. I swallowed, choking down my fears, recalling Hilda's earlier reassurance of our safety.

"We have no other choice," I said, trying to keep my voice steady. "We have no other leads. The sooner we get what little information we have to Father, the better."

Hilda nodded. "I'll send a note to Father. Catherine, can you, uh work your magic on this?" She gestured to the corpse. I let out a breath and stepped toward it, the others backing away.

I rolled my neck as my power built. With another breath, I centered it on the chest of the man lying on the ground. I felt inside his body for any sliver of spirit, but there was none; it had long dispersed. Pushing more of my power into him, I began to feel the heat grow. Soon, there was steam and the slight sizzle of burning flesh. Then, a bright light burst from his chest, engulfing the body. Moments later, there was nothing but ash in its place and the smell of burnt flesh in the air.

CHAPTER TWENTY-SIX

We made our way back to the inn in a near-silent parade, each of us debating the weight of our actions and the consequences of a failed mission. Once in my room, I made quick work of peeling off my leathers and slipping into one of the thin night dresses in the bursting armoire. Reaching for the bottle of wine that I swiped off the dining table in the common room, I pulled the red velvet chair in front of the fire, which I sparked to life with my magic. Using my teeth, I pulled the cork out of the top of the bottle and spat it into the flames before taking a long swig.

Every muscle in my body felt as if it had been pulled tight. I rolled my neck to relieve the pressure before leaning my head on the back of the chair. A long sigh spilled out of me. My mind drifted to the last conversation I had with Daren. He had warned me not to come home if I failed this mission, and here I was doing it on purpose. I took another long swig and stood to find my satchel.

Rummaging through it one-handed, I pulled out the small tin of fire paper I kept on hand. I sat back in the chair, setting the wine on the floor at my feet. I scrawled out a message to Daren, praying he could use his powers of persuasion to soften the blow of our failure before our arrival. With a few whispered words, I held the message over the fire watching the ink dissipate into the air and to Daren's own tin of fire paper.

There was a light knock at the door, and Adrien poked his head in. I nodded to him, not capable of willing my face into a smile. He prowled to me, standing behind the chair and sliding his hands over my shoulders in soft circles.

"You are all so tense."

"You aren't?" I looked up at him over my shoulder with raised brows. He shrugged one shoulder while he continued to rub ever-widening circles down my back, my twisted muscles aching softly from the pressure.

"I'm indispensable," he said finally.

"And if the rest of us die?"

"I try not to worry about things that are out of my control. Not that you will. It's as Hilda said, you are the five best Saithes they have, and with the threat of war, they cannot risk the loss." He stopped rubbing and came around the chair, extending a hand.

"Come to bed; let me rub those worries away," he said in a husky voice.

I took his hand and let him lead me to the bed, a welcome distraction.

***

The following morning, I left Adrien lounging in bed and dressed in a gown that Lady Lenna would likely wear before casually strolling the few honeycombs to Princess Ameria's residence. I hadn't spoken to her since the offer she had made to me at the libraries, and I knew that I couldn't leave without at least letting her know.

I was greeted at the entry by a disgruntled-looking servant who motioned to the parlor rather than exchange words with me. Shrugging her off, I found Ameria seated at a table loaded with books and parchments. She looked up when I entered, casually sliding the sheet she had been scribbling on under another.

"Find what you were looking for?" I asked with a tilt of my head.

She rubbed her eyes, leaning back in her chair. "Only more questions than answers."

"I'm sorry to hear that." I sat in the chair opposite her. "We've finished our business and will be leaving in the morning."

Her eyebrows shot up. "So soon?"

I wet my lips and nodded.

"Have you considered my offer?" She sat up, bracing her elbows on the desk and interlacing her fingers. I looked away, out the window, gathering my thoughts.

"I want to know more about what you actually want from me." I paused, putting a hand up before she could speak. "But there are things I must face first. I will find you when the time is right."

She nodded, dropping her hands to the desk and straightening her back.

"What name should I keep my eyes out for?"

I couldn't help but smile at that. "Lenna will be fine for now."

"Don't you trust me by now?"

"Says the woman hiding parchments when I walked through the door," I scoffed. Her cheeks turned pink, and she leaned back, crossing her arms.

I stood shaking my head. "Thank you for everything, princess. I hope to see you soon." I gave a low bow and made my way to the door, stopping over its threshold. "Oh, don't expect to find the answers you are seeking in Verone. You aren't likely to find them," I said and left.

***

The carriages were nearly done being loaded when I returned, and we were on our way within the hour. I had changed into my leathers and used a glamour to walk the few paces from the house to the carriage. The one-hour ride to the no-man's land outside the city, where we could shadowjump freely, felt like an eternity. All of us jostled along in silent anticipation.

Reikka stayed behind to see the caravan to its final destination, along with some goods she had procured in the city for the crown. Unfortunately, there were no shadowjumpers capable of moving large amounts of cargo.

Hilda jumped Adrien and me first from Verone to Bernitra, then to the waygate. When her mist cleared on the wind-whipped island, we found Daren leaning on one of the pillars, hands in his pockets, looking out to the sea.

Hilda wasted no time heading back to the others, leaving us to deal with whatever he came to tell us. I didn't miss the scowl he gave Adrien as we neared, nor did I miss the way Adrien tried to appear relaxed, and confident, even though every muscle in his body was pulled tight as a bowstring.

"Go ahead, Adrien, we will meet you on the other side," I

223

yelled over the wind for him to hear me. He gave a withering look over his shoulder at the warder as he stepped in front of me and went through the door.

For his part, Daren kept his expression even, but his eyes tracked Adrien until he disappeared with the slam of the door. The muscles of his jaw ticked like he was chewing on some thought. I closed the distance between us, coming close enough that we could speak in normal voices.

"Aelthor is at the manor," he said ominously. I winced. It was incredibly rare for Aelthor to come to the manor, and usually only under the guise of some special event. I swore under my breath. "What did you expect?" He turned his dark gaze on me, the wind shoving his hair into his eyes.

"Do I need to run?" I asked sincerely. If my life was on the line, maybe it was my only choice.

He pursed his lips. "They won't kill you now. You're worth too much."

"Me or my child?" I spat before I could think better of it. Daren's eyes went wide, his body tensing in a way that made him seem to grow before my eyes. I put my hands up instinctively. "I'm not with child, and I don't intend to be, but I expect you to know that's what's expected of me."

He nodded, looking into the wind again, the muscle of his jaw working. His hands, freed of pockets now, clenching and unclenching at his sides.

"Pterol said there would be a punishment, and that can't be avoided, but you'll get through it, and we can figure out the rest after." His voice turned soft in a way I hadn't heard before. I took a step closer to him, resting my hand on his muscled chest. He looked down at me, his eyes dancing with emotions that I could not place.

Just then, the rush of Hilda's magic sounded behind us, and she emerged with Tris and Adelay in tow.

"Let's get this over with," he said, pushing off the wall and away from me.

CHAPTER TWENTY-SEVEN

On the island, another carriage waited for us at the rock, taking us straight to the manor house.

When we pulled up to the main door, I could already feel the tension hanging heavy in the air. The large ornate doors had been left open, and nothing emanated from within but silence. With the number of sisters, warders, animals, and other staff, the manor was never silent.

Leon stood tall in the foyer, his dark lips pulled down into a scowl, hands folded behind his back. His black leathers were so clean they shone in the sunlight streaming in from the tall windows. He gave us no greeting, just silently turned, and we followed him past the stairs and the secret door to the formal ballroom beyond that was sometimes used as a sparring room.

A hand on my elbow gave me pause on the threshold. I turned to see Tris staring at me with a determined look I couldn't quite place. My heart jumped into my throat.

"Before we go in there, I need you to know that I trust you." The hair on the back of my neck stood on end. I let the shock show on my face, willing her to go on. "The body was cold, Catherine," she said in a voice so low I could barely hear it. "I know you would have seen that, and I know you wouldn't lie to me unless it was to protect me, so I'm trusting you."

Her eyes bore into me for a moment before she pursed her lips and walked into the room. My whole body went stiff, my mouth dry, and it took everything I had in me to follow her. I wet my lips, counting my steps, and then cataloging the weapons I had on me in my head, anything to calm my mind and my breathing. Until a few weeks ago, I wasn't sure I even knew what fear felt like. Now, I was well aware.

The ballroom had been cleared of everything, and a raised dais was placed against the back wall where the king sat in a large, highbacked chair. Father stood beside him; stoic as usual. In front of the dais, most of the members of the Harridan Society stood, the young and the old, from teachers and warders to active members. Some of the elder ladies even held the hands of small children or rocked them in their arms.

The tightness in my body loosened ever so slightly. There was no way Father would risk killing us in front of the other sisters, especially the young ones. It would shatter the illusion of comfort and safety they had here. Leon stopped a few feet from the dais, motioning us to form a line in front of it.

We each took our place, standing at attention before him. His eyes flicked from one end of the row to the other, then he turned, bowing to the king. He took two long strides to the side, furling his fingers at Adrien on the end to follow him. Adrien bowed to the king as well and obeyed the order, moving to the side with the audience. This would be our failure alone.

A long moment passed where no one spoke. I stood with both hands at either side, tucked in close to my body, pushing my chest out and holding my shoulders back like a good soldier.

"Kneel." Finally, Aelthor broke the silence. His voice was thick with anger; my stomach flipped at the sound of it. We lowered ourselves as a unit, quickly and silently.

"It has come to my attention that the four of you have failed me," he rumbled, loud enough to shake the walls. Despite my efforts, my breathing became shallow, and my palms slick with sweat.

"We are on the precipice of altering the entire world as we know it," he continued. "Banishing the chains that have kept us starving and fighting on this island for centuries. You were sent to retrieve vital information from the elf, and you have utterly failed. What do you have to say for yourselves?"

"We found him against the odds twice, Your Majesty." Hilda dared to speak. Her voice, clear and deep. "The first time we were ambushed, and he escaped. The second we had him cornered, he took poison before we could question him."

"You had a Mindwalker with you. Why didn't you allow him to take the elf's memories before he died?" I couldn't see his face, with my eyes trained on the ground in front of me, but I imagined those grey-blue eyes narrowing on Hilda, our brave Hilda, his own flesh and blood.

"Adrien did not arrive until after he had passed."

I did not dare to turn my head or look up at Adrien and see what was happening. Silently, I thanked Hilda for her bravery and counted the moments until we could leave this room.

"This is unacceptable," Father said. He took one step forward and then another, his shoes clicking on the polished wood as he slowly made his way down the dais. "Moving forward, we must recognize that times are changing. The time for leniency has passed."

His words made my stomach plummet. The clicking of his shoes echoed around me, like a tightening noose. My eyes narrowed in on what was before me. My boot, with its twelve riveted holes on each side and woven laces that were tied up tight. Inside those were a pair of lightweight wool socks, a small leather holster with a dagger, and a few coins.

The sound of a pop rang through the silent hall, followed by a splat. A spray of warm liquid splashed across the side of my face and body, causing me to flinch and squeeze my eyes shut. I didn't have to open them to know it was Tris' blood sprayed across me. A sickening thud told me she was down. There were gasps behind us and a few muffled cries from the younger girls. The soft sounds of shuffling feet and a few whispers escaped before all was quiet again; an eerie quiet that threatened to devour me whole.

Then another pop and splat.

This time, a lighter rain of blood peppered my side.

It had to be Adelay.

I squeezed my eyes tighter as bile rose in the back of my throat, and tears pricked my eyes. My beautiful, vibrant sisters were killed with the flick of a wrist. Now, there were shrieks and cries from the crowd, but Father's voice rang out over them.

"Let this all be a lesson to you, daughters of the Harridans; failure will not be tolerated. Insubordination will not be tolerated."

"You," the king spoke up now. A swishing sound told me he had stood, but I could not look up at him. I could not move. "You are my chosen few. The warriors who will decide the fate of the whole of Wraithland. This is for your well-being so that you can understand the gravity of our situation. We need you all to be at your best if we are going to accomplish what our people have been fighting for since the wards were placed fifteen thousand years ago."

His voice rose in a frenzied crescendo as he spoke, his excitement filling the room, pressing against the horror emanating from behind me. All of us were utterly destroyed at having seen our sisters ripped apart in front of us.

The king moved from his makeshift throne and sauntered down the dais. I heard a squelch as he walked through the gore, stepping on bits of my sister. He was still speaking, but I could no longer hear him. It took everything in me to stay upright, to hold still while I waited for my own death.

I had no recollection of when the king left, or the warders, or my other sisters. Time seemed to stop, hanging on that moment when Father had ripped the life from them. An ache echoed through my bones from kneeling on the hard floor, but I could not move from the spot, as if moving would somehow make it all real.

A firm hand on my shoulder jolted my eyes up. Hilda was there, her red-rimmed eyes and deeply lined face grim but steady. She took my elbow with a gory hand and pulled me upright. I felt and saw her magic, the beautiful gray strands of it, wrapping around me, holding me up, and escorting me out of the ballroom as we left our broken sisters there on the floor.

Hilda took me to the bathing chamber, where she drew us each a bath. I stepped into the warm water, not bothering to take my leathers off first. The water swirled with red as the blood and carnage washed from me. I sank beneath the water, laying in its depths until my lungs burned, and my body finally took over, forcing me up for air.

A gurgle escaped my throat, a horrible, aching sound that I had never heard before. I pushed my hands into my hair gripping it hard at the roots. Squeezing my eyes shut and pulling a new cocoon around myself, I let out a strangled scream, but it wasn't enough to quell the rising tide of rage inside me. I understood my place here, and I knew what servitude was, but this wasn't service; this was slavery. It was manipulation of the worst kind. Everything I thought I was; I thought I had achieved, meant nothing. These men would never let our people be free, and they would never let my sisters or the humans on the continent be free, either.

CHAPTER TWENTY-EIGHT

I sat there in the bath until the water went cold, and my hands trembled with it. Hilda had left long ago, leaving me at peace with my pain. I scrubbed the remaining blood from my hair and face before raising myself out of the tub, ignoring the water that slopped across the floor. There would be some other woman, some slave like me to clean it. I left my leathers in a heap by the tub as well, my stomach churning at the sight of them.

There were towels stacked in cupboards, and I wrapped one around myself. I found piles of extra clothing in the sewing room a few doors down, opting for the simple brown linen pants and the white tunic of the novices. I didn't bother to collect my weapons, wanting nothing given to me from this place.

I found Ash in the arena, running drills with some of the younger sisters. The cavernous space was full to bursting, with sisters, novices, staff, and warders. The only sounds were the heavy breathing and soft grunts of effort with the occasional shout of direction. This is how we were taught to deal with emotions, to bury them, and focus on training or work or the mission. This was one of the ways they controlled us, by keeping our minds from wandering.

I came to her side and fluidly stepped into the motions of the sequence they were working through, albeit with no weapon in hand. She did not so much as look in my direction until the sequence was complete. She shouted a command for the girls to move into a new sequence and we moved to the side. Ash crossed her arms over her chest, her eyes staring blankly ahead.

"Why did he spare you?" she asked finally through gritted teeth.

"Because they want me to carry a child for them."

Her head snapped in my direction; her expression enraged. There was enough noise around us that I continued without dropping a cocoon, my eyes pinned to a spot on the wall across the arena. It was all I could do to keep myself standing let alone prevent the tears that threatened to fall.

"They want me to bear the Mindwalker's child with the hope that it will have a greater power than either of us."

"Well fuck," she said, stepping forward, slapping the arm of one of the girls who had raised it too high.

"These are not the first deaths by Father, just the first they let us witness," I mumbled, keeping my voice low. A wash of memories fell over me, and I added, "At least the first by their hands."

There were many more sisters and novices whose lives were cut short by training accidents, injuries, or missions gone poorly. Some of these were even by my own hands. So many times, we were pushed past our limits, and only the strongest survived. My heart guttered, my breath catching as the vines around my heart squeezed tight. My vision tunneled as I imagined the thorns that had pierced the flesh there, blood oozing out of me to pool in the black depths of my soul.

Ash gave another command, and I shook the thoughts from my head.

"The Harridan Society isn't all we thought it was," I whispered. "All we were raised to believe it was and now things are only going to get worse. Once Aelthor breaks the wards, we will be at war—whether it is with the Elves or the humans. We will be first on the chopping block. Us, the warders, the Gasyters, we will all die by the dozens. And even if we prevail, he will continue to rule like this. There is no hope for a future different than what we have."

"What are you saying, Catherine?" she hissed.

"We have to stop them."

She shook her head. "No, no, we don't."

"No, you don't understand Ash." I turned to her with one hand going to her arm. I didn't even care if the warders saw it, I doubted any of them would reprimand us at this moment, but I dropped a cocoon around us to be safe. "It's not just about us. It's about them." I waved a hand to the girls moving in front of us. "Together, we can make a difference. We can change this as long as we have each other. We will be fine. We will figure out a new way. A way for us all to be safe, maybe even happy."

"Stop right there." Ash's voice came out deep, booming even. She ripped herself away from me. Her large blue eyes blazed bright, and a shock of ice snaked down my spine.

"We would not be here without them. Father took every single one of us in, feeding us, clothing us, training us. Where would we go without them? What would we do, and who would we be? You may not agree with every mission you're given, but it doesn't matter. Aelthor is privy to the knowledge that we don't have. How can you presume that you are smarter, better, more capable than the king? The king of Elven-blood, centuries older than us. What kind of arrogance do you have? What happened to you on that continent that made you think this was the right path?"

"It's not my arrogance, Ash, listen," I begged.

"No, you, listen, Catherine. It's not about us. None of this is about us. It is about the good of the whole of Wraithland. We suffer for their freedom, and we do it with pride." She beat her chest with one hand, squaring herself to me as if she were ready to fight.

"But they won't be free, ever, so long as a power-hungry, vengeance-seeking ruler like Aelthor leads us."

"Enough." She shoved me away this time. I fell back into the cocoon, breaking its magic. A few eyes turned to us, but they all looked away quickly, not wanting to take part in whatever was happening between us.

Ash stepped forward, her hair swaying. "It should have been you that died today. Not Adelay, not Tris. They were both loyal, loving sisters. They would, and did, lay down their lives for us, but you are a selfish whore. I should kill you where you stand." She spit the words in a vengeful whisper, still trying to keep this between us.

Tension gripped me as I realized there was no convincing Ash, the woman I had thought was my best friend for most of my life, would never be on my side. It wasn't her fault. She was a shell of a person, a woman beyond broken, just as Adrien had described. How many of my sisters had grown into this?

Her eyes flickered, the light going out of them. She took a deep breath.

"Consider this my debt paid," she said, crossing her arms again.

My mind reeled, hurtling me back to childhood, back to one of the many tests we faced as children. It was a yearly competition, a week of sparring, culminating in a single winner. None of us were permitted to eat on the first day, and after that, only the winners ate. The idea was that hunger would sharpen our senses. Those who lost would continue to spar until the final day when the lowest ranked would take on the winner. The final results were never pleasant.

I had won that year and was set to spar against the loser, Ash. She was scrawny even before the week of starvation. In recent weeks, she had grown a lot and was still trying to figure out how to use her new body. The match didn't last long, but something in me made me pull back on the last blow, stopping myself from ending her life. Father had seen it, my hesitation. After Ash had been sent to the infirmary, he had the rest of the class beat me within an inch of my own life for insubordination. This was how they fettered out the weak, disposing of them, *through us*. Training us to be cold and unfeeling.

Ash spent the subsequent years honing her skills, spending every waking moment working toward becoming one of the best and earning herself a spot as one of the Society's top Saithes, just behind me.

I had never realized she considered that moment a debt that she owed me.

"What are you saying?" I asked, my voice raw, as every ounce of strength I had left flowed out of me.

She dropped a cocoon around us again. "I'm saying I won't tell anyone what you've said here. You have until dawn to leave and never come back. I won't let you risk the lives of my sisters, but I will let you live. Go to your precious continent and stay out of our way."

Her eyes trailed my body, a sneer distorting her face before she turned and stalked away.

I didn't stay, not wanting her or anyone else to see me react, to see my heart crushed in my chest. Pushing out my magic, I felt for Daren. I hadn't seen him in the arena, but his presence was here, in his room on the second floor. There were two other females there, but I didn't care. I stomped straight to his room and threw the door open, all three sets of eyes landing on me.

Daren stood shirtless in the center of the room, with two acolytes naked, prostrating on the bed before him. These were girls who had ascended but not been assigned missions yet; their sexualization was all a part of the training. My stomach lurched; this wasn't training. It was rape. Another way to control us.

His face went from grim to concerned, and he dismissed the girls with a flick of his eyes. They grabbed their clothes and scuttled around me to get to the door. Everything in me wound tighter until my hands began to tremble.

"I needed a distraction," he said to me as if it was an excuse. Why had I come here? Daren had always said he wanted to be different and a better ruler, but what had he really done to show me that over the years? Acting as every other warder, worse sometimes, more like Father. I rubbed my temples, realizing there was no one here I could trust, not truly.

"I'm sorry. I shouldn't have come." It was all I could do to hide the tremor from my voice as I turned to leave. The weight of his hand on my arm stopped me.

"I did everything I could to save all of you," he said, his face contorting as if in pain. "I didn't know they were going to do that until it was done. It was meant to be a lesson for me as much as it was for you." He turned me to face him, whispering. "Catherine. I am so sorry."

Everything I had been holding in flooded out of me at that moment, silent tears trickling down my cheeks and my shoulders shaking. Daren took a deep breath and pulled me into his bare chest, wrapping his long, muscled arms around me, one hand stroking my hair. I wanted to hate him for his part in it all. The ways he used us, tortured us, beat us, in the name of training, but at this moment, I couldn't pull away.

We stood there for a long time until, eventually, my tears waned. I took a steadying breath and leaned back, wiping my eyes.

"I have to go." The words came out ragged.

Daren's brow furrowed, the post in his eyebrow straining. His arms came back around me pulling me in as if his strength would be enough to stop me.

"I can't stay here knowing what I know, feeling the way I do. It will be the death of me." I was pleading with him as if I needed his permission, like that would somehow make all this easier. My emotions warred inside me, my head clouding with frustration.

He took a deep breath, dropping his head to my hair and nuzzling me.

"It's not easy, but I've been doing it for years," he said finally. "You walking away is just leaving the rest of us to fight alone. You are more useful to us here. Besides, they won't let you just leave, you will be hunted."

I shook my head, pulling away again, just enough to look up into his eyes, now dark and glistening.

"I'm no use to anyone here," I said more firmly. "And I doubt they will have the manpower to send anyone after me."

"I can't do it without you." His voice cracked. "You have

always steadied me, given me strength when I needed it, and I will need all the strength I can get in the coming months." Something in my gut twisted. He was asking me to stay, to endure, for him. Hadn't I given enough already?

"This is a house full of girls who can give you what you need," I hissed. He pulled his lip ring between his teeth, watching me with sad eyes. My comment had hit a nerve.

"I shouldn't have come here," I said, pulling away fully and turning to the door.

"Do you love him?"

I whipped back, unsure I heard correctly. My hand hovered just over the door handle.

"What do you mean?"

"Do you love the Mindwalker?" He was looking at the floor, chewing on the ring in his lip, his hand scratching the back of his neck. The tattoos on his chest stretched and contorted with the movement.

"Daren, please, love is a fairy tale that exists in daydreams and books." I scolded him with the same words used against us.

"Then why was I about to throw my life away to save you in there?" He dropped his hand from his neck, his eyes met mine, dark and stormy and utterly shattering any strength I had left in me. "I was ready; if Pterol so much as looked at you, I would have destroyed him. I could do it. I've known for a long time that I'm more powerful."

I sucked in a breath. Pterol was one of the strongest Elven-blooded on the island, second only to his brother, Aelthor. If Daren could rival the king's power, he could be seen as a threat. Aelthor had a long life in front of him yet, he wouldn't let any of his successors show their power before his last breath. He wouldn't allow the threat to his power to exist.

"Daren, you can't talk like that," I said, my voice cracking, tears pricking the back of my eyes again. "If anyone heard you, you'd -it's dangerous. People like us don't get choices, they don't fall in love, and they don't give up their lives for one another. You can't do that, especially for me."

He stood clenching his fists at his side. "Then I guess it's just another reason you have to go."

I could almost see the wall he was building between us, shutting out his feelings for me with each brick he placed.

"Maleathe's second, his name is Grimmoth, he will help you go," he bit out. Turning to his desk, he pulled out a parchment and scribbled a note. "There's a place in town, a bar with green-painted doors and windows. Give this to the barmaid, Sam. She will take care of you."

I took the note, nodding.

"You could come with me, you know." The words came out as a whisper before I could think better of it. His face turned sad, nostrils flaring as he took a long, deep breath.

"The other contenders... I can't." He scrubbed a hand down his face. "If there is any chance at all that I can take the throne after Aelthor, I have to stay. The others will be worse than he is." He looked at me with eyes full of emotion. "If there is any hope of helping our people, I have a duty to stay."

I nodded again, feeling something wrenched apart inside me. With one last look, I turned to go.

CHAPTER TWENTY-NINE

Walking away from Daren's room, I traversed the second floor to the main stair that led to the front entry. My satchel was there by the door where we had all dropped them upon seeing Leon. Hilda and Adrien's were gone, but Tris and Adelay's were still there along with mine. I stopped short thinking of Adrien and how I hadn't thought of him in my time of need. With no recollection from the end of the assembly, I didn't know if he was even still here in the manor. Daren's question echoed in my mind and I felt the tension build in my chest again. There was no time for this nonsense. Shrugging off the thoughts, I grabbed all three packs and strode out the door. It wasn't quite midday, but the sun was already strong.

The front yard was empty, but I still did what I could to move quickly into the shadow of the forest. A lump in my throat began building as I entered the wood, finding the lightly worn path easily. I hugged the bags to my chest tightly, my nails digging into the leather and canvas. My eyes blurred as memories surfaced, reminding me of how I had come to be here. There were moments of laughter with my sisters, times of sadness, and times of triumph. I remembered a rare moment of praise when I had won a sparring competition after being locked in the dungeon and starved for days. The Ascension Ceremony, where Father initiated our training in seduction, a long-buried memory that made rage course through my veins anew.

Adrien had been right when he said the choice had been beaten, raped, and starved out of us. They had spent lifetimes manipulating us into believing it was for our own good and the good of Wraithland, but how much of it was just for their own twisted pleasures? Daren thought he loved me; how could he love someone he had never been truly allowed to know? I thought of my sisters with love, but there were so many secrets between us that I didn't believe I knew them truly either.

A dull ache began to form at the back of my head as I forced my thoughts to more practical matters, like where I would go from here. Even if I could make it to the continent, I had no money and nowhere to go. I knew no one but my sisters. There was a possibility of working for Ameria, but I would have to find her in whatever city she happened to be in. I had no way to contact her.

I stumbled over a root, nearly falling face-first into a tree, barely catching myself with a shaking hand. Choking down a few breaths, I pushed back the tears and tried to calm myself. There was no time to break down now. It wasn't safe to stay here, this close to the manor with bags in my hands, fleeing.

I had only made it a few more feet when my senses prickled, indicating something in the forest with me. I paused listening then pushing out my magic only to see the rose-pink fog of another's magic building in the brush to my right. I cursed myself for leaving my weapons behind and dropped the packs where I stood. In the span of a single heartbeat, I launched myself forward.

With three long strides, I thrust myself upward, using a

nearby tree to push myself over the brush. Kicking my feet apart in mid-air, I flipped myself over, gaining more ground so that I landed behind my would-be attacker throwing them off guard. I landed softly on the ground and moved to swipe the dagger from her hand, but she was faster.

Whipping around, she loosed the knife, causing me to dodge to the side. She was older, gray, and withered, but fast and cunning. Her dark eyes narrowed on me, but she didn't pause. I saw the pink smoke build as she turned to run. Reaching out, I pulled her rosy magic into me before laying chase at speeds I had never experienced before. The trees shot past in a blur, and I wasn't sure how my feet were even finding purchase on the uneven ground.

She threw a look over her shoulder at me, slowing just enough for me to overtake her. Unused to the speed, I was unable to stop, colliding with her, causing us both to tumble to the ground in a thudding heap. A searing pain slashed across my face as I realized she was dragging her nails across it. I batted her hand away and landed a good punch to the jaw with my other hand. The woman's head snapped back, and she groaned, trying to push me off wildly.

The pink fog of her magic started to build again. My hands were occupied with her flailing, forcing me to pull her magic away through other means. Blowing out a long breath, I sucked her magic in through my mouth, the bitter tang of it coating my tongue and throat. It filled my lungs, burning me from the inside. Her mouth dropped open, terror filling her wrinkled brown eyes.

"Sister, please," she pleaded. "Don't!"

The use of the moniker gave me pause. My eyes shot to her right hand, which I held by her side. She didn't fight as I flipped it up. There, over the spot where the stone should be, were two gnarled little scars that formed a cross over a circular depression. I let my thumb slide over the uneven skin, feeling it as I pushed her magic back out, blowing it away over my shoulder.

"What is this? What do you know?" I leaned over her, my face inches away. The woman wet her lips, her mind working, likely weighing which response would save her life. "Just be honest; you've got nothing left to lose," I growled, shoving her scared hand under my knee. I reached for the knife in my boot holster, but it was empty. Cursing myself again for leaving my weapons behind, I wrapped the hand around her neck instead.

"My granddaughter," she croaked, and I loosened my grip just enough for her to speak. "One of you took her." She swallowed and took a shuddering breath. "You murdered my daughter and her family. I want my granddaughter back."

My face crinkled in confusion for a moment before the realization hit me.

"Isadora," I whispered. Looking away for a moment, I sucked in the cool evening air, soothing my scarred lungs. How had this woman made it here from the continent? How had she even thought to come here? To find us? My brows knit together, and I sat back, loosening my grip on her neck just a bit more.

"How do you know about us?"

"I was one of you once." She held my gaze, her dark eyes hard and unyielding. It wasn't possible. There were no past sisters. There were plenty of jobs for older sisters, even ones as withered and bent as this. Leaving was never an option, never something we were even allowed to entertain. Any attempt would likely mean death anyway. My eyes narrowed.

"Lies," I hissed, squeezing tight again.

"My name is Tyanna Harridan." She pushed the words out over the pressure on her windpipe. Her voice rang in my ears. "I am a Saithe in the King's Harridan Society under the grace of Father Pterol Lockheed. *Beao fadgha ey Harridan.* Long live the Harridans."

All of the air blew out of my lungs, and I sputtered as she repeated part of the oath that we all took every morning before we began training as children. Something I hadn't heard outside the manor in all my life.

"That's not possible. Your child, you, you can't have—"

"I left The Society; let them believe I was dead all these years." She cut me off, confident and unyielding, now that my hesitation was visible.

"No one leaves." I pushed off her, stepping back as if she was contagious with some infectious disease. My head was spinning, emotion and logic battling for purchase in my ravaged psyche. She sat up but made no move to stand, a hand going to her throat. "No one leaves because they are connected to us by blood. They can track us anywhere we go. This makes no sense."

"Lies," she scoffed with a wave of her other hand. "Remove that stone, and they'll never find you unless you want to be found."

I blinked, staring at her, then blinked again, almost paralyzed. None of this seemed right. Nothing she was saying, nothing that had happened, nothing I was doing, none of it. I tried to shake some sense into my head before taking a deep breath. I looked back at the woman, still sitting there, watching me warily.

"You did a poor job of protecting your family," I said, flopping onto the ground, exhausted. My mind reeled, trying to piece together an understanding of what I was doing now, what I had seen earlier, and what I had just learned. This new information was too much. I didn't have it in me to keep trying to make sense of it all.

The woman nodded sadly. "After thirty years, I thought we were safe. I thought we were beyond the eye of this place." She shuddered. "But now I understand that the sisters don't just come from the island, do they?"

I shook my head gravely. "I didn't know it until, until Isadora, but I too was taken from my family. There's no telling how many of us were." I pressed my lips together to hold back the scream building in my throat, anger suddenly taking the place of my confusion. "They told us we were given up by our families for the greater good, but they lied. They made us think it was our duty to be there, to serve them, to fuck them, and to kill for them." My hands gripped the ground below me, tearing the plants up by their roots. My eyes locked onto hers, and I watched my anger reflected there. "And today, they killed my sisters for something they couldn't stop."

"Who killed them?" she whispered.

"Father and Aelthor."

Her eyes widened, her lips making a thin line. She scrunched her nose, tearing her eyes away to look out at the forest.

"I'm not surprised. Those bastards." She dropped the hand on her throat and let out a heavy sigh. "I didn't leave for so noble a reason. I was selfish. I wanted to keep the baby, to be a mother, to live like a simple farm wife. I was just tired of it all. I had the feeling they would either take the baby or strip the memories from me. A single mother with no memories wouldn't survive on this island; my baby wouldn't survive. So, I left, swearing I would never set foot in this place again.

"I was such a fool to think we were safe after all these years." Her voice cracked. "Father must have a way to sense potential power, to find girls like us, and when Izzy's power manifested, I should have realized she would be in danger. I should have known we would never truly be safe."

We sat in silence for a moment, both of us locked in our own torments.

"So, what now?" I pulled her attention back to me. "Are you just going to storm in there and demand your granddaughter back?"

"I had hoped I could be a little more stealthy than that," she chuckled, then her face turned solemn. "But the nearer I got to this place, the more I felt it wouldn't be enough. I can't leave here without removing Father as well."

"You'll never survive a battle with him," I said flatly. None of us could; his power was far greater than ours.

"Not on my own." She leveled her gaze at me. "But the gods brought us both here for a reason, no doubt."

I took a moment to consider her words. I never put much stock into the gods, not believing they gave a damn about us and our daily struggles. However, I couldn't deny this might be the only shot either of us had to make a difference. Once I left this island, it was unlikely I would ever make it back. I could help Ameria find the boy in the prophecy, and possibly help the continent prepare to go to war with Wraithland, but what else could be done?

Father wasn't even the solution to the biggest concerns that I had. For me, it was about stopping Aelthor's war, saving thousands of lives on both sides and making it possible for the banished to live in harmony with the continent. For all I had done to upset the balance of power on the continent, to smooth the road for Aelthor, for all the lives I had taken in his name, I wanted to do more. Removing father would do little to stop Aelthor, but it would slow him down. Father was his right hand in all things, not just The Society.

Perhaps ending him would give Hilda, Adrien, and whomever they had on their side enough time to figure out a real plan. A real way to stop the king, even if I didn't survive this, at least there would be that. Maybe it would shake Aelthor, his confidence, and his plans. Aelthor may be the king, but I was quite certain much of his strategy came from Father. Removing him would be a serious blow to the throne.

"If we attack together, there may be a chance, and then we can go for Isadora," I said at last.

The woman's eyes crinkled as her face broke into a wide grin. "We will need a solid plan and possibly some refreshment if we are to go about this correctly."

I nodded, standing. "I was just on my way to find someone whom I was told could help me." I stood and put out a hand for her to take. "I'm Catherine."

"Tyanna," she said through gritted teeth as she pulled herself up. "Let's go get our things and get out of here before one of the other sisters comes along."

I nodded, following her lead.

Without magic to bolster her, the woman shuffled more than strode, and it took us a while to get back to the spot where I had run into her and dropped my bags. As we ambled, she told me a little about her time there, asking questions about some of the elder sisters and warders. All of which I answered carefully. She may be my ally at the moment, but there was no telling what her true ambitions were just yet. The small glimpse I had seen of her magic told me she had enough power to be wary of.

"Where will we go after we gather our things?" Her voice was husky with the effort. "We will need a place where we can get that stone out of you, and they won't hear your screams while we do it."

"It's a small cut, I won't scream."

The woman spun on me. "It's more than a tracking beacon, girl," she said, her voice ominous. I swallowed and nodded, motioning for her to keep moving while she talked. She turned slowly, keeping her eyes on me, and I stepped beside her to show my full attention. "They tell you it enhances your powers, but in truth, it dulls them. They blend the stones: moonstone enchanted to mark your presence when connected to your blood and cobalt to dull your magic. The cobalt-tipped weapons can sever a man's powers, but when it sits under the skin, poisoning your blood, it's like a siphon on your magic." My heart began to ratchet up in speed as she spoke, and I realized the depth of their deception knew no bounds.

"Magic does not band itself to specific species; it exists in all things. They don't want us to know that we can be as powerful as them." She shook her head. "When I cut my stone out, there was only the smallest drop of cobalt, and I was overwhelmed by my powers. I thought it would kill me. It took me years to figure out how to control them fully."

"We don't have years," I said shakily.

"Maybe not, but with that power that you have to take from others." She took my shaking hand, squeezing it as we walked. "That is a special thing and may be the only way to take on the likes of Father Pterol. Power like that is unrivaled."

Tears pricked the back of my eyes. "What if I can't control my powers?"

I felt like a child, unable to control my emotions, my head throbbing. I wanted to tear my heart out and fall to the forest floor. It was all too much already, and now a new challenge was rearing its head.

"One thing at a time, girly," she said with a soft smile.

I looked down at my wrist, to the stone there, trying to string my thoughts out into orderly lines that made sense. These stones lay under our skin, mixing with our blood, keeping us tethered to them. Without our blood touching the stone, they couldn't track us. I thought back to Daren, he knew he was more powerful than Father. I had never used my power against Father prior to the Ascension, and the placing of the stone, not even in training. While he worked with some of the girls, he had always put me with Daren or Leon when working with magic. I had always thought it was because I needed less help than the others, but now I wondered if it was because he didn't want me to have an inkling that I could challenge him.

Rage began to bubble inside me again, only now I had an outlet. Now, I had a way to find out the truth. I looked up at the older woman, her brown eyes soft and warm as she watched me. Perhaps the gods may have had some influence on this chance meeting with a woman who had changed everything for me in my time of desperation.

"Let's do it," I said finally. "There is no safe place here, but Daren gave me a contact, and I trust him."

"Daren Aellonson?" The woman looked up at me, her face crumpled in disgust. "You trust that fool?"

Daren was in his eighties at least; he would have been a young man when this woman was still a young Saithe. She would have known him, possibly as intimately as me. How much could someone change in that time?

"I don't know about the man that you knew then, but the one that I know now is no fool. He sits on Aelthor's council but despises his cruelty and hopes for a way to find peace with the continent where Wraiths can live free and magic is embraced."

Tyanna looked incredulous, scrunching her nose. "I find that hard to believe, but I suppose if I have changed so much in as many years it's possible, he could have as well." She shrugged, looking up at me. Her eyes swam with emotions that I couldn't read. "What have I got to lose?"

CHAPTER THIRTY

As I had suspected, the bar with green-painted doors and windows was the same place I had gone with my sisters the night before leaving the continent on the ill-fated hunt for the elf. It was dark, and the sign on the door said it was closed, but I tried the handle anyway, finding it unlocked.

I pushed it open and stepped in, squinting in the dim light.

"We're closed." A woman's voice I recognized shouted from a back room, behind the bar.

"I thought you told me I was welcome here, any time?" I shouted in response.

Sam's head popped around the corner, her face lighting up when her smoky eyes landed on me. She shook her head, her wild curls swaying with the movement, and her face broke into a broad smile.

"I don't think I've ever said that to anyone in my entire life, but I suppose if anyone is welcome around here, it is you," she laughed. "Have a seat; I'll be right out."

Tyanna and I followed her direction, pulling up two stools at the bar, which was much less sticky than I remembered.

Moments later, Sam came out with stacks of glasses on trays, which she carefully set down on the bar beside us before wiping her brow and smiling at us broadly.

"What is it I can get you ladies?" she asked. In the bright light of day, I could see her features more clearly. She had high cheekbones, slanted eyes, and smooth skin that was a deep blue. She was beautiful, and her smile was dazzling.

I took the note Daren had given me from my pocket and slid it across the bar top to her. Her eyes flitted down to the note and back up to me. Looking down, I saw the paper was stamped with a seal I didn't recognize. It was a set of five diamonds oriented like a star, each representing a different element.

She snatched it up and opened it, watching me suspiciously. When she was done, she nodded to herself and folded it back up before turning and setting it aflame on a wall sconce.

"Well, you need to get to the continent?" she said flatly. Her lips made a thin line that caused tension to creep up my spine.

"Maybe, maybe not." I shrugged, trying to appear relaxed. "We have something to do first, and if we survive, then I'm sure we will need a ride out of here."

She nodded again with unexpected seriousness. "Well, there's a boat leaving in the early afternoon tomorrow. I can get you on it, but if you are caught before then, that's on you, and there's nothing to be done about it."

"That'll do," I said. "You'll know one way or another by then."

"In the meantime, there are some things we need to do that include a bed and some restraints." Tyanna chimed in from beside me. Both Sam and I turned to her, mouths agape. She put her hand up. "I'll explain it all when we are in a private room. And we should bring one of those as well." She pointed to the wall behind Sam that held an array of bottles of alcohol. "Strongest you have."

***

Sam led us up the stairs carrying a bottle of something clear and strong smelling. The room was similar to the one I had seen before but smaller. She set the bottle on the bedside table and went to find restraints while Tyanna and I settled ourselves.

I set both mine and Tris's satchel on the floor and slipped off my shoes, sitting on the bed with Adelay's bag first. Now seemed as good a time as any to see what was in them. Adelay's was designed like a pack that could be carried on your back. It was made of black canvas that had been waxed to prevent water damage. It was simple and didn't look like it got much use, though I suppose the purpose of the Tachdre was to maintain a safe house, which implied remaining in one place.

I emptied the contents onto the bed. There were plenty of the things I expected. An extra set of leathers, a few knives, candles, matches, an aid kit, a fire note tin, a leather binder for notes, a comb, and some pins for her hair. Then, there was a small velvet pouch. Inside it was a necklace with a single clear bead that sat inside a silver ring. There was nothing remarkable about it, but clearly, it meant something, or she wouldn't have carried it with her all this way. It was frowned upon to keep sentimental items of any kind, though I had seen many of my sisters disregard this rule. I held up the necklace and inspected it for a moment before placing it back in its bag and sliding it into my pocket.

Sam reentered the room with a set of leather straps in hand

253

and a wry smile on her face. Neither Tyanna nor I asked where she got them. It didn't matter. I shoved everything on the bed back into the bag and set it down beside the others.

"Are the restraints really necessary?" I said, eyeing them from my spot on the bed.

Tyanna nodded, coming to the side of the bed. She uncorked the bottle of liquor and handed it to me. I took a long swig, savoring the strong burn as it slid down my throat.

"The straps are to protect you from yourself." She motioned for me to take another swig, and I did. "When the stone is removed, it will unleash magic you haven't had access to. It will assault your senses. For me, it felt like my skin was on fire, and I clawed at it until I bled. My head pounded and my body was so sore it took days for me to even get out of bed. I can't say it will be like that for you, but we must expect something similar."

I wet my lips, gritting my teeth with determination. "Let's get it over with."

Taking another big swig of the alcohol, I laid back on the bed, letting the women strap down my arms and legs in the soft leather straps. Sam took up a spot in the corner, by the door, arms crossed over her chest. Tyanna pulled a chair up to the side of the bed, her eyes on me the whole time. I gave her a reassuring nod and turned my eyes to the ceiling.

The initial cut of the knife barely tickled my skin. The second cut hurt a little more, but nothing I wasn't expecting.

"This might hurt a bit," Tyanna said as she slipped the end of the knife under the stone and pried it out of its place. I bit my tongue as the pain radiated up my arm, and then there was nothing.

I looked down to see Tyanna's wide eyes, her mouth agape. She was holding the stone up, looking at it in the light. It was no bigger than a thumbnail, but it was nearly solid cobalt, with the exception of a small clear spot in the middle. My eyes darted from hers to the stone, wondering at her surprise as cold began to glide up my arm. It was as if my blood had been replaced by ice, the searing pain of frost etching its way over my body. I swallowed as my vision blurred, and my heart raced. The pain stretched across my chest, encapsulating my heat, and I screamed.

Through my blurred vision, fuzzy colors began blasting from every corner, dull and vivid all at once. It overwhelmed my senses, and I squeezed my eyes shut, but it did little to quell the onslaught of my magic. Even from behind my eyelids, I saw colors moving and exploding in time with the intense sounds assaulting my ears from every direction. I could smell damp earth and taste the metal tang of blood. I tried to spit it out, but nothing left my mouth. My skin felt like it was on fire, and I tried to itch it away only to be restrained by the straps. I began thrashing wildly. In my mind, I willed myself to calm down, but the burn was agonizing, and then there was pressure. It came from all around, squeezing me tight so that I couldn't breathe. I knew in the back of my mind that I was tethered to the bed, but it felt like I was sinking into the depths of the deepest lake, the pressure pushing down on me as I sunk lower.

Another scream exploded from me as fire raced down my spine, spreading down my limbs. Now, my mouth went dry and salty as if it were full of sand. Then there was the smell of burning flesh. It was so strong that my stomach turned, and I thought I would throw up. Just then, the pounding in my ears crescendoed to a height so intense I screamed again.

My voice seemed to echo as it faded, as everything faded and fell away.

I was floating in a dark abyss, unable to see my own hand at the end of my arms. There was a pull at my middle as if I was tethered by something I couldn't see. I reached out a hand, feeling in the air for anything. My hand slipped over something fine and silky. A vibration reverberated out into the dark as if I had just plucked the string of an instrument. I followed the movement with my eyes to its origin point. I moved toward it, willing myself forward.

A form began to appear in the distance, getting closer and closer until I recognized Adrien. His face was calm with a slight smile playing on his lips. He held out a hand for me. He was so handsome, and I could feel the warmth and comfort in his touch. Something tugged on my tether, pulling me closer to him.

I looked up into those blue-gray eyes I had become familiar with. His smile broadened, and they crinkled at the edges. There was something different about them. I took a step back as his features altered in front of me. Two long scars began to form under his right eye. His hair lightened, and suddenly, it wasn't Adrien but Father.

CHAPTER THIRTY-ONE

Horror washed over me, and I jumped awake, finding myself on the bed of the small room at Sam's bar. I was no longer restrained, and the sheets had been soaked through from my sweat. Sam sat in a chair near the end of the bed, rubbing her eyes as if she had just woken up. I tried to ask her what happened but began coughing instead. Sam got up and rushed to the bedside table to hand me a glass of water, which I chugged down greedily.

"You had me worried," she said with a smile. "I've never seen anyone thrash and scream and fight in their dreams like you. Seems you are feisty in all parts of your life, huh?" Her voice was loud, ringing in my ears.

I smiled at her and then winced at a sudden pain in my lip as it cracked. "How long was I out for?" I asked, my voice hoarse.

"Well, it's nearly dawn now, so quite a while," she said, pulling the chair closer. It scraped against the wood, making me wince.

She sat back down, and I noticed a faint glow about her like a light yellow ring was just hovering there. I reached out to touch it, my fingertips electrified, and I pulled back quickly. She looked sideways at my hand, and her brows lowered in confusion.

"You have magic." The words came out like a reverent whisper.

Now, her eyebrows shot up. "How can you know that?"

"I-I can see it, but it used to only be when, uh, are you pulling it in now?" My eyes trailed the glow that still hovered there. It didn't move like most other magic when beings would build it up to use it. This magic just stayed there at the ready. She shook her head.

"Well, I've never called it that, but no, I'm not, and don't go around telling everyone I've got it." She leaned back in the seat and rubbed her arms. "Most other Gasyters don't like magic wielders. There is an elf way back in my line somewhere, which no one needs to know about."

I couldn't help my smirk before mirroring Tyanna's words from before. "Magic exists in the earth, that means any being can wield it."

"Tell that to the elders," she scoffed, waving a hand at me.

"Where is Tyanna anyway?" I said, pushing myself to a sitting position. My head was fuzzy, and every muscle in my body ached. I pushed the blanket off, the movement nearly making me scream again. My skin felt raw, like my clothes were made of grit, and every motion rubbed the wound open again.

"Resting herself in the room next door." Sam leaned forward with a smile. "That broad might be an old lady, but she has got nerves of steel. I don't know much about your sisters, just what Daren has mentioned in our work, but from just the two of you, I know that I never want to be on your ladies' bad side."

"That's probably wise," I laughed, regretting it immediately as my head throbbed. Sam refilled my glass with a pitcher and handed it to me. Something about this girl just made me like her. "Unfortunately, we need to get moving. Who knows what Father Pterol has been told about me by now, the whole sisterhood could be hunting me."

"Excuse me." Sam held up a hand, her eyebrows shooting up her forehead. "Hunting you? I thought I was on Daren's side here."

"It is far too complicated to explain." I rolled my shoulders, trying to loosen up the stiffness. There was no time for this. "Daren's not aware of my plans. I don't know what he would think of them honestly, but if what I plan to do works, it will bring him closer to the throne. None of it will fall back on him, and no one will know that you're involved either."

She crossed her blue arms over her chest and pursed her lips. "Who said I didn't want to be involved exactly?"

My lips quirked into a smile, and I shook my head, fighting the urge to wince again. "You haven't a clue what's going on, and even if you did, I would not ask you to take part in this; we are not likely to see the sunrise."

She shrugged. "I don't know what your deal is, but I do know that me and Daren go way back. I know Daren ain't like the others, and I think you know that too, or he wouldn't have sent you here. And while you might have your own thing going on, we're clearly on the same side so whatever you need, I'm in. You just tell me where to aim." She pointed two fingers across the room like she was eying a target.

I laughed, but found it hard to digest her words. Daren had lived a long time, had been to many places, and seen many things, but even I didn't hold that kind of loyalty to him. Sam's excitement to help was either naivety or something else I couldn't quite place. Even then, I doubted he would agree with what Tyanna and I had planned to do. It was true that he had his reservations, but he was still loyal to the king; at least, that's how he appeared to be.

Maybe I didn't really know Daren at all, just like he didn't really know me. We both had secrets, secrets we kept to protect not only ourselves but also each other. Maybe he had an entire army waiting in the wings to take down the king. It didn't matter; either way, he wasn't here now.

"Thank you," I whispered. "That means more than you know, but this isn't your fight."

"I get it," she sighed. "I'm here for you when you're done. If you need to get out or whatever." She stood and poured me another glass of water from the pitcher, setting it on the table. "I'll wake Tyanna."

"Thanks," I said, taking the drink and slugging it back, noticing that the glow she once held had begun to fade already.

I set the glass down and picked up a candle from the table. Focusing on the wick, I blew a thin line of air toward it until it ignited with a spark and a flash. It was a bit more enthusiastic than I had intended, but nothing I couldn't account for. I rolled my neck and stretched my shoulders, moving my limbs here and there, feeling my muscles and working the ache out of them.

Sitting up, I swung my feet over the side of the bed and set them gingerly on the cool wooden floor. It was rough, more rough than I remembered, but I pushed the feeling away until it felt smooth. Controlling that part of my innate magic before it overwhelmed me. Next, I reached for a different magic, feeling for the presence of other beings. It came quickly, and I wasn't prepared for the abundance of numerous heartbeats, the electric energy of their magic and the thrum of their life forces. I had forgotten that I was in a guest room over a bar that had just closed. There were still beings here, in the rented rooms, cleaning, and loitering in corners. It was too much. A sharp pain shot through my already pounding head, and I pulled it back with a wince, digging the heels of my hands into my eyes.

"Don't push yourself just yet, girly." Tyanna's voice cut through the fog in my brain.

I looked up to see her shuffling into the room, followed by Sam and a Gasyter male, so large he had to turn sideways to get through the door. He was wearing the same plain leather trousers and white tunic that he had worn the first night we met a few weeks ago. It hadn't occurred to me that Grim would be short for Grimmoth, the man that Daren had said was General Maleathe's second and one of the two men I had enjoyed before the ill-fated mission to the continent.

He gave me a quick glance before looking to the ground, his hands shoved deep into his pockets. In the light of day, he was more handsome than I remembered, with a chiseled jaw and shaggy black hair that fell into his eyes. There was a hint of dark stubble on his sapphire chin and two long scars that arced up from his eyebrow into his hair. He was well-muscled, with the stance and breadth of a seasoned warrior. At his open collar, I saw the edges of a large marking that, I knew, spread across his chest and shoulder. My cheeks flushed, and I pushed the thoughts away. Now was not the time to relive those moments.

Tyanna came and sat on the bed beside me, her brows lowered as she inspected me. With a wrinkled hand, she turned my head this way and that, moved one arm, then the other, before placing one hand on my back and the other on my chest.

"How do you feel?" she asked, handing me a dropper bottle.

"I have a headache." I shrugged. Taking the bottle and placing two full droppers delicately under my tongue. "It's more like a hangover. Everything is a little more sensitive, but I don't feel all that different."

The older sister pursed her lips and shook her head. "You two go find us some food, will you?"

Sam gave an annoyed face but turned to go with Grim following silently behind.

Tyanna held up the stone she had removed from my skin. Instinctively, I looked down at my bandaged wrist and back up at the stone. It was bigger than I thought it would be and a lot more blue. Cobalt was known to be harmful to magic. If it was able to get into the blood, like on the tip of a blade, it would prevent the injured from utilizing their magic until it cleared their system. Even just the tiniest powder could incapacitate a skilled magic wielder, I had used it myself on prisoners, but this much, sitting beneath my skin for years, was something I had never imagined.

She put the stone in my hand and then pulled a necklace out of her shirt. It was a small locket that she opened. Inside was a very similar stone but with the opposite coloring. Where mine was all cobalt, hers was nearly all moonstone, with a small dot of blue in the middle.

"This was my stone." She said grimly. "I wasn't the strongest Saithe of my time; that was Hilda, but I wasn't far behind her. That much cobalt should have killed you long ago." She shook her head, her eyes getting misty. "The power you have inside you is likely to rival Father's own, maybe even Aelthor himself.

"How is that possible?" My words came out as a strangled whisper.

"I don't know. There's so much we don't know because of them," she said grimly. "We should be resting a few more days, give you time to figure out your abilities, but I worry for Isadora and what's happening to her even now."

I nodded, fighting the tears that prickled the back of my eyelids. "No, I'm ready now." I forced myself to stand, arching my back and stretching my arms over my head. "At this point, there is no telling what has been said about me. For all we know there could be a price on my head. Staying risks the lives of everyone here, in addition to Isadora." Every movement was like a torment. I wanted nothing more than to lay back down and sleep for days, but that wasn't an option. "We go now."

"You mean after you eat all this food, I just threw together for you," Sam said from the doorway, again followed by Grim, who carried a tray of tea and a roll of papers in his hands. Tyanna and I made room for them to set everything on the bed. Grim pulled up the chairs and sat with us, offering one to Sam before he opened the papers in his hands.

"These are the plans for the Lockheed Manor," he said, his deep voice sending chills down my spine. He smoothed them out on the bed and looked up at me through impossibly long lashes. I looked away, taking a bite of my bread and ignoring the smirk that crossed Sam's face as she watched us. "I haven't been able to get in touch with Daren, but Sam says we are to give you anything you ask for," he said coolly. "Don't make me regret this."

"Then you best back out now, young man," Tyanna cut in.

Grim turned his attention to her, a muscle feathering in his jaw. He wet his lips before speaking. "I'm not meaning to be dramatic, ma'am, but this can't fall on me. I've worked too hard to gain my position in the capital. It would ruin all the plans we have set in place. So if you fail, you'd best be ready to sacrifice yourselves."

He held her stare for a moment before turning back to the

papers before him. Tyanna raised her brows and gave a smile of acceptance before also bending her head over the papers.

"Now, I haven't heard exactly what you're planning to do, but judging by the way those stones have been removed, I've got plenty of ideas," he continued. "These are the blueprints for the manor, including a number of secret passages and hidden rooms. It may not be one hundred percent accurate, but it's the closest thing we've got."

"How did you even get this?" I said, my breath hitching in surprise. This was the place I had spent most of my life, and there were so many parts of it I had never even known existed. It was a labyrinth hiding just under the surface. "This is the kind of thing that would be under lock and key."

"We have our ways." Sam winked at me. "But it's the only one we have, so you have to do your best to memorize it because you aren't walking away with it."

I nodded, taking another bite of bread. Grim proceeded to lay out the entire building, including places to hide and pathways for escape. He had clearly spent some time studying the manor for whatever plan he was working on.

A wave of apprehension washed over me as I listened to him speak. How long had Daren been working with them? What kind of plans had they devised in that time? Had my sisters and I been at risk of attack this whole time? How many others knew about our existence? My heartbeat began to race and I took a deep breath, pushing the thoughts away. It didn't matter now; we were about to change everything.

Eventually, Grim finished his explanations and left to gather some weapons while we finished eating, and I changed into Adelay's leathers. While she was shorter and more stout than me, all the leathers we were given by The Society had been enchanted, and they immediately conformed to my physique. I had no room for carrying bags, so I left everything else in Sam's care, with the exception of Adelay's necklace, which I clasped around my own neck.

An hour later, we were rested, fed, loaded down with weapons, and an intimate knowledge of the manor. We said our goodbyes to both Sam and Grim, expressing our thanks for everything. Turning, I followed Tyanna as we slipped out the back door of the bar. On the threshold, a hand on my elbow stopped me. Before I turned around, I felt Grim's firm chest leaning into my shoulder as he bent his head toward my ear.

"Good luck," he said in that deep, rumbling voice of his that made every hair in my body stand on end. I gave him a smile over my shoulder and shook off the feeling, wondering as I stepped away how much of that was my heightened senses and how much of it was just the effect he had on me. Perhaps if I died today, I could use the image of our last encounter to die happy.

CHAPTER THIRTY-TWO

Getting to the manor was the easy part, albeit slow. I wondered how much help Tyanna would be in a fight, but her magic had to do some good.

We both glamoured ourselves as we approached the front door, the only entrance not warded against those outside The Society. The glamours wouldn't hold up if we came across anyone up close, but from a distance, it was enough to get us by.

The entrance hall was as empty as it ever was and we were able to slip in easily. I felt a tingle slide down my spine as I crossed the threshold, my pulse quickening as we slunk around the outer edge of the large room. We chose to take the hall past the kitchen to the second stair instead of the main one, which was visible from many rooms. Moving silently together, we carefully made our way down the hall.

"I thought we had a deal, Catherine." Ash's singsong voice called out from behind us. I let out a breath, realizing that someone had warded the house to warn them if I came back. The tingle I felt might not have been apprehension, but my heightened senses. I spun, seeing only Ash standing there, a purple glow emanating from her. Could she have been the one to set the ward?

"I'm not staying, Ash. I just have to take care of something first."

"Then you won't mind if I join you?" She strutted down the hall toward us, her head held high. We had been best friends for most of our lives, and though we had never been permitted to share as much as I would have liked, no one knew me better than her. And now we both knew damn well that I had not come back to the manor without a mission, and she was going to do everything in her power to thwart it.

"Who is your friend?" She paused beside me, cocking her head to the side and eyeing Tyanna. The elderly woman remained silent, standing tall despite her shrunken frame. She stared back at Ash with dead eyes, giving away nothing.

"Don't do this, Ashlynn," I whispered. Her head snapped to me, our eyes level. She took a long breath in through her nose, her chest rising and falling with the sound.

"What do you expect me to do, Catherine?" she hissed. "Walk away and let you roam the estate? What are you going to do?"

"Ash," I pleaded, feeling a knot form in my stomach. "It's got nothing to do with me. If we keep going down this path, thousands will die, and it doesn't have to be that way."

"Says who?" She shook her head, her hair swaying. "I won't have this argument again, get out. I'm giving you one more chance, sister. Just fucking get out."

Her magic pulsed in the air around her, fingertips crackling with it. I had never experienced the sights and sounds of magic like this, and it was overwhelming. My chest tightened, my hands shaking as I watched her expression change and her magic build.

"Go ahead, Tyanna, I will meet you there," I said with as much steadiness as I could muster, keeping my eyes on my friend.

Tyanna turned and shuffled forward even slower than before. I was surprised Ash let her go, but perhaps she didn't consider the older woman a real threat. My eyes trailed over Ash's features, the sincerity and rage roiling in her face, the pout of her lip, the bright cerulean of her eyes, and the blunt ends of her hair. She had been my classmate, my friend, my partner, and finally, my sister. A lifetime of memories washed over me, and I thought my knees would buckle under their weight, but just then, Ash drew a large dagger, and I jumped back into the familiar stance of readiness, drawing my own weapon.

She lunged forward with a scream, and I slapped a cocoon of protection around us as I blocked it. I couldn't risk others finding us now. I ducked away and spun, running to the library, only a few doors away. She swore and followed me. I used my magic to shut the door behind her and ward it off from sound. She came at me as I was distracted, resulting in a slash at my arm. Nothing deep, but it stung. She could have done worse.

"Come on, Ash," I pleaded. "You don't want to do this as much as I don't."

"Fucking the Mindwalker teaches you how to read minds now?" she spat, drawing another dagger and coming at me with both hands slashing.

"I don't want to hurt you," I said, blocking the blows. The clang of our blades scraping against my ears. She was walking me backward and soon I would have my back against the wall.

Moving to the offensive, I pulled my second blade and slashed it at her abdomen. She jumped back just in time, but it was enough for me to slide out of her reach. I lunged before she could regroup, and she was forced to defend herself. I backed her into the side of a chair, and before she fell, she used her magic to fling it at me. I had to duck nearly to the floor to avoid it, and she was there before I could get on my feet again. At this point, our many years of training together kicked in, and we went back and forth, each of us gaining the upper hand only to lose it again until we were both breathing heavily.

My nerves began to fray. There could only be so much time before someone discovered us or Tyanna in the house. My chest constricted as tears welled in my eyes. I pulled at my magic, pushing it into my arms, and the blade in my hand. When I struck the next blow, there was a sickening crack as Ash's arm broke from the force.

She stumbled back, wiping the hair from her face, now damp with sweat. Her eyes went wide in shock. Then her brows drew down over them as she pulled at her own magic. It billowed from every corner of the room, fueled by her rage.

I dashed toward her, reaching for her magic. I had only scooped up a small wisp when she sent a blow toward me. Her magic was the unique kind bestowed on the water people. She could pull the liquid out of anything and the blast she sent at me was meant to do that. It would have put me on my knees, near to death if I hadn't sent the same blast back to her. That small wisp of magic magnified by my own and slammed into her stream of bright purple, causing an explosion on impact. I ducked my head and threw my hands up as the blast rained liquid and smoke down around me.

Moments later, I opened my eyes to the destruction and my ears ringing. Furniture had flown across the room into shelves, books had been scattered, covers ripped and pages shredded. Around me was a small clear space, as if I had been shielded. A few feet away, Ash lay on the ground, blood dripping from the corner of her mouth, her broken arm flopped at an odd angle. She blinked and groaned as I stood. Thanking whatever it was inside me that caused my magic to shield me on its own.

Taking a step closer, I saw she was reaching for her dagger with her good hand, her body stiff and non-responsive. With a few quick steps, I kicked it away.

"I'm sorry." I knelt beside her, my voice shaking. I reached out a hand, calling to the healing magic that lived deep inside me. I wasn't the most skilled healer, but I could help.

"Fuck you." She coughed, pushing my hand away. "I don't want your help."

I swallowed hard and stood. She was badly injured but would survive. With the destruction around me, I knew someone had heard, no ward could cover all this, and I needed to move.

"I'm sorry," I whispered again as I turned to leave.

CHAPTER THIRTY-THREE

I crept out of the office, pushing my magic out. There were dozens of beings in the manor. Too many for my addled brain to comprehend. Many were already moving swiftly toward the library. I raced up the narrow back stairs, taking them two at a time. On the landing, I was confronted with two of the younger sisters who recently ascended. They were running down the hall, stopping short when they saw me. I paused, not sure what they were going to do, but they stood at attention, expectantly waiting for orders.

"Ash, the library, go." I pointed down the stairs from which I had just come and continued down the hall as they rushed past me.

I caught a movement in a small drawing room beside Father's office and slipped inside to find Tyanna there, alone.

"He came out and went toward the main stair seconds ago.

Now is our chance," she said. I nodded and watched as she pulled at her magic. With her speed, no one would see her go into Father's office; even if someone was waiting inside, she could get in and out before they noticed her. It was the one location in the manor that my magic couldn't reach into, and we had prepared for it. If she didn't appear back in front of me in three seconds, it was safe for me to enter.

Shaking out my limbs, I counted off the three seconds in my head. Again, I used my magic to make sure the hall was empty and slipped out. This time I felt the slight prick of the wards as I crossed the threshold of the room, noting it to analyze later if I had the opportunity.

It had been decided that Tyanna would hide in a secret room attached to Father's office. The doorway was hidden in the massive bookshelf that lined the entire western wall. I had to use my magic again to feel for the latch. Unfortunately, Grim's plans only showed that it existed, not how to get into it, but I had seen enough secrets in my life to know where to look and in a few moments, I had it.

Hooking my finger on the spine of a book, I pulled it back, and the door swung inward. Wasting no time, Tyanna slipped in and closed the door behind her. As soon as she was settled, I moved to the large windows, ducking behind the massive velvet curtains. I glamoured to cover my presence and waited.

More than likely, Father would sense me through the glamour. His superior powers had always made him capable of such things, but hopefully, without the cobalt in my system, my magic would be stronger. I felt for the stone in my pocket, rubbing it with my thumb. The element of surprise was all we had going for us.

Father's magic was only rivaled by the king and his ilk. I

couldn't imagine my new strength would be that much more impressive against him. Even if it could rival his, he had decades of practice on his side. I took a deep breath to steady my nerves, wishing I had some of Sam's liquor to help take the edge off.

The minutes seemed to drag on as I stood there, waiting. My throat began to feel parched, and my legs stiff from lack of movement. I tried to occupy my mind by counting the threads in the curtain near my face or daydreaming about what life would be like after I left this house for a final time.

After what seemed like hours, my senses finally began to tingle. There were beings nearing the door. I pushed my magic out further, feeling for them as the door opened. One I recognized immediately as Adrien, another Father, and finally Hilda. They moved across the room slowly, Father grumbling to himself about the waste of Ash's death.

My blood ran cold at his words. When I left her, she was alive —hurt, but nothing she wouldn't recover from. I clenched my teeth and dug my nails into my palms. Had he killed her because she failed him, even after she had been so unfailingly loyal?

I had told Tyanna we would wait for him to be alone, but now I had rage burning through my veins. I didn't stop to think if Hilda and Adrien would be with us as I thrust my magic out, reaching for Father's presence. If I could grasp the essence of him, there was a chance I could sever his connection to magic for a moment. I heard the scrape of his chair on the floor as he pulled it back. I felt my magic take hold, there was a pause in his speaking.

Lunging from my hiding spot behind the curtain, I threw a set of throwing stars in the direction of Father's desk. Hilda and Adrien jumped into action, swatting them away with ease. Adrien pulled a dagger from his hip as they both turned, jaws dropping in shock at the sight of me.

Ignoring them, I charged forward toward Father, pulling a blade as I ran with a screeching battle cry. This was the signal for Tyanna, who burst from her hiding spot behind the door, throwing a bolt of her electric magic at him. The sudden movement and the hold I had on him were enough to distract him for a moment.

I threw a blast of fire in his direction as it landed on his desk, scattering papers everywhere. He dodged both blasts but was unprepared for the blade I thrust down on him. The grasp I had on his essence shattered, and a blast of his magic threw me backward and onto the floor, but not before my blade struck his arm. I scrambled up and launched another assault.

With one hand, I threw a dagger and pulled another from its sheath while the other hand launched another blast of fire. From the other side, Tyanna launched bolt after bolt of electricity in the same direction. Father had backed up against the wall behind his desk, using his magic to defend himself, while also building more of his blood-red magic for an assault.

The adrenaline in my veins gave me a strength I had never felt before, and everything slowed down as if I was watching it happen in slow motion. Tyanna was a force using her unbridled rage to drive Father back. Hilda stood beside her at the ready but motionless in shocked silence, watching everything unfold. Adrien was behind me, his eyes dark and his lips twisted into a cruel smile. Perhaps they were with us after all.

Throwing out another blast of fire, I pushed all the air out of my lungs. In a few long strides, I was close enough to suck his magic in with my breath. It burned, scalding me from the inside like I had never experienced. I continued to pull it in through the pain as the edges of my vision began to go fuzzy.

Our eyes met. His familiar blue-gray eyes, hard with anger,

suddenly softened with shock when he realized what had happened, that I had overpowered him. A smile twisted across my face as I held his power inside me, even as it shredded my lungs. I threw his own power back at him with the added strength of my own behind it.

Time sped forward as his body was blasted sideways into the wall of books with a sickening crack. Then everything paused for a moment as he slid down the wall, crumpling onto the floor. Could this truly be so easy? I took a step forward, and his head snapped up, his face pinched in fury. He made to stand, and I readied myself to continue the fight, but his legs wobbled, his eyes searching behind me.

Spinning, I found Adrien with his eyes locked on Father. He walked forward slowly, his face solemn, focused. The sound of a thud pulled my attention back. Father was now kneeling before me, his eyes clouded over, unseeing. Adrien had broken into his mind during the fray while I had my hands on his power. My heart thrummed with excitement; we could win this.

"End him," Hilda shouted from the side. "We don't torture people."

Adrien put up a hand to silence her, his lip curling into a sneer as Father fell to the floor and began writhing there. Now, my heart leaped into my throat as I realized what was happening. A horrifying scream gurgled out of him as his breeches darkened with liquid. The fine line Adrien had talked of was now crossed, and he was actively torturing Father of his own volition.

"Adrien, stop," Hilda protested again, walking toward her son. She halted mid-stride, frozen in place. Blood began to seep from Father's eyes, ears, and nose.

I looked at Adrien; his face was twisted into a vicious grin. While I couldn't see it, I could feel the immense power he wielded.

It thrummed in the air around him. He was torturing the man and enjoying it. He had rendered his own mother's mind openly, preventing her from so much as speaking to him. A single man was now in control of some of the strongest beings on the island.

The sight of his darkened eyes standing over the broken man quelled all the built-up rage I had felt only moments ago. It ebbed away replaced with heartache and something like fear. I took a tentative step forward, then another, easing my way closer to him.

"He deserves worse," Adrien seethed. He wasn't looking at me, but I knew it was to me he was speaking.

"Maybe, but you are better than this," I said, taking another tentative step and reaching toward him. "Look at me, Adrien."

Gently, I rested my hand on his arm and pulled him toward me. He resisted at first, but then, slowly, he turned in my direction, his expression hard and angry, his eyes stormy.

"He is the cause of every scar I bear, every heartbreak, everything for me and hundreds of others."

I nodded. "His pain does nothing to change that. It just reflects on you." The words came out more stern than I intended. "Let him go."

We stood there for a long time. I held his gaze, willing him to stop, while Father lay on the floor beside us, his screams echoing off the walls of the room. Adriens's nostrils flared, and Father made a gurgling noise. Hilda screamed through clenched teeth, still frozen in place. Then there was silence.

Adrien ripped his gaze away from mine to the floor where Father lay. Daren knelt beside him, his hands dripping with blood from where he had slit the man's throat. He looked up at us as blood pooled around him, his face stern, hardened as if he had suddenly aged years. My brain tried to make sense of where he had come from, but before I could, Adrien shouted a curse and launched himself at the larger man.

I grabbed his wrist as he brandished a knife, and Daren jumped to his feet and out of reach. Hilda appeared in front of her son like a wall to block him. I watched as Adrien's eyes darted from her to Daren and back.

"Get him out of here," Daren commanded, shaking the hair from his face.

Before I could gather myself to react, Hilda's gray-black magic was whisking them away, and I was left there with Daren and Tyanna. The three of us looked between each other, unsure of what to do or say. The minutes stretched out like hours until Tyanna shuffled her way to a chair and sat.

"Where's my granddaughter, Aellonson?" she said with a huff.

Daren's brows furrowed as he looked her over. Slowly, his face changed as her identity dawned on him. "Tyanna?" he whispered. She nodded, stretching her legs in the chair. "You died."

"No, I was pregnant, and I left." She held up the scarred wrist where her stone would have been. "And then you lot killed my girl and took her baby, Isadora. And I'm not leaving without her."

Daren sucked his lip ring between his teeth and looked away, letting out a long sigh. He looked to the shelves along the wall, the muscles of his jaw pulsing. I was still unsure of what to do. Was Daren on our side? Would he turn us in? Had he killed Father out of kindness or his own devices?

"It's fine," he said, finally turning back to us. "This is all fine. You were never here." He pointed at me without looking in my direction, then Tyanna. "It was you who did all this, alone. We will get Isadora, and then the two of you will leave. Go to the continent and let me clean this up. Do not show your faces back here for any reason."

Just then, Hilda appeared, her expression somber, and her hands clenched into fists.

"What is your part in all this?" Daren snapped at her before her smoke even cleared.

"None." I stepped forward, finally finding my voice. My brain finally catching up to the moment. "She and Adrien were just here in the room when Tyanna and I attacked."

"And you didn't intervene?" he asked Hilda with steely reserve, anger bubbling just below the surface.

"You know more than most what I have endured at the hands of that man," she said, eerily calm, almost defiant.

Daren sighed again, clenching his fists at his sides. A knock at the door startled me so much that I jumped. Daren cursed and turned toward us; his eyes focused on Hilda only.

"Take them to the dungeon, cell three hundred four. Get the girl and take them to the continent. Then come see me. We have a lot to discuss," he hissed and began walking toward the door. None of us moved immediately, still stunned by the events that had just occurred. "Now!" he shouted, back over his shoulder and reaching for the door.

I rushed forward lifting Tyanna off the chair as Hilda's magic swirled and she took hold of us. We disappeared just as Daren turned the handle.

When the mist cleared, we found ourselves in the lowest parts of the manor where the darkness was eternal and the dampness was bone-chilling. The hallways here were narrow, illuminated by enchanted torches every few feet. Large iron doors with no windows lined the walls. This was the prison ward. My stomach clenched. I had no idea this place held children. I had only ever been down here on occasion to bring a prisoner down or extract information from one. How many little girls had I walked by, unaware and completely ignored?

"What cause is there to keep an innocent child in a place like this?" Tyanna cried beside me.

Hilda sighed, her voice cracking as she spoke. "It's usually only a day or two before the girls are brought out. It's part of the process for severing them from the lives they led before, part of forgetting their pasts."

"It's been weeks," I said, bile rising in my throat.

Hilda's voice was barely a whisper. "Some are more difficult to break than others."

Whatever was left of my heart shattered. How many girls were kept here? Was I kept here? How long was it before I gave in? How had I forgotten all this?

Refusing to dwell on it more, I swallowed and grabbed a torch from the wall to begin the search. There weren't regular guards down here, but a patrol did make the rounds every few hours. I had no idea what time it was, it would be best if we could make this quick. Luckily, it was the second door I checked. Like the others, it was not locked but simply bolted from the outside. Pulling the bolt back, I threw the door open.

It was dark in the cell, the only light coming from the torch in my hand. I raised it up over my head, casting a faint glow over the space. In the corner was a small being, curled into a little ball, unmoving. Her hair was matted and slick with filth, the little dress she had been wearing when we captured her tattered and torn.

Tyanna rushed forward, collapsing beside the little figure and taking the girl's face in her hands. She was groggy but alive, her eyes fluttering open. She made a screeching noise before collapsing into tears and burying her face in her grandmother's chest. Behind us, the door swung shut with a thud.

"Someone's coming," Hilda whispered, moving closer; her magic was already winding around us.

This time, when the mist cleared, we were in the arena, one level above. I looked to Hilda in confusion; she had to know we needed to get away from here quickly.

"My magic is waning, and there's three of you." Her brows knit together in concern.

"It's fine, follow me." I scooped up a new dagger from the training rack, having lost mine in the fray, and led the way down the corridor to the main stair. Behind me, Tyanna shuffled as quickly as she could, and Hilda carried the weakened girl.

We made it to the stairs and up to the main level without a problem. I pushed my magic out through the wall, feeling for anyone nearby before pulling the latch that released the secret door. I pushed it open the rest of the way and slipped around the corner, securing the entry. Hilda held the door with her back for Tyanna to come through. I had nearly reached the main door when Leon came through, followed by Daren, who was barking out orders. They both stopped dead in their tracks when they saw me.

There was no telling what my position was with Leon, what Ash or Daren had told him, it was possible that I could have played it off but Tyanna rounded the corner before I could stop her. I threw a pulse of magic to Hilda to keep her and the girl hidden. Leon's head cocked to the side assessing us.

"Who is this?" He asked, his deep voice resonating in the open space. I didn't have an answer for him.

Daren's eyes darted between me and Leon, and with an almost imperceptible shake of his head, he signaled. Leon would not be with us, and so Daren could not protect us now. I swallowed heavily. Leon's power had always rivaled Daren's; this battle would not be easy.

Tyanna grabbed my arm, pushing me back behind her, a pink fog building in her presence.

"Get my granddaughter out of here," she shouted, pulling her bent back straight. I hesitated.

Even with her unbridled powers, she would not survive a battle with Leon and Daren together. I would be leaving her to die.

"Go Damit" she yelled, her pink fog prickling with magenta streaks of lightning.

I looked up at Leon and Daren, both standing ready, but something in Daren's eyes tugged at my heart as I turned and trotted back around the corner.

Hilda was kneeling, holding the flailing arms of Isadora, who was screaming and fighting to get away, her face stained with tears. Then, Hilda's dark magic began to swirl inside the cocoon she built around them as I stepped forward, breaking its barrier, and together, we vanished.

CHAPTER THIRTY-FOUR

Hilda got us as far as the woods outside the manor, where I got us a set of horses to take to the waygate. We crossed to the island and Hilda jumped us to an inn in Renialie. It took the last of Hilda's reserves to then jump us one last time to Velreign, a riverside city in the heart of Liagheria. Somewhere along the line, Isadora stopped crying for her grandmother, taking a stony, mute stance beside me.

We appeared in an ornate dining room in what I later found out was Princess Ameria's main residence. Adrien was there with Reikka; they both stood from the table as we appeared, both of them looking grim.

"What the hell was that?" Adrien spat before any of us could speak. "And what is she doing here?" He gestured to the girl who cowered behind me.

"I could ask you the same," I said coldly, hardening my gaze and holding tightly to Isadora's hand. Hilda stepped away from us, reaching for a glass of wine on the table before sitting heavily in Reikka's vacated chair. She looked paler and wearier than I had ever seen her. The mental barrier she held had been broken by her own son. A man she had known her whole life had been tortured and killed before her. Then, she had used so much of her magic to get us out of there. The last hour had been hard on her possibly more than the rest of us.

"Calm down," she said, taking a sip and savoring it. "I need food, and then we can discuss this civilly." She looked up to Reikka, who simply nodded and stalked off.

I moved forward but was stopped when Isadora remained planted on the spot. She was still filthy; her eyes, now red-rimmed, were vacant as she stared straight ahead. I tried to think of something to say, something I could tell her to make it better, but nothing came. It was me who had first taken her from her home, who had killed her family, and then allowed her grandmother to sacrifice herself. An ache in my chest reminded me of the thorns of a rose squeezing tightly around my heart, the image that impregnated itself in my mind in Father's office days ago. Kneeling in front of her, I spoke as softly as I could.

"It's okay, Isadora, you are safe now." A moment passed. She sniffled and looked down at her bare feet.

"Is my gram dead?" Her voice was so small, so high-pitched, it tore at my heart.

"I don't know for sure, but I think so," I said. She nodded, her expression still vacant.

"Come sit at the table, and we will get you something to eat and some new clothes."

She nodded again and let me lead her to the table. A moment later, Reikka reappeared, followed by a handful of servants carrying trays of food and tea. I heaped piles of food in front of the girl and encouraged her to eat before turning to the others.

I told them the story, sparing a few details of course. I did admit that we had not planned for them to be there, or Daren or Ash. After my story, Reikka took the girl to get her cleaned up, and Hilda went to rest before jumping back to talk to Daren. There was no telling what would happen next; we were just left to wait it out.

Adrien and I sat silently at the table for a long time. The adrenaline had worn off sometime during the story, leaving me feeling like a hollow shell. Everything had been ripped apart inside me and I didn't know how it would all fit back together. My entire body ached with fatigue, my head pounded, and my chest felt as if it would cave in at any moment. I reached across the table for the bottle of wine, hoping it could provide some relief, but Adrien slipped it from my grasp.

He stood, putting out his hand to me. I took it, following him into a parlor and a large bed chamber. There, he poured us each a glass of wine and then slowly undressed me. It wasn't in the same way as he had before. This time, he moved carefully as if I were a child. Then he led me to the bed, and I slid under the covers without a word. He undressed himself and got in, wrapping both arms around me. All of the emotions I had over the last few days and weeks bubbled to the surface, and my eyes began to well with tears.

"Let it out," he whispered into my hair.

***

I didn't leave the room for two days, spending all that time either sleeping, drinking, or fucking Adrien. We didn't talk about the events of the last few weeks, what happened at the manor, the girl, or what either of our futures would look like.

On the third day, Reikka pulled me out of bed and marched me down to my own set of chambers a level below, where she had a bath and new clothes waiting. The princess had arrived from her visit to Verone, and I was expected to assume a position in her household. I would be a lady-in-waiting to Her Highness, again taking the name of Lady Lenna Vongale.

Once I was cleaned and dressed, she sat me in a chair to braid my hair.

"Isadora is doing well if you care," she said. I looked at her in the mirror. She had always been stern and monotone, giving away nothing when she spoke, but now I noticed a hint of inflection.

"What are we going to do with her?" I asked hesitantly, not sure I wanted or deserved to know.

"I'm going to keep her with me." Her eyes, so dark they were almost black, met mine in the mirror. "I will train her and keep her safe from Aelthor. She is powerful, maybe even more so than you," she said, her hands working deftly as she curled a few loose tendrils of hair around my face. This was the most I had ever heard Reikka talk.

"How can you do that though? You will have to go to Wraithland eventually."

"I go once a year at most, and now with Daren fully on our side." She shrugged as if in answer.

"Are we sure he is on our side completely? Does he know about what you have been doing here with the humans and the Elves?"

She shook her head.

"I suppose he will now," I said.

Reikka gave a shrug. "The princess has just arrived and is cleaning up in her rooms. You are free to do as you please until dinner when you will be presented to Her Majesty." She turned from the mirror and made her way to the fireplace. There, she pressed a stone in the wall, and a door swung inward. "These stairs follow the chimney up to Adrien's room since ladies in waiting can't be seen coming and going from men's bedrooms at all hours." She gave a wink, and I laughed.

"Thank you."

"No," she said as she made her way to the door. "Thank you for removing that scum from the face of Primthera." She nodded and left.

I wasted no time going to the wall and closing the door, only to open it again, making sure I understood how it worked. Then, I made my way up the dark, winding staircase. At the top, there was a small crack in the stone that let just enough light through to see the outline of the top step. It looked large enough to see through, and though I had to bend down, I was able to. Adrien was at the high table in the middle of the room, where he had maps and books strewn about. He was pouring over them with intense concentration.

I grabbed the frayed rope next to it and pulled the door open. Adrien looked up in surprise which quickly turned into a broad grin when he saw me.

"Ahh, Reikka planned well, I see," he said.

"That she did," I said, swaying my hips as I strolled toward him, my new dress dusting the floor as I moved. "What has got you so captivated over here?"

"Oh, just making plans," he said, bending over the table again. "Since someone had to go and upend everything by killing Pterol."

"Oops," I chuckled, planting a kiss on his cheek and coming around the side of the table.

He smirked at me beneath his lashes. "It may not end up doing much if Aelthor just puts one of his other cronies in his place. So, we should move fast and take out some of his other council members." He rubbed his chin, where a fine stubble had begun to grow. "You are acquainted with Maleathe, yes?"

"I am."

"He frequents a tavern outside the castle; you can meet him there and lure him to a room where I can extract the information we need before you end him."

He said it so casually I was momentarily confused.

"You want me to go back to Wraithland?"

"Aelthor won't want anyone to know it was one of his own that killed Pterol, so he won't tell Maleathe, at least not right away. We will go tonight." He still hadn't looked up from the papers while he spoke to me.

"I'm not doing that," I said, firmness lining each word.

"Why not?" He looked up finally, his brows knit together.

"Adrien," I sighed. "All my life, I've been a tool to be used by others, and I know we are fighting something bigger than just me, but I can't just keep doing this. I want a different life." I thought briefly of my magic, the new abilities I had yet to uncover.

He rolled his eyes and looked back down at his papers. I felt anger begin to blossom deep in my gut.

"We all want a different life, Brigitta," he said casually. "And we will all need to sacrifice something for it."

"Like you going into people's minds even though you hate it?" I asked. His cheek twitched lightly and he looked up at me again.

"Yes, like that," he said with a sigh. "We need to take advantage of the chaos that you've created. There will be time to heal and learn and build the life you want when this is all over."

"Will it ever be over?" I threw my hands up. "It's not as simple as you make it sound. Even if we kill Aelthor, there are dozens of men vying for his position. Then there are thousands of people on Wraithland who have been raised on hate and don't know there's another way. This is not some small, easy task to be taken all at once."

He stepped forward as I spoke, reaching out and taking me by the elbows, rubbing his hands up and down my arms. An overwhelming sense of calm billowed down on me, and I let it roll over my body. I took a deep breath, fighting the tears that prickled at the back of my eyelids.

"It will be okay," he said. "You can do this."

The words echoed in my mind, and I felt myself become ignited with the desire to please him, to finish the task. I nodded.

"You're right," I said, letting my tears well in my eyes. "You're always right; I don't know how you do it." I sighed, and he smiled, leaning in to kiss my forehead. It was that large, genuine smile that I loved so much.

"We will get through this, and then we will decide the new leader of Wraithland." He rubbed my arm and turned back to the table of papers.

I turned toward the window, feeling cold creeping in where his hands had touched me. Keeping my expression stoic, I checked the walls I had built around my mind, reinforcing them with my newfound powers. Next, I rolled a glamour down over myself, masking all scents and sounds that emanated from my body before I began to replay the last few weeks in my mind.

From the moment I had first met Adrien, when he looked up at me with those hooded eyes, I had felt something, a pull toward him. I remembered the moment we first touched, his hand brushing mine as he slipped the knife from my hand when he killed those children. The top of the stairs the night we took Isadora. The evening we spent together and the morning when he told me I was broken. The feelings I had felt then, and the way I wanted to give myself to him on the roof in Verone. I wanted to see what happiness felt like as if he could just hand it to me. And then the words he used, the little manipulations, he had been weaseling his way into my mind this whole time. Frost tingled under my skin as my blood ran cold.

This wasn't the first time he had entered my mind or used his powers to calm me, to coerce me to do things. How many of my decisions these last weeks were truly mine? How many of Hilda's? Or Reikka's? It dawned on me that everyone would be at risk to him and his manipulations. I continued to stare out the window, keeping my face even, as I felt pure, unadulterated rage building deep into the marrow of my bones. I let out a sigh, knowing what had to be done now.

Moving towards the table of papers, I went to the hot pot of tea he had resting there, with two cups. Had he expected me? Had he manipulated this situation as well? I bit back the curse twisting on my tongue and held my face even.

Carefully, I picked up the teapot and poured myself a cup of tea. It took everything I had in me to keep my hands steady as I lifted the dainty teacup to my lips. I took a sip, noting how it felt cold in my mouth despite the steam that rose from it. Adrien still hadn't looked up from his papers.

"So, after Maleathe, what are we meant to do? We still don't have a way to kill Aelthor," I asked sweetly, cocking my head to the side.

"We will figure that out; for now, we just have to keep him busy." His eyes only flicked up from the papers in front of him for a moment.

"And how is that to be done?" I stepped around the table, closer to him.

"We interrupt his missions, halt trade, use the same tactics he used to cause upset on the continent," he mumbled, not bothering to look up at all this time. I should step away, give him his peace to think, but I didn't want him to have peace. He needed to be thrown off balance, to get agitated and let his truth slip, a truth that would be the end of him.

"Interrupting missions could end in more deaths for my sisters." I pushed.

He pursed his lips. "It's an unfortunate cost that we may have to pay."

"Why not reach out to the Elves? There must be someone powerful enough to take him down."

"The Elves have been in hibernation for ten thousand years; they hardly have any magic left."

I had to choke back my shock, taking a sip of my tea, to cover it. Was he so agitated already that he was giving himself up? Did he think his hold on me was so strong that it didn't matter? He had told me only days before that he wasn't privy to this kind of information.

"Even the mighty Eldrid?"

"Yes," he said curtly, his hands tracing a path across a map of the continent.

"We can still use them to scare Aelthor—they would help us, wouldn't they?"

"No, Eldrid wants nothing to do with us. He's only allowing Weilson to chase the prophecy in an attempt to protect himself."

"So, he's not hibernating anymore?"

"Correct."

"Are all the Elves awake?"

"No."

"So, Hilda is fine with sacrificing the sisters?"

"She will be."

"Have you had to make her before?"

"Yes."

"And Reikka?"

"Yes," he sighed in exasperation, finally looking up at me. "I'm sorry, love; I know you have questions and this is all new for you, but I need to focus. Sit, drink your tea, and give me a moment." I felt that same overwhelming sense of calm slide over my body. I smiled at him.

"I'm sorry," I said, reaching for the teapot. I refreshed my cup, watching the steam waft upward as he went back to his work. He didn't even realize what he had admitted. He had manipulated his own mother with his powers, Reikka too, and obviously me. Who else had he done this to? And how many times?

I took another step around the table, resting my free hand on his shoulder and then rubbing it gently down his back in the quiet, intimate way of lovers. Again, he didn't even look up, completely entranced now. He spoke, saying something about movements and weak places to target, but I wasn't listening. Setting the teacup down, I leaned forward on the table, my hands sliding along the edge and scooping up the letter opener that sat there.

There was no hesitation in my movements. I took a long step forward, using the momentum to thrust the knife into his throat. He turned to me, those blue-gray eyes wide with shock. My face crumpled as the tears spilled down my face. I ripped the knife out, stepping back and letting the blood spurt across the table. His eyes softened as he reached a hand toward me. His mouth began working like a fish gasping for air. I felt the claws of his mind reaching for mine, my new walls holding firm against them.

His legs collapsed beneath him, and he fell to the ground in a heap. My heart lurched, and I had to put my elbow on the table to steady myself.

"I told you to stay out of my mind, Adrien. There's no place in this new world for manipulation like yours," I said as I dropped the letter opener onto his chest. I stood still watching as the blood pooled beneath him, stretching away from his body. Finally, his chest shuddered and stopped moving, and then his head fell to the side. His presence wafted upward, brushing past me and sending an icy chill down my spine.

I wanted to scream, shout, or break things. Needing to let out everything that had built inside me but I couldn't. There were others milling around the common rooms. Now that the princess was back, there would be no hiding a tantrum. I couldn't risk someone connecting me to this.

Taking a deep breath, I stepped back, running my clean hand over my hair. I didn't know whether it was the rage or the training that had propelled my actions. Adrien had gone from friend to enemy so quickly, but if I had taken the time to stop and think, his manipulations could have blinded me, perhaps permanently. There may not have been another moment of clarity. There wasn't time to second guess myself now. No magic could bring the dead back, and I had to deal with what I had done now.

I went to the window and with my bloody hand, pushed it open, leaving a print on both the sill and the stone on the outside. Next, I moved toward the table, flipping through the papers and maps, cataloging as much as I could into my brain before crumbling it and tossing it to the fireplace. All the missives, notes, and anything that could be of any use to anyone was tossed away before I used magic to set it ablaze, turning it to ash. I checked all the drawers, and secret compartments taking what I wanted, and leaving the place disheveled.

With one last look at the prostrate body of my former lover, I went through the secret door to my own rooms, using my magic to slam it shut behind me.

293

CHAPTER THIRTY-FIVE

Back in my room, I scrubbed my hands clean, changed dresses, blotted the blood spatter with cold water, and hung the old one to dry. After a quick check in the mirror, I made my way out, down the hall past several loitering courtiers, and a set of guards that stood watch over the entrance to the wing that Adrien's room was in. I made sure to give them a warm hello when I went by.

I didn't hesitate as I walked up to his door, knocking and then pushing it open like a woman on a mission like I had something to say. Only instead of speaking, I let out the shriek that had been pent up in my throat since I had realized his betrayal. It barreled out of me with such force I was sure the walls shook. Throwing myself to the ground beside him, I screamed and cried and thrashed, pounding his chest as if to wake him. In those moments, I let it go. I let out the pain, anger, betrayal, and utter sadness. It took both of the guards to pull me out of the room, as I flailed incoherently, screaming his name.

In the sitting room, Hilda appeared from another door and rushed forward, only to stop short, falling against the door frame. She didn't scream or cry; instead, she put a hand to her mouth as the tears welled in her eyes and turned her gaze on me.

My heart stopped for a moment at the look on her face. I had seen death so many times, seen the heartbroken loved ones, the lovers, the mothers, the children, but never had I seen so much regret filled in a single look. I stood as she stumbled toward me, putting out my arms to catch her. She gripped me, her nails digging into my flesh.

"What happened?" she seethed through gritted teeth.

"Come," I said, wrenching my arm from her grip and wrapping it around her shoulders. I led her into a small parlor, leaving the door open but dropping a cocoon of silence around us.

"He was using his magic on me," I blurted before she had the chance to sit down. The usually silent, stoic, brave Hilda fell into a chair as if the ground had fallen out from under her. I knelt at her feet, taking her hands in mind. "I'm so sorry, Hilda. I had no choice."

She looked down at me with those same blue-gray eyes as his. Bile rose in my throat, and tears began streaming down my face anew.

"He had been doing it for a while, I just put the pieces together," I tried to explain. "I didn't want to do it, but I didn't see another way."

"Because there wasn't another way," she whispered. "I thought that I could keep him safe from this. That if I could keep a thread of goodness in him, it would be worth it." She swallowed and shook her head. "It might be worth the innocents I've killed, the sisters I let die in my place, the people I tortured and hunted because I was selfish. Because I wanted to protect my children. But I was a fool." She looked away, her teeth grinding against each other.

"I saw it before, you know." She swallowed and turned back to me. "I tried to ignore it. I tried to help push him in the right direction, but what did I expect? When he was used as a tool to break others this way, exposed over and over and over again to the evil that lives in us all. I should have known that someday it would overtake him. I knew in Pterol's office, I knew then that he had gone too far." She put her face in her hands. "My poor innocent boy, this is all my fault."

"No, Hilda." My voice cracked, and I had to clear my throat to continue. "It's not your fault. You had hope; all this time, you had hope. You built this resistance. You saved my life. We have a chance to change things. None of this would have happened if you hadn't done what you needed to do to keep him alive. I am so sorry that I was the one to take him from you."

"I want to hate you, Catherine." She took a deep breath, rubbing her hands on her leathers. I sat back on my heels and waited for her to continue. "But if anyone would be able to fight his magic, it would be you. I had hoped whatever feelings were growing between you could tether him back down. He had true feelings for you, however twisted they may have been. That much I could see."

Her words made the tears come again. Any reserve I had left to stop them was long gone. I got up and went to the chair beside her, wiping my eyes.

"I'm going to go for a while," she stood.

"Go where?"

"I don't know, but The Society has nothing to hold over me

anymore. There is so much blood on my hands. Why am I the one still here, when they are gone? Why have the gods chosen me to punish?"

"You can't leave now," I said in shock. "Everything has changed, I don't know enough. Who will represent us with the Elves and the humans? What about your daughter? Adrien told me about his sister. We need you; I need you."

She tilted her head to the side and looked me over, giving me a faint smile.

"Leeta is dead." Her voice was raw. My jaw dropped in shock, a faint image of Leeta's face flashing in my mind. How had I not seen the resemblance? I had known her all my life and had never seen it. She shook her head and continued. "You and Reikka, and Moreanne, together, I have no doubts that you can conquer anything."

There will be others now who will join, and Darren might even be on our side after all. I need time, right now I won't be any good to anyone." She took a few steps back, out of view from the open door, the black-gray tendrils of her magic beginning to swirl around her. "Keep an eye on the princess; if it is her child who is the key to taking down Aelthor, she will need your protection."

And before I could respond, she was gone.

CHAPTER THIRTY-SIX

I sat there for a moment, completely bewildered. Hilda had just left us, left me. After everything I had done, I couldn't blame her. I was the reason Adelay and Tris were dead, and Ash, and Father, and now her son. Without my stone, I had no connection to the sisterhood and no way of knowing what was going on there. Reikka might have some answers, but her ties with the sisters were tenuous at best after spending so much time away. There was no way of telling which of my sisters would be with us. I leaned back in the chair and looked around the room, cataloging the furniture and artwork in it to try and calm myself.

"Lady Lenna?" I turned to find a male servant standing stiffly by the door. "Her Highness has requested your presence."

Letting out a long sigh, I nodded, wiped my eyes, and stood. The servant led me through the main sitting room that was attached to Adrien's, which was now teaming with people. All of them vying for a better look, the women pretending to swoon and looking for moral support from the men in the room. It was typical of courtiers to seek advantage even in the death of another. I grit my teeth as I moved past them and down the hall to the princess's private wing.

She was out on a balcony off of her main sitting room, leaning over the rail, her long loose curls trailing down her back. She was just as lovely as the last time I saw her, though her expression left some to be desired.

The servant introduced me before turning sharply and leaving. I gave an elegant curtsy and stepped toward the railing. Ameria didn't look at me, keeping her eyes on the horizon. A cocoon snapped down around us, and I couldn't stop the chuckle as I realized she had been practicing.

"Why is the scholar dead?" she asked flatly.

"He lied to me," I responded just as flatly. I wouldn't begin this new life based on the same series of lies.

Her head snapped to me. "That's all it takes?"

I sighed, looking away from her and to the distant hills. "I'm not sure how much you know, but he had these powers, and he used them to manipulate me, and if he did it to me, he could have been doing it to anyone. I couldn't trust him anymore."

She nodded, turning back to the scenery.

"I could have you arrested, tried, and hung for such an offense."

"I'm sure you could do much worse."

She turned back now, her eyes stern, almost cold. "He was the sole source of information that we had on the movements of Aelthor. I know he can remove the wards and is planning an attack on the continent; without Adrien, we are at a loss."

"There's more to the story than you know." I swallowed,

reminding myself that half-truths were not the way forward. "Reikka has contacts with The Society. I have others. We will get the information we need."

"So, I'm just supposed to look the other way and ignore the murder on my doorstep?"

"It's not the first and is likely not to be the last," I said, keeping my voice steady and turning again to the horizon. "You can go ahead and arrest me. I won't stop you, but I'll be gone before any trial can take place."

She pinched her lips into a flat line and squinted her eyes at me. "I'd rather you take my offer."

I chuckled again at her bravado. "I want to," I said. "On one condition."

Now, the princess turned around fully, leaning back against the balcony rail and crossing her arms over her chest.

"I'm no lady in waiting. Let me be your personal guard."

She pursed her lips, looking me up and down; I could almost see the wheels in her mind turning over.

"Done," she said finally.

I nodded but stayed silent, waiting for whatever was on her mind to spill out.

"What is your name?" she asked, leveling her gaze at me. "The real one you want to be called. And be sure to answer wisely since this is the name you are taking to your new future with me."

I mulled it over in my mind, having never had the opportunity to choose a name of my own. I had worn the names and faces of dozens of others, but none of them felt like home. Even Catherine, the name my true mother had given me, seemed to have been marred by the life I had led until now, yet I didn't want to leave that last vestige of my first self behind completely. Perhaps someday, I would be able to make it back to the place of innocence that that little girl had. Then it came to me.

"Call me Rin."

Glossary of Terms & Creatures

Agyros (Ag-ir-os) – The family name of the rulers of Wreabarroth.

Braithe (Bray-th) – A classification of Harridan Sister, ranked below a Saithe. They are typically used as spies and messengers on the continent but do not interact with targets as Saithes do.

Borreagor (Bore -a-gore) – The name of a large desert in the central part of the continent, mostly within the borders of Wreabarroth. Also, the name of a city at the northern tip of the desert in Liagheria.

Elf (Elves) - Encompasses many species that derive from the immortals of the third moon. Often the most human-looking (aside from pointed ears) and most powerful are considered Elves (sometimes Noble Elves), while other species are considered lesser Elves.

Dragon – Large flying reptilian beings with four legs and wings. As incredibly powerful beings they were hunted and it is thought driven to extinction shortly after the Elves' appearance on Primthera. Little is known about them.

Gasyter (Guh-sey-ter)- A species of lesser elf. They are large and broad with blue-tinted skin, thick black hair, and goat-type horns. They have a warrior-based culture and are some of the strongest, fastest healing beings on the planet, though they prefer brute strength and look down on the use of magic as cheating or weakness.

Giants - Humanoid beings that are two to three times the size of a human, with thicker muscles and an affinity for crafting detailed/intricate things with their hands. They tend to be kind and intelligent but were mostly driven from the continent by the Elves who believed they required too many resources to support due to their large size.

Goin Elves - A species of lesser elf with dark grey skin and silver or white hair. They are known for their abilities with elemental magic and are strong fighters.

Immortals – Beings that do not die and preside on the third moon in abject luxury. The most powerful of them are considered Gods. Wraithen is the god of Ether, Leaghaire is the god of Water, Tienen is the god of Fire, Cretalanh is the god of Earth, Adhairig is the god of Air.

Liagheria (ly-hair-ee-a) – The name of a country on the eastern half of the continent, that lies between Streyland, Wreabarroth, and the sea.

Little people (Dwarves) - Humanoid beings that are half the height of an average man. They are good cooks, and very family-oriented. Driven into the mountains by the Elves long ago they have created a thriving culture despite the harsh terrain. Because of this, they have learned to mine precious metals and crystals, honing their skills as craftsmen, however, they refuse to trade with the humans because of the thousands of years of poor treatment by them and the Elves.

Maleathe (mal-a-th) – Top General of Wraithland.

Naiad (Nai-ad)- A species of lesser elf that thrives in water. They have a humanoid appearance but with webbed hands and feet. They also have overly large eyes with extra lids to see in under the water, and gills behind their pointed ears. They have a green or blue tint to their skin.

Noble Elf – A humanoid-appearing elf that hails from a royal bloodline. They are thought to contain more power and wisdom than other Elves. It is believed that they are derived directly from the Immortals of the third moon.

Pterol (T-air-el) – Head of the Harridan Society.

Reinalie (Ren – aa - lee) – A largeish town on the eastern coast of Wreabarroth.

Saithe (Say-th) – The highest classification of Harridan sister, utilized for specialized and dangerous missions.

Third Moon – Believed to be a small moon that only appears near Primthera once every 17 thousand years. It is believed to be the home of the immortals.

Tachdre (Tack-dr-ay) – A classification of Harridan Sister, ranked below a Saithe. They are typically assigned long-term missions to maintain safe houses, and important locations, as well as transfer of information.

Waterfolk - Includes numerous humanoid species that thrive in the water including Merpeople, Naiads, and the like.

Witch – A human who has learned how to utilize magic.

Wraiths – Slang term for anyone from the exiled island of Wraithland, including Gasyters, Goin Elves, Waterfolk, Witches, and Noble Elves.

Wreabarroth (Wray-bar – roth) – The name of a country on the eastern half of the continent, that lies between Liagheria, Chiotania, and the sea.

Claire A. Brower

Acknowledgments

This book was a labor of love that I could have never completed without the support of numerous people, but most importantly my husband. Eric, you have always been my biggest supporter and comedic relief. Thank you for always being there.

Thank you also to my amazing cousin and lifelong friend Nikki. I can't tell you what it means that no matter what the distance and time between us you are always so loving and supportive.

To my friends, alphas, and betas; Christine, Shay, Jennifer, Lindsey, Jillian, Millie, Maggie, Vanessa, Carmen, Jen B., and several more, I'm so thankful that the bookstagram community has brought such love and support into my life through you all.

To my amazing street team and their fearless leader Kerri Markham, thank you so much for all you have done in support of me and this book. Kerri, you have been an amazing asset and friend to have in my corner and I would truly never have gotten anyone to read this book without you.

Brittany Gossins, thank you for not only being an amazing editor but also for being the one to inspire me to actually do this self-publishing thing. It was you who put the idea into my head, and for that I will be forever grateful.

Tabitha Chandler thank you for being so easy to work with and giving Rin the final polish.

Andrea Aguirre – Your ability to take my idea and bring it to life in such a beautiful and masterful way was completely beyond my expectations. Thank you for lending me some of your skills and talent for this project.

About the Author

Claire A. Brower is an author, mom, and business owner, who resides in the foothills of the Adirondacks in Upstate, NY. She is an avid reader, crafter, adventurer, and home cook, who loves spending time with family and relaxing in the woods. She began writing early in life but has only recently begun the process of sharing her work with the world at large. Learn more about her and her work online.

www.ClaireABrower.com